TWO NOVELS BY ROBBE-GRILLET

Two Novels
by Robbe-Grillet

Jealousy
& In the Labyrinth

Translated by Richard Howard

GROVE PRESS, INC.   NEW YORK

Library of Congress Catalog Card Number: 65-16711

ACKNOWLEDGMENTS: The essay by Bruce Morrissette is a
revised adaptation of an article which appeared originally in
The French Review, Vol. XXXI, no. 5 (April 1958) under the
title *"Surfaces et structures dans les romans de Robbe-Grillet,"*
and is printed with the author's permission. Roland Barthe's
essay appeared originally in *Critique*, nos. 86-87 (juillet-août
1954) under the title *"Littérature objective: Alain Robbe-
Grillet,"* and was subsequently translated in *Evergreen Review*,
No. 5 (Summer 1958). It is reprinted with the author's permission. Mme. Anne Minor's review of *Jealousy* originally
appeared in *The French Review*, Vol. XXXII (April 1959)
under the title *"La Jalousie,"* and is printed with the author's
permission.

First Evergreen Black Cat Edition 1965

Seventh Printing

DISTRIBUTED BY RANDOM HOUSE, INC., NEW YORK

MANUFACTURED IN THE UNITED STATES OF AMERICA

CONTENTS

INTRODUCTORY ESSAYS

SURFACES AND STRUCTURES IN ROBBE-GRILLET'S NOVELS

by Bruce Morrissette

The rising curve of Alain Robbe-Grillet's literary star continues its dazzling ascent. As early as 1953, when Robbe-Grillet launched his career with *The Erasers* (*Les Gommes*), Roland Barthes saw in the young author's work a revolutionary aspect comparable to that of the "surrealist attack on rationality." His second novel, *The Voyeur* (*Le Voyeur,* 1955), amazed the critics, won an important literary prize, and gained the attention of the literary public. Robbe-Grillet thereupon began to reveal his talents as a theorist of the novel form, publishing a series of articles in *L'Express* and two remarkable essays, "A Fresh Start for Fiction" (*Evergreen Review,* No. 3) and "Old 'Values' and the New Novel" (*Evergreen Review,* No. 9) which led to his being designated widely as the leader of the "school" of the New Novel in France. It is thus that Jean-Louis Curtis depicts him in *À la recherche du temps posthume*. This witty book describes Marcel Proust's return to earth to conduct an inquiry into the state of modern literature. In the milieu where the master of the psychological novel had expected to hear discussions of Henry James and his disciples, Marcel is astonished to find even Gilberte Swann agreeing that "today we ask something quite different of the novel," and that "psychology nowadays is out of style, obsolete, no longer possible," since modern readers have only scorn

1

for the sacrosanct "characters" of the traditional novel. To prove to Marcel *redivivus* that the modern novel "can no longer be psychological, it *has* to be phenomenological," Mme. de Guermantes introduces him to Robbe-Grillet ("with hair and mustache the color of anthracite") who promptly recites, in parodied style, the "new doctrine." One could also cite to illustrate the uneasiness caused in certain literary quarters by this disturbing new force, a cartoon showing the Tree of Literature with numerous well-known Novelists and Critics clinging to its branches, while below, sawing away at the trunk, stands a smiling Robbe-Grillet.

Things were at this stage when, in 1957, *Jealousy* appeared. Hostile critics threw themselves on the novel. The old guard, with André Rousseaux and Robert Kemp, hastened to denounce it, and to assure the reading public that the so-called "new path" for fiction promised by Robbe-Grillet in reality led nowhere. Robbe-Grillet was called a competitor with the "cadastre" or record book of county property lines, because of his minute, geometric descriptions, some of which (like the notorious "counting the banana trees" passage in *Jealousy*) were read over the radio, for laughs. Well, the critics seemed to say, if that's the renewal of the novel, the new objectivity or the "realism of presence," there is no need to get excited. A flood of articles, mostly antagonistic, inundated Paris. Critics on the whole (but with some notable exceptions) showed a complete lack of understanding of the new work. Shortly, copies of *Jealousy* disappeared from bookstore windows, unsold and returned to the shelves or the publisher. The 6th *arrondissement,* the center of literary activities, buzzed with rumors of Robbe-Grillet's "failure," in which a number of well-known proponents of the conventional novel took an ill-concealed delight. Yet the impression was inescapable that some of these hostile critics sought to disguise a disturbing uneasiness created in them by a profoundly original creation. Thus André Rousseaux declared, in revealing fashion, toward the end of a long article, "This is a rather extended commentary for a book that I detest."

For then, as now, Robbe-Grillet's works conveyed a powerful impression that "something," as Samuel Beckett says in *Endgame,* "is taking its course." This "something" has taken time to reveal itself, and its meaning is still not finally determined, but one can, with some confidence, survey the path covered thus far. If many early critical problems seem to have been at least partially solved, other new ones have risen. Space is lacking here to do more than indicate the principal ones, and to suggest possible critical approaches to their solution.

Take the example of *The Erasers* (1953). The baroque plot of this novel may be briefly summarized: In an atmosphere reminiscent of many *films noirs* or crime movies, the detective Wallas arrives in an Amsterdam-like Flemish city, traversed by canals and surrounded by a Circular Boulevard. His story unfolds in an overlay of actions by other characters, seen at oblique angles and in reciprocal relationships, in the midst of images twisting in a turmoil of syncopations, displacements, and echoes of a kind that many critics did not hesitate to call "metaphysical." Wallas is seeking an assassin; he does not know, as we do, that there has been no murder. Twenty-four hours after this imaginary crime, Wallas believes that he has found the criminal. He fires at this ambiguous murderer, and kills him. But it is not the assassin, it is the presumed victim, finally slain by the very hand which sought to effect a premature vengeance.

Fascinated by the various *objets troublants* of the novel, by the author's art of *description* (in which some critics, like François Mauriac, saw a parallel with the poems of Francis Ponge describing pebbles, wicker baskets, and the like), the reviewers, following the lead of

3

Roland Barthes' early essays on Robbe-Grillet, directed their attention especially to the depictions of drawbridges in motion, wall posters in series, the arrangement of the seeds in a miraculously described section of tomato, etc. Even here much remained to be said about the true nature of these "realist" presences: distinctions to be made between objective reality and literary reality, between the "Einsteinian dimension of the object" in which Barthes saw a new "mixture of space and time" on one hand and the purely literary dimensions of a new artistic universe on the other. Furthermore, *The Erasers* contains a hidden "second plot," which most critics allowed to pass unnoticed — namely, the story of Oedipus. The author himself, in a little-known brochure, revealed the presence of this "much older story which is reconstituted" in the novel; but the reviewers made only superficial references to the Oedipal inner structure. Since Robbe-Grillet's aversion to allegory, symbol, and concealed meaning is fundamental, how could the mythical "depth" of *The Erasers* be reconciled with its author's theory of pure "surfaces"? Obviously, a clearer view was needed of the legendary parallel so knowingly developed in the novel. This involved deciphering elements that remained unrecognized despite Robbe-Grillet's efforts to alert the critics to their existence: as to the form of the novel, its division into five acts, prologue, and epilogue, with the chorus transformed into an "omniscient narrator"; as to its decor, the temples, palaces, streets, hills, and ruins of Thebes reflected throughout, in the water of the canals, in the painting of the ruins of Thebes standing on an easel in front of a dummy in the window of a stationery store (where Wallas tries to find that elusive gum eraser which is surely stamped with the name "Oedipus," though Wallas can only recall the syllable "di," the others having been "erased" on the rubber cube that he once saw), the theme of a child rescued by shepherds in a pattern embroidered on the curtains of the city's monotonously identical houses, the image of the Sphinx formed by debris floating on a canal, the statue of Laius' chariot at the crossroads, and the statuette of a blind man led by a boy; as to the plot, Wallas-Oedipus who swears to discover a murderer who is none other than himself, the assassin of his father who is "not unresponsive" to the attractions of his father's wife, the man who remains blind before the evidence of his own identity, who understands neither the deformed riddles of the drunkard-Tiresias nor the disguised version of his own destiny related by women in a tramway, Wallas-Oedipus who, from excessive walking through labyrinthine streets and on the Circular Boulevard, returns, "his feet swollen," to close the twenty-four hour circle of the eternal solar myth of night and day, by killing, in a reversal of time that causes no alteration of the basic story, his father-victim. The "various meanings" that the author himself admits putting into *The Erasers* include all these things, brought together with a new art of synthesis of plot and formal structure, involving objects, time, space, and myth.

The title itself of Robbe-Grillet's prize-winning next novel, *The Voyeur,* is something of a problem, and its faulty interpretations have spoiled several critics' treatment of the work. Mathias, the protagonist, is a traveling salesman who lands on an off-shore island, like Ouessant near Brest, rents a bicycle, and sets out on its roads to sell wrist watches. The author has called Mathias a "character who does not coincide with himself." He is, we realize gradually, a schizophrenic criminal, who, on the so-called "blank page" which constitutes a hole in the action, commits the sadistic murder, accompanied perhaps by torture and rape, of a thirteen-year-old girl. One is reminded of the suppressed crime of Svidrigailov in Dostoevski's *Crime and Punishment,* as well as that hidden episode in the life of Stavrogin whose "confession"

5

remained so long unpublished. Certain critics, like Maurice Blanchot, deny the "truth" of the crime of *The Voyeur,* though such an interpretation seems impossible to reconcile with the images of murder that break through into Mathias' consciousness toward the end of the narrative. *The Voyeur* is ostensibly written in the third-person mode, but this third person blends into the "personality" of the protagonist. At the same time, chronological inversions, repetitions, variations on scenes, "false" scenes, discontinuities, and other new effects involve the reader in the action with surprising force. The unusual density or "presence" of the outside world in *The Voyeur* and the use of *visual* elements (geometry, measurements, objective and falsely objective descriptions) led critics to state almost unanimously that Mathias is the *voyeur* of the title: a *"voyant,"* as Pierre Gascar phrased it, or "a man," in Émile Henriot's words, "on whose retina objects acquire a relief and an intensity of an obsessive or hallucinatory character." This idea is almost certainly erroneous, since the *voyeur* of the title, as a careful examination of the text proves, is undoubtedly the young Julien, who has "seen everything" during the crime, and whose disquieting attitude provokes a psychic syncope in Mathias at the climax of the plot. Robert Champigny accuses the author of something approaching bad faith in choosing his title: "Commercial reasons may have played a part in the choice of the title. *Le Voyeur* is a misleading title. It may even appear as shockingly ironical when the reader realizes, after 100 pages or so, that he has been made the unsuspecting accomplice of a homicidal maniac." But the truth about the title is quite different: far from creating a false track, *voyeur* indicates a structural center, a focus of visual lines of force.

The Voyeur also contains a fascinating series of objects and images in figure-of-eight form, recurring like leitmotives in a Wagnerian opera. Here, too, some critics would see symbols, though what is really involved is a different kind of correlation (rather than "correspondence") between elements of the plot and exterior reality: a cord rolled in an eight is used by Mathias to bind his girl victim, the watching (voyeur) sea gulls wheel above in eights, the smoke of Mathias' cigarette (used to burn the girl, perhaps) describes an eight, the doors of the houses on the island are decorated with an eight pattern like eyeglasses, etc.

If one had to name Robbe-Grillet's finest novel to date, it would probably be *Jealousy*. Once again, the dominant feature is the work's formal structure. A first-person narrator who, however, never says "I" and whom one never sees or hears, draws us into an identification with him, installs us in the "hole" that he occupies in the center of the text, so that we see, hear, move, and feel with him. The brief, dense, triangular plot, which has no conventional denouement, unfolds in a rectangular tropical plantation house whose porch columns cast upon the terrace shadows like those of a sun dial, cutting time and action into slices. All the characteristics of Robbe-Grillet's special universe are present: repetitions, minute descriptions, studies of gestures and movements of objects, "aberrant" things with ambiguous functions that are stubbornly persistent in their "being-there," reversals of external chronology (but following an inner order of associative causality), absence of any attempt at psychological *analysis* or any use of the vocabulary of psychology, total rejection of introspection, interior monologues, "thoughts," or descriptions of states of mind; and a systematic use, almost like that of music, of "objective themes," including a network of *stains*, whose chief example is the spot left by the centipede crushed on the dining-room wall by Franck, the presumptive lover of the jealous narrator-husband's wife A, whom we often see, with the husband's eyes, though the *jalousie* or sun blind of a window. . . .

7

The scene of the crushing of the centipede against the wall, which is repeated at crucial moments in significant variants throughout the novel, forming the emotional center of the novel, raises once more the question of symbolism. The centipede incident *grows* in the narrator's mind (and in ours), taking on monstrous proportions full of erotic meaning. Such neosymbols or, to use Eliot's phrase, "objective correlatives" are encountered everywhere among Robbe-Grillet's "surfaces" of objects, gestures, and actions. Yet it would be a mistake to accuse the author of "betraying" in his works the hatred for the "metaphysical depths" of things that he has expressed in his theoretical articles, or to argue, as many have done, that the novelist is himself plunging into the "fog of meaning" (sentimental, sociological, Freudian, etc.) that he has so often denounced. It would be especially simplistic to conclude that Robbe-Grillet's "realism of presence" only conceals, beneath cunning symbols, signs, analogies, motifs, and correspondences, an even deeper "depth."

If a single critic (Bernard Dort) called *Jealousy* an "allegory," many were tempted to term thus the story of *In the Labyrinth* (*Dans le labyrinthe,* 1959). Robbe-Grillet felt impelled to take special precautions against this danger, stating in a foreword that the novel had "no allegorical value" and that it was a "fiction" of "strictly material reality." Without violating this principle, it is nevertheless possible to argue that the work is, like some of Mallarmé's poetry, "allegorical of itself," that is, that it embodies, rather than symbolizes, the creative process that the novelist goes through to invent, incarnate, and structure a novel. The narrative "presence" who says "I" in the first line, but never again refers to himself until near the end, when a "my" is followed by the final word "me," seems to be elaborating against the odds of multiple possibilities a story which will satisfy the implicit requirements of a number of elements assembled in his room: a shoe box containing as yet undescribed objects, a bayonet, patterns like falling snow on the wallpaper, criss-cross paths left by slippers on the floor, and — above all — the various soldiers and civilians depicted in the café scene shown in a steel engraving of "The Defeat of Reichenfels," whose materialization into a living, moving narrative is one of the marvels of the novel. Nowhere is Robbe-Grillet's technique of concordances more evident than here: the principle of the *labyrinth,* of impasses, reversals, new tentatives, blind pursuit of a goal so remote and so hidden behind unimaginable entanglements of the mind and senses that any outcome seems impossible, is applied not only to the story of the soldier and his box, but to the physical labyrinth of the city, with its identical and unidentifiable intersections, its buildings full of blind corridors lined with doors that open and close, its false soldier's refuge with covered windows, its enigmatic café, and to the style of the writing itself: its balanced ternary phrases, swinging between alternatives, its negations and retreats, its flashing on and off of lights, its materializations and dematerializations of buildings, and the like.

The quest of the wounded, feverish soldier to deliver his box takes on something of the aspect of the action of a medieval novel by Chrétien de Troyes, such as *Perceval* whose scenes in the hall of the Fisher King have a similar mysterious quality of unsolved symbolism. Even the disclosure of the "neutral," anodyne nature of the contents of this box, following the soldier's death, failed to prevent some readers from seeing the box as containing the soldier's soul, handed over to a doctor representing a priest. But readers experiencing the story in the *innocent* manner prescribed by the author may find in the revelations which constitute the denouement of the novel (which is exceptional in Robbe-Grillet's practice) a process of appeasement of tension serving to reinforce, with a lyricism that is rare in the author's works, the unsentimental

9

pathos of an unusually touching end. Do the "scattered pages" left on the table of the unseen narrator, as the book closes, represent *In the Labyrinth* itself? If so, the novel indeed approaches the Flaubertian ideal of the *livre sur rien,* the self-contained work that is its own form and substance.

Those who have seen Robbe-Grillet's films, *Last Year at Marienbad* and *L'Immortelle,* or who have read their scenarios, can verify the assertion that most of their author's novelistic techniques recur, in more or less modified form, as cinematic structures. The whole realm of the relationship between novel and cinema remains largely open to investigation. The art of Robbe-Grillet, with its objectification of mental images, its use of psychic chronology, its development of "objectal" sequences or series related formally and functionally to plot and to the implicit psychology of characters, its refusal to engage in logical discourse or analytical commentary, is as ideally suited to film as to narrative, and may well serve as the basis for a "unified field" theory of novel-film relationships in the future. "Nouveau roman, nouveau cinéma," says Robbe-Grillet: after the new novel, the new cinema. But, at the same time, let us be prepared for new novelistic surprises, for Robbe-Grillet is, and will remain, essentially a creator of *fiction,* whose structures will require the novel as well as the film to attain their fullest development.

OBJECTIVE LITERATURE:
ALAIN ROBBE-GRILLET

by Roland Barthes

> **Objective n.** In optics, the lens situated nearest the object to be observed and receiving the rays of light directly from it. — *Oxford English Dictionary*

High on the pediment of the Gare Montparnasse is a tremendous neon sign that would read *Bons-Kilomètres* if several of its letters were not regularly out of commission. For Alain Robbe-Grillet, this sign would be an object par excellence, especially appealing for the various dilapidations that mysteriously change place with each other from one day to the next. There are, in fact, many such objects — extremely complicated, somewhat unreliable — in Robbe-Grillet's books. They generally occur in urban landscapes (street directories, postal schedules, professional-service signs, traffic signals, gatehouse fences, bridge superstructures) or else in commonplace interiors (light switches, erasers, a pair of glasses, percolators, dressmaker's dummies, packaged sandwiches). "Natural" objects are rare (the tree of the third "Reflected Vision," [1] the tidal estuary of *Le Chemin du Retour*), immediately abstracted from man and nature alike, and

---

[1] See "Three Reflected Visions," *Evergreen Review* Vol. I, No. 3.

primarily represented as the instruments of an "optical" perception of the world.

All these objects are described with an application apparently out of all proportion to their insignificant — or at least purely functional — character. Description for Robbe-Grillet is always "anthological" — a matter of presenting the object as if in a mirror, as if it were in itself a *spectacle,* permitting it to make demands on our attention without regard for its relation to the dialectic of the story. The indiscrete object is simply *there*, enjoying the same freedom of exposition as one of Balzac's portraits, though without the same excuse of psychological necessity. Furthermore, Robbe-Grillet's descriptions are never allusive, never attempt, for all their aggregation of outlines and substances, to concentrate the entire significance of the object into a single metaphorical attribute (Racine: "Dans l'Orient *désert,* quel devint mon ennui." [2] Or Hugo: "Londres, une *rumeur* sous une *fumèe.*" [3]) His writing has no alibis, no resonance, no depth, keeping to the surface of things, examining without emphasis, favoring no one quality at the expense of another — it is as far as possible from poetry, or from "poetic" prose. It does not explode, this language, or explore, nor it is obliged to charge upon the object and pluck from the very heart of its substance the one ambiguous name that will sum it up forever. For Robbe-Grillet, the function of language is not a raid on the absolute, a violation of the abyss, but a progression of names over a surface, a patient unfolding that will gradually "paint" the object, caress it, and along its whole extent deposit a patina of tentative identifications, no single term of which could stand by itself for the presented object.

On the other hand, Robbe-Grillet's descriptive tech-

---

[2] In the *empty* Orient, how great my suffering became.

[3] London, a *murmur* beneath a *fog.*

nique has nothing in common with the painstaking artis-
anry of the naturalistic novelist. Traditionally, the latter
accumulates observations and instances qualities as a
function of an implicit judgment: the object has not only
form, but odor, tactile properties, associations, analogies
— it bristles with *signals* that have a thousand means of
gaining our attention, and never with impunity, since they
invariably involve a human impulse of appetency or rejection. But instead of the naturalist's syncretism of the
senses, which is anarchic yet ultimately oriented toward
judgment, Robbe-Grillet requires only one mode of
perception: the sense of sight. For him the object is no
longer a common-room of correspondences, a welter of
sensations and symbols, but merely the occasion of a certain optical resistance.

This preference for the visual enforces some curious
consequences, the primary one being that Robbe-Grillet's
object is never drawn in three dimensions, in depth: it
never conceals a secret, vulnerable heart beneath its
shell (and in our society is not the writer traditionally the
man who penetrates beneath the surface to the heart of
the matter?). But for Robbe-Grillet the object has no
being beyond *phenomenon*: it is not ambiguous, not allegorical, not even opaque, for opacity somehow implies a
corresponding transparency, a dualism in nature. The
scrupulosity with which Robbe-Grillet describes an object has nothing to do with such doctrinal matters: instead he establishes the existence of an object so that
once its appearance is described it will be quite drained,
consumed, used up. And if the author then lays it aside,
it is not out of any respect for rhetorical proportion, but
because the object has no further resistance than that of
its surfaces, and once these are exploited language must
withdraw from an engagement that can only be alien to
the object — henceforth a matter of mere literature, of
poetry or rhetoric. Robbe-Grillet's silence about the

"romantic" heart of the matter is neither allusive nor ritual, but *limiting*: forcibly determining the boundaries of a thing, not searching for what lies beyond them. A slice of tomato in an automat sandwich, described according to this method, constitutes an object without heredity, without associations, and without references, an object rigorously confined to the order of its components, and refusing with all the stubbornness of its *there*ness to involve the reader in an *elsewhere,* whether functional or substantial. "The human condition," Heidegger has said, "is to be *there."* Robbe-Grillet himself has quoted this remark apropos of *Waiting for Godot,* and it applies no less to his own objects, of which the chief condition, too, is to be *there.* The whole purpose of this author's work, in fact, is to confer upon an object its "being *there,"* to keep it from being "something."

Robbe-Grillet's object has therefore neither function nor substance. More precisely, both its function and substance are absorbed by its optical nature. For example, we would ordinarily say, "So-and-so's dinner was ready: some ham." This would be an adequate representation of the function of an object — the alimentary function of the ham. Here is how Robbe-Grillet says it: "On the kitchen table there are three thin slices of ham laid across a white plate." Here function is treacherously usurped by the object's sheer existence: thinness, position, and color establish it far less as an article of food than as a complex organization of space; far less in relation to its natural function (to be eaten) than as a point in a visual itinerary, a site in the murderer's route from object to object, from surface to surface. Robbe-Grillet's object, in fact, invariably possesses this mystifying, almost hoaxing power: its technological nature, so to speak, is immediately apparent, of course — the sandwiches are to be eaten, the erasers to rub out lines, the bridges to be crossed — it is never in itself remarkable, its *apparent* function readily makes it a part of the urban landscape or commonplace interior in which it is to be found. But the *description* of the object somehow exceeds its function in every case, and at the very moment we expect the author's interest to lapse, having exhausted the object's instrumentality, that interest persists, *insists,* bringing the narrative to a sudden, untimely halt and transforming a simple implement into space. Its usefulness, we discover, was merely an illusion, only its optical extension is real — its humanity begins where its function leaves off.

Substance, in Robbe-Grillet's work, suffers the same queer misappropriation. We must remember that for every writer of the nineteenth century — Flaubert is an excellent example — the "coenesthesia" of substance — its undifferentiated mass of organic sensation — is the source of all sensibility. Since the beginning of the romantic movement it has been possible to establish a kind of thematic index of substance for each writer precisely to the degree that an object is not visual for him but tactile, thereby involving his reader in a *visceral* sense of matter (appetite or nausea). For Robbe-Grillet, on the contrary, the supremacy of the visual, the sacrifice of all the "inner" attributes of an object to its "superficial" existence (consider, by the way, the moral discredit traditionally attached to this mode of perception) eliminates every chance of an effective or "humoral" relation with it. The sense of sight produces an existential impulse only to the degree that it serves as a shorthand for a sense of touch, of chewing, hiding, or burying. Robbe-Grillet, however, never permits the visual sense to be overrun by the visceral, but mercilessly severs it from its usual associations.

In the entire published work of this author, I can think of only one metaphor, a single adjective suggesting *substance* rather than superficies, and applied, moreover, to the only psychoanalytic object in his repertoire: the softness of erasers ("I want a very *soft* eraser"). Except for this unique tactile qualification, more or less called for by the peculiar gratuitousness of the object for which *The Erasers* is so scandalously or so enigmatically named, the work of Robbe-Grillet is susceptible to no thematic index whatsoever: the visual apprehension which entirely permeates his writing cannot establish metaphorical correspondences, or even institute reductions of qualities to some common symbol; it can, in fact, propose only symmetries.

By his exclusive and tyrannical appeal to the sense of sight, Robbe-Grillet undoubtedly intends the assassination of the object, at least as literature has traditionally represented it. His undertaking is an arduous one, however, for in literature, at least, we live, without even taking the fact into account, in a world based on an organic, not a visual order. Therefore the first step of this knowing murder must be to isolate objects, to alienate them as much from their usual functions as from our own biology. Our author allows them a merely *superficial* relation to their situation in space, deprives them of all possibility of metaphor, withdraws them from that state of corresponding forms and analogous states which has always been the poet's hunting ground (and who can be in much doubt today as to what extent the myth of poetic "power" has contaminated every order of literary activity?).

But what is most difficult to kill off in the classical treatment of the object is the temptation to use the particular term, the singular, the — one might almost say — *gestaltist* adjective that ties up all its metaphysical threads in a single subsuming knot ("Dans l'Orient *désert* . . ."). What Robbe-Grillet is trying to destroy is, in the widest sense of the word, the adjective itself: the realm of qualification, for him, can be only spatial or situational, but in no case can it be a matter of analogy. Perhaps painting can provide us (taking all the precautions this kind of comparison imposes) with a relevant opposition: an ideal example of the classical treatment of the object is the school of Dutch still-life painting, in which variety and minuteness of detail are made subservient to a dominant quality that transforms all the materials of vision into a single visceral sensation: *luster,* the sheen of things, for example, is the real subject matter of all those compositions of oysters and glasses and wine and silver so familiar in Dutch painting. One might describe the whole effect of this art as an attempt to endow its object with an adjectival *skin,* so that the half-visual, half-substantial glaze we ingest from these pictures by a kind of sixth, coenesthetic sense is no longer a question of surface, no longer "superficial." As if the painter had succeeded in furnishing the object with some warm name that dizzily seizes us, clings to us, and implicates us in its continuity until we perceive the homogeneous texture of a new ideal substance woven from the superlative qualities of all possible matter. This, too, is the secret of Baudelaire's admirable rhetoric, in which each name, summoned from the most discrepant orders of being, surrenders its tribute of ideal sensation to a universal perception of *radiant* matter ("Mais les bijoux perdus de la mer," etc.[4]).

In opposition to this concept, Robbe-Grillet's description of an object finds its analogies with modern painting (in its broadest acceptation), for the latter has abandoned the qualification of space by substance in favor of a simultaneous "reading" of the planes and perspectives of its subject, thereby restoring the object to its "essential bareness." Robbe-Grillet destroys the object's dominion-by-substance because it would frustrate his major intention, which is to insert the object in a dialectic of space. Not that this space is Euclidean — the extreme care Robbe-

---

[4] But the lost jewels of ancient Palmyra, the unknown metals, the pearls of the sea. . . .

Grillet takes to situate the object in a proliferation of perspectives, to find within the elasticity of our field of vision a singularly fragile point of resistance, has nothing whatever to do with the classic concern to establish the dimensions and depths of academic perspective.

It will be recalled that according to the classical concept of description, a picture is always a motionless spectacle, a *site* frozen into eternity: the spectator (or the reader) has accorded the painter power of attorney to circulate around the object, to explore with his delegated eyes its shadows and — to use Poussin's word — its "prospect," thereby effecting the simultaneity of all possible approaches, since every spectator after the painter himself must look at the picture with the painter's eyes. This is the source of the imaginary supremacy of the spectator's "situation" in classical painting (so clearly expressed by the very nomenclature of its orientations: "on the right . . . to the left . . . in the foreground . . . in the background . . ."). The descriptive technique of modern painting, however, nails the *spectator* to a single place and releases the *spectacle* upon him, adjusting it to several angles of vision at once. It has often been remarked that modern canvases seem to leap from the wall, rushing out at the spectator, overwhelming him by their aggressive pre-emption of space: the painting is no longer a prospect, then, but a "project." And this is precisely the effect of Robbe-Grillet's descriptions. They set themselves in motion spatially, the object is released without losing sight of its earlier positions, and somehow, for a moment, exists in depth without ceasing to be merely flat. There is recognizably the same revolution at work here that the cinema has effected upon the visual reflexes.

In *The Erasers,* in fact, Robbe-Grillet has had the coquetry to include one scene in which a man's relation to this new space is described in an exemplary fashion. Bona is sitting in the middle of a vast, empty room, and he describes the field of space before his eyes: it includes the window, behind which he can make out a horizon of roofs and moving clouds, so that the spatial field actually moves past the motionless man; space becomes non-Euclidean while remaining just as it was. In this little scene, furthermore, we have all the experimental conditions of cinematographic vision: the cubical room as the theater; its bareness as the darkness requisite to the emergence of the new, motionless vision; and the window, of course, as the screen itself, flat and yet accessible to every dimension of movement, even that of time.

Of course all this is not, ordinarily, vouchsafed to us *just like that*. Robbe-Grillet's camera is also something of a magic lantern, a real camera obscura. For example, consider the persistence with which this author arranges the elements of his picture according to the classic orientation of the imaginary spectator. Like any traditional scenario-writer, he throws in a good many *on the right's* and *to the left's,* whose propulsive role in academic composition we have just examined. But in the case of Robbe-Grillet, such purely adverbial terms indicate nothing at all: linguistically, of course, they are gestural commands and have no more dimension than a cybernetic message. It has, perhaps, been one of the grand illusions of classical rhetoric to believe that a scene's verbal orientation has any power of suggestion or representation whatever. In literature, beyond a certain crudely operative procedure (in the theater), these notions are completely interchangeable and, of course, quite useless, having no other excuse for existing except to justify the spectator's ideal mobility.

If Robbe-Grillet chooses, with all the deliberation of a good craftsman, to employ such devices, it is in the cause of mockery, in behalf of the destruction of classical space and the dispersion of concrete substance, the high-pressure volatilization of a supersaturated universe, an over-constructed space. His multiplication of details, his obsession with topography, his entire demonstrative apparatus actually tend to destroy the object's unity by giving it an exaggeratedly precise location in space, by drowning it in a deluge of outlines, coordinates, and orientations, by the eventual abuse of perspective — still under its academic denominations — by exploding the traditional notion of space and substituting for it a new space, provided, as we shall soon see, with a new depth and dimension in time.

Robbe-Grillet's descriptive strategy, then, can be summarized as follows: destroy Baudelaire by an absurd appeal to Lamartine, and at the same time, of course, destroy Lamartine (the comparison is not entirely gratuitous, if you agree that our literary "sensibility" is wholly adjusted by ancestral reflexes to a "Lamartinian" vision of space). Robbe-Grillet's analyses, minute and patient enough to be taken for imitations of Flaubert or Balzac, unceasingly corrode the object by their very precision, attack the adjectival skin classical art deposits on a picture to induce in its spectator the euphoria of a restored unity. The classic object fatally secretes its adjective (the Dutch *luster,* the Racinian *désert,* Baudelaire's *radiant* substance), and it is just such a fatality which Robbe-Grillet is hunting down, subjecting it to the anticoagulating effects of his own description. At any cost this skin, this carapace must be destroyed, the object must be kept "open" to the circulation of its new dimension: Time.

To understand the temporal nature of the characteristic Robbe-Grillet object, we must observe the mutations he compels it to undergo, and here again confront the revolutionary nature of his endeavors with the norm of classical description. The latter, of course, has had its means of subjecting objects to the forces of breakdown and collapse. But always in such a way that the object, so firmly settled within its space or its substance, merely encountered a sort of Ulterior Necessity that fell upon it from the

Empyrean. The classical concept of time has no other countenance than that of the Destroyer of perfection (Chronos with his scythe). For Balzac, for Flaubert, for Baudelaire, for Proust himself (the mode merely inverted), the object is the hero of a melodrama, decaying, disappearing, or rediscovering its final glory, ultimately participating in a real eschatology of matter. One might say the classical object is nothing but the archetype of its own ruin, forever opposing its spatial essence to the action of an ulterior (and therefore exterior) Time which operates as a destiny, not as an internal dimension.

The classical concept of time thus inevitably encounters the classical object as its catastrophe or its deliquescence. The mutability Robbe-Grillet accords his objects is of an altogether different kind — a mutability of which the *process* is invisible: an object, described for the first time at a certain moment in the novel's progress, reappears later on, but with a barely perceptible difference. It is a difference of a situational or spatial order — what was on the right, for example, is now on the left. Time dislocates space, arranging the object like a series of slices that almost completely cover one another: and it is this spatial "almost" which contains the temporal dimension of Robbe-Grillet's object. It is the kind of variation crudely — but recognizably — indicated from frame to frame in old films, or from drawing to drawing in a comic strip.

Thus we can readily understand the profound motive that has compelled this novelist to represent his object from what must always be a *point of view*. Sight is the only sense in which continuity is sustained by the addition of tiny but integral units: space can be constructed only from *completed* variations. Visually it is impossible for a man to participate in the *internal process* of dilapidation — no matter how fine you slice the units of decay, he cannot see in them anything but their effects. The visual dispensation of the object is the only one that can include within it a *forgotten* time, perceived by its effects rather than by its duration, and hence deprived of its pathos.

The whole endeavor of Robbe-Grillet has been to locate his object in a space provided in advance with these points of mutation, so that it seems merely out of joint rather than actually in the process of decay. The neon sign on the Gare Montparnasse would be a good object for Robbe-Grillet because its presented complexity of structure is entirely visual in effect, composed of a certain number of *sites* which have no other freedom but to annihilate themselves or change places. On the other hand, it is easy to conceive of things that would be bad objects for Robbe-Grillet: a lump of sugar dipped in water and gradually melting down (furnishing geographers their image of erosion) — here the continuity of decay would be inacceptable to Robbe-Grillet's intentions, since it restores a sense of the menace of time, the contagion of matter. On the contrary. Robbe-Grillet's objects never decay: they mystify or they disappear; time is never a corruption or even a catastrophe, but merely a change of place, a hideout for data.

The point is most explicitly made in his "Three Reflected Visions," where Robbe-Grillet uses the phenomenon of mirror reflection to account for this kind of break in the temporal circuit: imagine the motionless changes of orientation produced by a mirror-image as being somehow decomposed and distributed throughout a certain period of time and you have the art of Alain Robbe-Grillet. But of course the virtual insertion of time into the vision of the object is an ambiguous matter: Robbe-Grillet's objects may have a temporal dimension, yet the concept of time in which they exist is scarcely a classical one — it is an unwonted sort of time, a time *for nothing*. If there is a sense in which Robbe-Grillet has restored time to his object, it would be nearer the truth to say that the kind of time he has restored is one in which an affirmative can be expressed only by a negative, a positive only by its contrary. Or better still, if more paradoxically, one might say that Robbe-Grillet has given his objects movement without that movement having taken place in time.

I have no intention of detailing the plot of *The Erasers* (Robbe-Grillet's first novel) here, but I cannot resist pointing out that this book is the story of a circular sense of time which somehow cancels itself out after having led its men and its objects along an itinerary at the end of which they find themselves *almost the same* as when they started. Everything happens as if the whole story were reflected in a mirror which sets what is actually on the right on the apparent left, and conversely, so that the "plot" development is nothing more than a mirror-image spaced out over a period of twenty-four hours. For the knitting-together of the parts to become truly significant, of course, the point of departure must be unusual, even sensational. Hence the detective-story nature of this novel in which the "almost-the-same" qualities of the *mirror-image* consist in the corpse's change of identity.

Thus even the plot of *The Erasers* enlarges this same ovoid (or overlooked) time that Robbe-Grillet has introduced among his objects. One might call it a mirror time — specular time. The development is even more flagrant, of course, in *Le Chemin de Retour,* in which sidereal time (in this case, the rhythm of the tide), by changing the shape of the land surrounding a tidal basin, represents the very gesture that causes the reflected object to succeed the direct one, welding them together where they meet. The tide modifies the hiker's field of vision as a mirror-image reverses the orientation of space — right becoming left, etc. Except that while the tide is rising, the hiker is on an offshore island, absent and unaware of the *duration* of the change: time *takes place* between parentheses. This

23

intermittent withdrawal is the definitive and central act of Robbe-Grillet's experiment: to keep man from participating in or even witnessing the *fabrication* or the *becoming* of objects, and ultimately to exile the world to the life of its own surface.

His endeavor is decisive to the degree that it has affected the one literary "substance" which still enjoys the privileges of the classic point of view: the object. Not that other contemporary writers have not already concerned themselves with this very problem, some of them to good effect — we have Cayrol, we have Ponge as our most notable examples. But Robbe-Grillet's method is more extreme and more experimental, for he intends nothing less than a definitive interrogation of the object, a cross-examination from which all lyric impulses are rigorously excluded. To find a comparable strictness of procedure, one must turn to modern painting, where the rational destruction of the classical object may readily be discerned in all its anguish. Robbe-Grillet is important because he has attacked the last bastion of the traditional art of writing: the organization of literary space. His struggles parallel in significance those of surrealism with rationalism, of the avant-garde theater (Beckett, Ionesco, Adamov) with the conventions of the middle-class stage.

Yet his solutions owe nothing to these corresponding conflicts. Robbe-Grillet's destruction of the classical concept of space is neither oneiric nor irrational; it is based on an entirely new notion of the structure of matter and movement. The proper analogy is neither the Freudian universe, nor the Newtonian — we must face instead an intellectual complex derived from contemporary art and science — from the new physics and the cinema. This can be only roughly sketched out, for here as in so many fields, we have no History of Forms. And since we lack as well an Esthetic of the Novel (by which I mean a history of its dispensation by its creators), we can only assign

Robbe-Grillet a purely approximate place in the evolution of the form. Let us remember once again the traditional background against which his struggles are enacted: the novel was secularly instituted as an experiment in depth: social depth with Balzac and Zola, "psychological" with Flaubert, memorial with Proust — in every case the degree of man's or society's *inwardness* has determined the novel's field of action. The novelist's task has been, correspondingly, a labor of locating, quarrying, and excavating in the dark. This endoscopic function has been sustained by a concomitant myth of a human essence *at the bottom of things* (if he can only dig deep enough), and is now so natural to the form that it is tempting to define its exercise (reading *or* writing) as what skin-divers call a delirium of the depths.

Robbe-Grillet's purpose, like that of some of his contemporaries — Cayrol and Pinget, for example, though in another direction — is to establish the novel on the surface: once you can set its inner nature, its "interiority," between parentheses, then objects in space, and the circulation of men among them, are promoted to the rank of subjects. The novel becomes man's direct experience of what surrounds him without his being able to shield himself with a psychology, a metaphysic, or a psychoanalytic method in his combat with the objective world he discovers. The novel is no longer a chthonian revelation, the book of hell, but of the earth — requiring that we no longer look at the world with the eyes of a confessor, of a doctor, or of God himself (all significant hypostases of the classical novelist), but with the eyes of a man walking in his city with no other horizon than the scene before him, no other power than that of his own eyes.

—Translated by Richard Howard

A NOTE ON *JEALOUSY*

by Anne Minor

In a witty article published in the January 1959 number of *La Revue de Paris* under the title "Le Cas de Robbe-Grillet," Denise Bourdet describes her visit to the young writer. She accounts "in the author's manner" for the precise details of construction, arrangement, dimension, and movement which define the site, the apartment house, the hallway, the elevator — in a word, the entire distance covered to the door of Robbe-Grillet's apartment, or more exactly to the door mat on which she wipes her feet, accidentally kicking it against the door, making a noise which announces her arrival and immediately provokes the appearance of Robbe-Grillet in his red sweater. One can imagine a game in which the players would have to guess which passage of this account is by the author and which by the imitator, so cleverly done is this exercise in Robbe-Grillet's style.

Are we to conclude that any gifted author can write like Robbe-Grillet, that his style is the model of a "genre," as the acting of Madeleine Renaud or Maurice Escande can serve as a model for a student graduating from the Conservatory? In other words, is Robbe-Grillet's style a method, or is it the valid, the irreplaceable and sole mode of expression suitable to the author's enterprise? To answer, let us reread his novel *Jealousy*. The action, or the absence of action, takes place in a tropical climate, in a

27

bungalow overlooking banana plantations, a stream on whose bank the natives are slowly shifting the tree trunks intended to rebuild a bridge, and a road leading to the town.

Five characters animate the narrative. First of all the narrator himself, or rather — since at no moment does he appear in the first person — his gaze, both impassive and tense, which takes the reader among the locales of an observation sometimes direct and sometimes reconstructed in the narrator's memory. The second and third characters are the narrator's wife, called A, and a neighbor, a planter named Franck who is seen alternately on the veranda, sitting at table in the white-walled dining room, at the wheel of his car. Christiane, Franck's wife, appears only in conversational references; she stays at home, taking care of her child. The houseboy, a mechanized character who obey's A's orders, brings the lamp, serves and clears the table, asks questions but does not wait to hear answers. Nothing happens. In the evening, in the silence and the darkness, the noise of the crickets or the cries of nocturnal beasts of prey can be heard — cries which express nothing but "the existence, the position, and the movements of each animal."

A and Franck are sitting in comfortable armchairs, their arms resting on the arms of the chairs, their hands parallel, motionless. Conversation? The narrator suggests one or two themes — commentaries by A and Franck on a novel with an African decor; the account of motor trouble. One day Franck announces a plan to go to town to buy a truck and visit certain agents: A will accompany him, to make several purchases. A and Franck have left in the car for town, 50 kilometers from the plantation, at six one morning. They were scheduled to return around midnight. Motor trouble has kept them from doing so, and they have spent the night at a hotel. Upon their return, they have offered no details. The next day, or perhaps two weeks or a month earlier — the narrator no longer knows — A and Franck are sitting at table. A notices a centipede on the white wall of the dining room. Franck gets up, wads his napkin and squashes the insect. The black stain remains on the wall, a few stumps of its limbs litter the tile floor. A watches, her clenched fist closes over her knife. The horror inspired by the insect, Franck's sadistic gesture, the motionless presence of the two observers — everything contributes to giving this incident the scope of a symbolic prefiguration. We are beholding the gesture of murder. Who has been killed? Who will be the killer?

But the observer turns to his task: he sees what his gaze chooses to include, he does more than observe — he measures distances, counts objects, specifies the structure of the house, the shape and orientation of the veranda, the garden, the courtyard, the green mass of the banana groves, he lists the trees and the plants and, turning to regard the people, seems to film their movements, to record their remarks. And then, as though to account for an unexpressed doubt, begins all over again, trains this invisible mechanism — his gaze — and records once again, scrutinizes, enumerates, collects. Thus there reappear at different times, in skillful rhythm of repetitions: on the bank of the stream, the crouching native, "leaning over the liquid surface of the muddy river," A's tapering fingers brushing her black curls or offering Franck, on the veranda, a glass filled to the brim. By a kind of enchantment, the reader gradually identifies himself with this gaze and breathlessly follows the slow, tormenting progress of jealousy. Is this a kind of justifying evidence? We reach the paroxysm, we lie in wait for the criminal, but nothing happens except the return to the miniscule details and their undecipherable mystery. From the position of A and of Franck, from their fugitive smiles, from the description of the hallway, of the office whose doors open onto the terrace, the reader reconstructs the scenes, the characters.

Thus without knowing how, and despite the irritation provoked by a deliberately systematic, supposedly objective description in which distances, depths, shadows are defined in the terms of a geometrician, an architect, an engineer, or an agronomist, we share in fear, in the obsessive need to know. As in Van Gogh's last paintings, the images turn, circling in the reader's head as in the narrator's. The centipede, the extended hands, the motor breakdown, Christiane's absence, A's swaying gait in the courtyard, the morning of the return . . . the centipede . . . the hands . . .

We close the book, we know that after this anything can happen, that the narrator can kill Franck, or perhaps it is Franck who will kill him, or else nothing will happen — the protagonists will remain the same, they will keep on sitting in their armchairs, arms and hands outstretched: the houseboy will serve the iced drinks; the banana groves will extend in front of the veranda with its trees planted in quincunxes; we will see the stream with its muddy water, the natives crouching near the logs. . . .

We wondered at the beginning of these lines what we were to think of the very special form a Robbe-Grillet novel assumes. There has been talk of a new realism, and Robbe-Grillet himself has discussed the necessity of allowing the object its own identity, of avoiding any humanization. But other reasons which relate more closely to the content of the work explain perhaps why the writer chooses to measure, to situate, to define with a rigor that seems to exceed the context of a literary work. It is because, in fact, the narrator seeks to convince himself of his own objectivity. If he uses technical and specific terms in the description of objects, trees, or characters, this is perhaps chiefly to assure himself of his own *sang-froid*, to be able to convince himself: "I am not mad, I am not suffering from an *idée fixe,* I have no prejudices; I am sane, calm, merely observing, I only say what I see, I only see what exists."

But perhaps, too, he is merely trying to divert himself, to exorcise an *idée fixe,* to give himself something to do, like someone tired of waiting and counting his steps as he paces back and forth on the road. And then, finally, is he not, by means of this exercise, about to discover a flaw in the supposed certainty of the figures or facts observed? Then doubt would give way to hope.

Thus the style of this novel which has been characterized as "icy and poignant" corresponds to the author's enterprise. At every moment, it translates the double level on which the work functions: the observation which has all the appearances of objectivity; the torment which reaches the point of obsession. A wager, certainly, but the fact is there: the author brings off his impossible demonstration: we have lived his anguish with him; we do not know, when we close this book, if the crime has been committed, or if each person is to return to his place, to act as if nothing had happened, while the narrator endlessly pursues his futile investigation.

— Translated by Richard Howard

JEALOUSY

CONTENTS

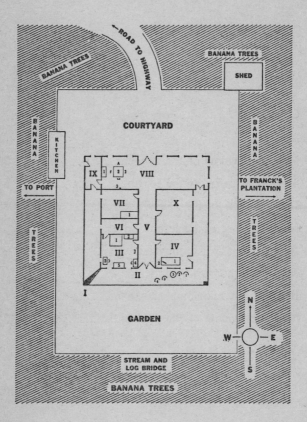

LEGEND

   I. Southwest pillar and its shadow at the beginning of the novel.

  II. Veranda: 1) Franck's chair. 2) A . . .'s chair. 3) Empty chair. 5) Cocktail table.

 III. A. . .'s room: 1) Bed. 2) Chest. 3) Dressing table. 4) Writing table. 5) Wardrobe.

  IV. Office: 1) Desk. 2) Photograph of A . . .

   V. Hallway

  VI. Bathroom

 VII. Small bedroom: 1) Bed.

VIII. Living room — dining room: 1) Sideboard. 2) Table. 3) Mark of centipede on wall.

  IX. Pantry.

   X. Storage room or other (not described).

Now the shadow of the column—the column which supports the southwest corner of the roof—divides the corresponding corner of the veranda into two equal parts. This veranda is a wide, covered gallery surrounding the house on three sides. Since its width is the same for the central portion as for the sides, the line of shadow cast by the column extends precisely to the corner of the house; but it stops there, for only the veranda flagstones are reached by the sun, which is still too high in the sky. The wooden walls of the house—that is, its front and west gable-end—are still protected from the sun by the roof (common to the house proper and the terrace). So at this moment the shadow of the outer edge of the roof coincides exactly with the right angle formed by the terrace and the two vertical surfaces of the corner of the house.

Now A . . . has come into the bedroom by the inside door opening onto the central hallway. She does not look at the wide open window through which—from the door—she would see this corner of the terrace. Now she has turned back toward the door to close it behind her. She still has on the light-colored, close-fitting dress with the high collar that she was wearing at lunch when Christiane reminded her again that loose-fitting clothes make the heat easier to bear. But A . . . merely smiled: she never suffered from the heat, she had known much worse climates than this—in Africa, for instance—and had always felt fine there. Besides, she doesn't feel the cold either. Wherever she is, she keeps quite comfortable. The black curls of her hair shift with a supple movement and brush her shoulders as she turns her head.

The heavy hand-rail of the balustrade has almost no

paint left on top. The gray of the wood shows through, streaked with tiny longitudinal cracks. On the other side of this rail, a good six feet below the level of the veranda, the garden begins.

But from the far side of the bedroom the eye carries over the balustrade and touches ground only much further away, on the opposite slope of the little valley, among the banana trees of the plantation. The sun cannot be seen between their thick clusters of wide green leaves. However, since this sector has been under cultivation only recently, the regular criss-crossing of the rows of trees can still be clearly followed. The same is true of almost all the property visible from here, for the older sectors—where confusion has gained the ascendancy—are located higher up on this side of the valley, that is, on the other side of the house.

It is on the other side, too, that the highway passes, just below the edge of the plateau. This highway, the only road that gives access to the property, marks its northern border. A dirt road leads from the highway to the sheds and, lower still, to the house, in front of which a large cleared area with a very slight slope permits cars to be turned around.

The house is built on a level with this courtyard, from which it is separated by no veranda or gallery. On the three other sides, however, it is enclosed by the veranda.

The slope of the terrain, more pronounced starting from the courtyard, causes the central portion of the veranda (which runs along the front of the house on the south) to stand at least six feet above the garden.

On all sides of the garden, as far as the borders of the plantation, stretches the green mass of the banana trees.

On the right and the left, their proximity is too great, combined with the veranda's relative lack of elevation, to permit an observer stationed there to distinguish the arrangement of the trees; while further down the valley, the quincunx can be made out at first glance. In certain very recently replanted sectors—those where the reddish earth is just beginning to yield supremacy to foliage—it is easy enough to follow the regular perspective of the four intersecting lanes along which the young trunks are aligned.

This exercise is not much more difficult, despite their more advanced growth, for those sectors of the plantation on the opposite hillside: this, in fact, is the place which offers itself most readily to inspection, the place over which surveillance can be maintained with the least difficulty (although the path to reach it is a long one), the place which the eye falls on quite naturally, of its own accord, when looking out of one or the other of the two open windows of the bedroom.

Her back to the hall door she has just closed, A . . . absently stares at the paint-flaked wood of the balustrade, nearer her the paint-flaked window frame, then, nearer still, the scrubbed wood of the floor.

She takes a few steps into the room, goes over to the heavy chest and opens its top drawer. She shifts the papers in the right-hand side of the drawer, leans over and, in order to see the rear of the drawer better, pulls it a little further out of the chest. After looking a little longer, she straightens up and remains motionless, elbows close to her body, forearms bent and hidden by the upper part of her body—probably holding a sheet of paper between her hands.

She turns toward the light now in order to continue reading without straining her eyes. Her inclined profile does not move any more. The paper is pale blue, the size of ordinary letter paper, and shows the creases where it has been folded into quarters.

Then, holding the letter in one hand, A . . . closes the drawer, moves toward the little work table (near the second window, against the partition separating the bedroom from the hallway) and sits down in front of the writing-case from which she removes a sheet of pale blue paper—similar to the first, but blank. She unscrews the cap of her pen, then, after a glance to the right (which does not include even the middle of the window-frame behind her), bends her head toward the writing-case in order to begin writing.

The lustrous black hair falls in motionless curls along the line of her back which the narrow metal fastening of her dress indicates a little lower down.

Now the shadow of the column—the column which supports the southwest corner of the roof—lengthens across the flagstones of this central part of the veranda, in front of the house where the chairs have been set out for the evening. Already the tip of the line of shadow almost touches the doorway which marks the center of the façade. Against the west gable-end of the house, the sun falls on the wood about a yard and a half above the flagstone. Through the third window, which looks out on this side, it would reach far into the bedroom if the blinds had not been lowered.

The pantry is at the other end of this west wing of the veranda. Through its half-open door can be heard A . . .'s voice, then that of the black cook, voluble and singsong, then again the clear, moderate voice, giving orders for the evening meal.

The sun has disappeared behind the rocky spur that ends the main section of the plateau.

Sitting facing the valley, in one of the armchairs of local manufacture, A . . . is reading the novel borrowed the day before; they have already spoken about it at noon. She continues reading, without raising her eyes, until the daylight becomes too faint. Then she raises her head, closes the book—which she puts within arm's reach on the low table—and remains staring straight in front of her, toward the openwork balustrade and the banana trees on the opposite slope, soon invisible in the darkness. She seems to be listening to the noise that rises on all sides from the thousands of crickets inhabiting the low ground. But it is a continuous, ear-splitting sound without variations, in which nothing can be distinguished.

Franck is here again for dinner, smiling, talkative,

affable. Christiane has not come with him this time; she has stayed home with the child, who is running a slight fever. It is not unusual, these days, for her husband to come without her like this: because of the child, because of Christiane's own ailments—for her health has difficulty adapting itself to this hot, humid climate—and also because of her domestic problems, her difficulties managing her too numerous and poorly organized servants.

Tonight, though, A . . . seemed to expect her. At least she had had four places set. She gives orders to have the one that will not be used taken away at once.

On the veranda, Franck drops into one of the low armchairs and utters his usual exclamation as to how comfortable they are. They are very simple chairs of wood and leather thongs, made according to A . . .'s instructions by a native craftsman. She leans toward Franck to hand him his glass.

Although it is quite dark now, she has given orders that the lamps should not be brought out, for—she says—they attract mosquitoes. The glasses are filled almost to the brim with a mixture of cognac and soda in which a little cube of ice is floating. In order to avoid the danger of upsetting the glasses in the darkness, A . . . has moved as near as possible to the armchair Franck is sitting in, her right hand carefully extending the glass with his drink in it. She rests her other hand on the arm of the chair and bends over him, so close that their heads touch. He murmurs a few words: probably thanking her.

She straightens up gracefully, picks up the third glass —which she is not afraid of spilling, for it is much less full—and sits down beside Franck, while he continues telling the story about his engine trouble, which he had begun the moment he arrived.

It was A . . . who arranged the chairs this evening, when she had them brought out on the veranda. The one she invited Franck to sit in and her own are side by side against the wall of the house—backs against this wall, of course—

43

beneath the office window. So that Franck's chair is on her left, and on her right—but farther forward—the little table where the bottles are. The two other chairs are placed on the other side of this table, still farther to the right, so that they do not block the view of the first two through the balustrade of the veranda. For the same reason these last two chairs are not turned to face the rest of the group: they have been set at an angle, obliquely oriented toward the openwork balustrade and the hillside opposite. This arrangement obliges anyone sitting there to turn his head around sharply toward the left if he wants to see A . . . —especially anyone in the fourth chair, which is the far-thest away.

The third, which is a folding chair made of canvas stretched on a metal frame, occupies a distinctly retired position between the fourth chair and the table. But it is this chair, less comfortable, which has remained empty.

Franck's voice continues describing the day's problems on his own plantation. A . . . seems to be interested in them. She encourages him from time to time by a few words indicating her attention. During a pause the sound of a glass being put down on the little table can be heard.

On the other side of the balustrade, toward the opposite hillside, there is only the sound of the crickets and the starless dark of the night.

In the dining room the two kerosene lamps are lit. One is at the edge of the long sideboard, toward its left end; the other on the table itself, in the empty place of the fourth guest.

The table is square, since extra leaves (unnecessary for so few people) have not been added. The three places set are on three sides, the lamp on the fourth. A . . . is at her usual place; Franck is sitting at her right—therefore with his back to the sideboard.

On the sideboard, to the left of the second lamp (that is, on the side of the open pantry door), are piled the clean plates which will be used during the meal. To the right of the lamp and behind it—against the wall—a native pitcher of terracotta marks the middle of the sideboard. Farther to the right, against the gray-painted wall, is outlined the magnified and blurred shadow of a man's head—Franck's. He is wearing neither jacket nor tie, and the collar of his shirt is unbuttoned; but the shirt itself is irreproachably white, made of a thin material of high quality, the French cuffs held together by detachable ivory links.

A . . . is wearing the same dress she wore at lunch. Franck almost had an argument with his wife about it, when Christiane criticized its cut as being "too hot for this country." A . . . merely smiled: "Besides, I don't find the climate here so bad as all that," she said, to change the subject. "If you could imagine how hot it was ten months out of the year in Kanda! . . ." Then the conversation had settled for a while on Africa.

The boy comes in through the open pantry door, holding the tureen full of soup in both hands. As soon as he puts it down, A . . . asks him to move the lamp on the table, whose glare—she says—hurts her eyes. The boy lifts the lamp by the handle and carries it to the other end of the room, setting it down on a piece of furniture A . . . points to with her left hand.

The table is immediately plunged into shadow. Its chief source of light has become the lamp on the sideboard, for the second lamp—in the opposite direction—is now much farther away.

On the wall, toward the pantry door, Franck's head has disappeared. His white shirt no longer gleams as it did just now beneath the direct light of the lamp on the table. Only his right sleeve is reached by the beams of the lamp three quarters of the way behind him: the shoulder and the arm are edged with a bright line, and similarly, higher up, the ear and neck. His face has the light almost directly behind it.

"Don't you think that's better?" A . . . asks, turning toward him.

45

"Certainly more *intime*," Franck answers.

He drinks his soup in rapid spoonfuls. Although he makes no excessive gestures, although he holds his spoon quite properly and swallows the liquid without making any noise, he seems to display, in this modest task, a disproportionate energy and zest. It would be difficult to specify exactly in what way he is neglecting some essential rule, at what particular point he is lacking in discretion.

Avoiding any notable defect, his behavior, nevertheless, does not pass unnoticed. And, by contrast, it accentuates the fact that A . . . has just completed the same operation without having seemed to move—but without attracting any attention, on the other hand, by an abnormal immobility. It takes a glance at her empty though stained plate to discover that she has not neglected to serve herself.

Memory succeeds, moreover, in reconstituting several movements of her right hand and her lips, several comings and goings of the spoon between the plate and her mouth, which might be considered as significant.

To be still more certain, it is enough to ask her if she doesn't think the cook has made the soup too salty.

"Oh no," she answers, "you have to eat salt so as not to sweat."

Which, on reflection, does not prove beyond a doubt that she tasted the soup today.

Now the boy clears away the plates. It then becomes impossible to check again the stains in A . . .'s plate—or their absence, if she has not served herself.

The conversation has returned to the story of the engine trouble: in the future Franck will not buy any more old military matériel; his latest acquisitions have given him too many problems; the next time he replaces one of his vehicles, it will be with a new one.

But he is wrong to trust modern trucks to the Negro drivers, who will wreck them just as fast, if not faster.

"All the same," Franck says, "if the motor is new, the driver will not have to fool with it."

Yet he should know that just the opposite is true: the new motor will be all the more attractive a toy, and what with speeding on bad roads and acrobatics behind the wheel . . .

On the strength of his three years' experience, Franck believes there are good drivers, even among the Negroes here. A . . . is also of this opinion, of course.

She has kept out of the discussion about the comparative quality of the machines, but the question of the drivers provokes a rather long and categorical intervention on her part.

Besides, she might be right. In that case, Franck would have to be right too.

Both are now talking about the novel A . . . is reading, whose action takes place in Africa. The heroine cannot bear the tropical climate (like Christiane). The heat actually seems to give her terrible attacks:

"It's all mental, things like that," Franck says.

He then makes a reference, obscure for anyone who has not even leafed through the book, to the husband's behavior. His sentence ends with "take apart" or "take a part," without its being possible to be sure who or what is meant. Franck looks at A . . ., who is looking at Franck. She gives him a quick smile that is quickly absorbed in the shadows. She has understood, since she knows the story.

No, her features have not moved. Their immobility is not so recent: the lips have remained set since her last words. The fugitive smile must have been a reflection of the lamp, or the shadow of a moth.

Besides, she was no longer facing Franck at that moment. She had just moved her head back and was looking straight ahead of her down the table, toward the bare wall where a blackish spot marks the place where a centipede was squashed last week, at the beginning of the month, perhaps the month before, or later.

Franck's face, with the light almost directly behind it, does not reveal the slightest expression.

The boy comes in to clear away the plates. A. . . . asks him, as usual, to serve the coffee on the veranda.

Here the darkness is complete. No one talks any more. The sound of the crickets has stopped. Only the shrill cry of some nocturnal carnivore can be heard from time to time, and the sudden drone of a beetle, the clink of a little porcelain cup being set on the low table.

Franck and A . . . have sat down in their same two chairs, backs against the wooden wall of the house. It is once again the chair with the metal frame which has remained unoccupied. The position of the fourth chair is still less justified, now that there is no view over the valley. (Even before dinner, during the brief twilight, the apertures of the balustrade were too narrow to permit a real view of the landscape; and above the hand-rail nothing but sky could be seen.)

The wood of the balustrade is smooth to the touch, when the fingers follow the direction of the grain and the tiny longitudinal cracks. A scaly zone comes next; then there is another smooth surface, but this time without lines of orientation and stippled here and there with slight roughnesses in the paint.

In broad daylight, the contrast of the two shades of gray—that of the naked wood and that, somewhat lighter, of the remaining paint—creates complicated figures with angular, almost serrated outlines. On the top of the hand-rail, there are only scattered, protruding islands formed by the last vestiges of paint. On the balusters, though, it is the unpainted areas, much smaller and generally located toward the middle of the uprights, which constitute the spots, here incised, where the fingers recognize the vertical grain of the wood. At the edge of the patches, new scales of the paint are easy to chip off; it is enough to slip a fingernail beneath the projecting edge and pry it up by bending the first joint of the finger; the resistance is scarcely perceptible.

On the other side of the veranda, once the eye is accustomed to the darkness, a paler form can be seen outlined against the wall of the house: Franck's white shirt. His forearms are lying on the elbow-rests. The upper part of his body is leaning back in the chair.

A . . . is humming a dance tune whose words remain unintelligible. But perhaps Franck understands them, if he already knows them, from having heard them often, perhaps with her. Perhaps it is one of her favorite records.

A . . .'s arms, a little less distinct than her neighbor's because of the color—though light—of the material of her dress, are also lying on the elbow-rests of her chair. The four hands are lying in a row, motionless. The space between A . . .'s left hand and Franck's right hand is approximately two inches. The shrill cry of some nocturnal carnivore, sharp and short, echoes again toward the bottom of the valley, at an unspecifiable distance.

"I think I'll be getting along," Franck says.

"Oh don't go," A . . . replies at once, "it's not late at all. It's so pleasant sitting out here."

If Franck wanted to leave, he would have a good excuse: his wife and child who are alone in the house. But he mentions only the hour he must get up the next morning, without making any reference to Christiane. The same shrill, short cry, which sounds closer, now seems to come from the garden, quite near the foot of the veranda on the east side.

As if echoing it, a similar cry follows, coming from the opposite direction. Others answer these, from higher up, toward the road; then still others, from the low ground.

Sometimes the sound is a little lower, or more prolonged. There are probably different kinds of animals. Still, all these cries are alike; not that their common characteristic is easy to decide, but rather their common lack of characteristics: they do not seem to be cries of fright, or pain, or intimidation, or even love. They sound like mechanical cries, uttered without perceptible motive, expressing nothing, indicating only the existence, the position, and the

49

respective movements of each animal, whose trajectory through the night they punctuate.

"All the same," Franck says, "I think I'll be getting along."

A . . . does not reply. Neither one has moved. They are sitting side by side, leaning back in their chairs, arms lying on the elbow-rests, their four hands in similar positions, at the same level, lined up parallel to the wall of the house.

Now the shadow of the southwest column—at the corner of the veranda on the bedroom side—falls across the garden. The sun, still low in the eastern sky, rakes the valley from the side. The rows of banana trees, growing at an angle to the direction of the valley, are everywhere quite distinct in this light.

From the bottom to the upper edge of the highest sectors, on the hillside facing the one the house is built on, it is relatively easy to count the trees; particularly opposite the house, thanks to the recent plantings of the patches located in this area.

The valley has been cleared over the greater part of its width here: there remains, at present, nothing but a border of brush (some thirty yards across at the top of the plateau) which joins the valley by a knoll with neither crest nor rocky fall.

The line of separation between the uncultivated zone and the banana plantation is not entirely straight. It is a zigzag line, with alternately protruding and receding angles, each belonging to a different patch of different age, but of a generally identical orientation.

Just opposite the house, a clump of trees marks the highest point the cultivation reaches in this sector. The patch that ends here is a rectangle. The ground is invisible, or virtually so, between the fronds. Still, the impeccable alignment of the boles shows that they have been planted only recently and that no stems have as yet been cut.

Starting from this clump of trees, the patch runs downhill with a slight divergence (toward the left) from the greatest angle of slope. There are thirty-two banana trees in the row, down to the lower edge of the patch.

Prolonging this patch toward the bottom, with the same arrangement of rows, another patch occupies the space included between the first patch and the little stream that flows through the valley bottom. This second patch is twenty-three trees deep, and only its more advanced vegetation distinguishes it from the preceding patch: the greater height of the trunks, the tangle of fronds, and the number of well-formed stems. Besides, some stems have already been cut. But the empty place where the bole has been cut is then as easily discernible as the tree itself would be with its tuft of wide, pale-green leaves, out of which comes the thick curving stem bearing the fruit.

Furthermore, instead of being rectangular like the one above it, this patch is trapezoidal; for the stream bank that constitutes its lower edge is not perpendicular to its two sides—running up the slope—which are parallel to each other. The row on the right side has no more than thirteen banana trees instead of twenty-three.

And finally, the lower edge of this patch is not straight, since the little stream is not: a slight bulge narrows the patch toward the middle of its width. The central row, which should have eighteen trees if it were to be a true trapezoid, has, in fact, only sixteen.

In the second row, starting from the far left, there would be twenty-two trees (because of the alternate arrangement) in the case of a rectangular patch. There would also be twenty-two for a patch that was precisely trapezoidal, the reduction being scarcely noticeable at such a short distance from its base. And, in fact, there are twenty-two trees there.

But the third row too has only twenty-two trees, instead of twenty-three which the alternately-arranged rectangle would have. No additional difference is introduced, at this level, by the bulge in the lower edge. The same is true for the fourth row, which includes twenty-one boles, that is, one less than an even row of the imaginary rectangle.

The bulge of the bank also begins to take effect starting from the fifth row: this row, as a matter of fact, also possesses only twenty-one trees, whereas it should have twenty-two for a true trapezoid and twenty-three for a rectangle (uneven row).

These numbers themselves are theoretical, since certain banana trees have already been cut at ground level, once the stem has matured. There are actually nineteen tufts of leaves and two empty spaces which constitute the fourth row; and in the fifth, twenty tufts and one space—that is, from bottom to top: eight tufts of leaves, an empty space, twelve tufts of leaves.

Without bothering with the order in which the actually visible banana trees and the cut banana trees occur, the sixth row gives the following numbers: twenty-two, twenty-one, twenty, nineteen—which represent respectively the rectangle, the true trapezoid, the trapezoid with a curved edge, and the same after subtracting the boles cut for the harvest.

And for the following rows: twenty-three, twenty-one, twenty-one, twenty-one. Twenty-two, twenty-one, twenty, twenty. Twenty-three, twenty-one, twenty, nineteen, etc. . . .

On the log bridge that crosses the stream at the bottom edge of this patch, there is a man crouching: a native, wearing blue trousers and a colorless undershirt that leaves his shoulders bare. He is leaning toward the liquid surface, as if he were trying to see something at the bottom, which is scarcely possible, the water never being transparent enough despite its extreme shallowness.

On the near slope of the valley, a single patch runs up-hill from the stream to the garden. Despite the rather slight declivity the slope appears to have, the banana trees are still easy to count here from the height of the veranda. As a matter of fact, the trees are very young in this zone, which has only recently been replanted. Not only is the regularity of the planting perfect here, but the trunks are no more than a foot and a half high, and the tufts of leaves that terminate them are still quite far apart from each other. Finally, the angle of the rows with the direction of the valley (about forty-five degrees) also favors their enumeration.

An oblique row begins at the log bridge, at the right, and reaches the left corner of the garden. It includes the thirty-six trees in its length. The alternate arrangement makes it possible to consider these same trees as being aligned in three other directions: first of all, the perpendicular to the first direction mentioned, then two others, also perpendicular to each other, and forming angles of forty-five degrees with the first two. These last two rows are therefore respectively parallel and perpendicular to the direction of the valley—and to the lower edge of the garden.

The garden is, at present, only a square of naked earth, recently spaded, out of which are growing perhaps a dozen thin young orange trees a little shorter than a man, planted at A . . .'s orders.

The house does not occupy the whole width of the garden. Therefore it is isolated on all sides from the green mass of the banana trees.

Across the bare ground, in front of the west gable-end, falls the warped shadow of the house. The shadow of the roof is linked to the shadow of the veranda by the oblique shadow of the corner column. The balustrade here forms a barely perforated strip, whereas the real distance between the balusters is scarcely smaller than the average thickness of the latter.

The balusters are of turned wood, with a median hip and two accessory smaller bulges, one at each end. The paint, which has almost completely disappeared from the top surface of the hand-rail, is also beginning to flake off the bulging portions of the balusters; they present, for the most part, a wide zone of naked wood halfway up the baluster, on the rounded part of the hip, on the veranda side. Between the gray paint that remains, faded with age, and the wood grayed by the action of humidity, appear little reddish-brown surfaces—the natural color of the wood— where it has been exposed by the recent fall of new flakes of paint. The whole balustrade is to be repainted bright yellow: that is what A . . . has decided.

The windows of her bedroom are still closed. However the blinds which replace the panes of glass are opened as far as possible, thus making the interior of the room bright enough. A . . . is standing in front of the right-hand window, looking out through one of the chinks in the blinds toward the veranda.

The man is still motionless, bending over the muddy water on the earth-covered log bridge. He has not moved an inch: crouching, head lowered, forearms resting on his thighs, hands hanging between his knees.

In front of him, in the patch along the opposite bank of the little stream, several stems look ripe for harvesting. Several boles have already been cut in this sector. Their empty places appear with perfect distinctness in the series of geometrical alignments. But on closer inspection it is possible to distinguish the sizeable shoot that will replace the severed banana tree a few inches away from the old stump, already beginning to spoil the perfect regularity of the alternate planting.

From the other side of the house can be heard the noise of a truck coming up the road on the near slope of the valley.

A . . .'s silhouette, outlined in horizontal strips against the blind of her bedroom window, has now disappeared.

Having reached the level portion of the road, just above the rocky outcrop that marks the end of the plateau, the truck shifts gears and continues with a less muffled rumble. Then the sound gradually fades as it drives off east, through the scorched brush dotted with motionless trees, toward the next plantation—Franck's.

The bedroom window—the one nearest the hallway—opens outward. The upper part of A . . .'s body is framed within it. She says "Hello" in the playful tone of someone who has slept well and awakened in a good mood; or of someone who prefers not to show what she is thinking about—if anything—and always flashes the same smile, on principle; the same smile, which can be interpreted as derision just as well as affection, or the total absence of any feeling whatever.

Besides, she has not awakened just now. It is obvious she has already taken her shower. She is still wearing her dressing gown, but her lips are freshly made up—the lipstick color the same as their natural color, a trifle deeper, and her carefully brushed hair gleams in the light from the window when she turns her head, shifting the soft, heavy curls whose black mass falls over the white silk of her shoulder.

She goes to the heavy chest against the rear partition. She opens the top drawer to take out a small object and turns back toward the light. On the log bridge the crouching native has disappeared. There is no one visible around the house. No cutting crew is working in this sector, for the moment.

A . . . is sitting at the little work table against the wall to her right that separates the bedroom from the hallway. She leans forward over some long and painstaking task: mending an extremely fine stocking, polishing her nails, a tiny pencil drawing. . . . But A . . . never draws: to mend

55

a run in her stocking she would have moved nearer the daylight; if she needed a table to do her nails on, she would not have chosen this one.

Despite the apparent immobility of her head and shoulders, a series of jolts disturbs the black mass of her hair. From time to time she straightens up and seems to lean back to judge her work from a distance. Her hand rising slowly, she puts into place a short curl that has emerged from this shifting mass. The hand lingers as it rearranges the waves of hair, the tapering fingers bend and straighten, one after the other, quickly though without abruptness, the movement communicating itself from one to the other continuously, as if they were driven by the same mechanism.

Leaning over again, she has now resumed her interrupted task. The lustrous hair gleams with reddish highlights in the hollow of the curls. Slight quivers, quickly absorbed, run through the hair from one shoulder to the other, without its being possible to see the rest of the body stir at all.

On the veranda in front of the office windows, Franck is sitting in his customary place, in one of the chairs of local manufacture. Only these three have been brought out this morning. They are arranged as usual: the first two next to each other under the window, the third slightly to one side, on the other side of the low table.

A . . . has gone to get the glasses, the soda water, and the cognac herself. She sets a tray with the two bottles and the three big glasses down on the table. Having uncorked the cognac she turns toward Franck and looks at him, while she begins making his drink. But Franck, instead of watching the rising level of the alcohol, fixes his eyes a little too high, on A . . .'s face. She has arranged her hair into a low knot whose skillful waves seem about to come undone; some hidden pins must be keeping it firmer than it looks.

Franck's voice has uttered an exclamation: "Hey there! That's much too much!" or else: "Stop! That's much too much!" or, "Ten times too much," "Half again too much," etc. . . . He holds up his right hand beside his head, the fingers slightly apart. A . . . begins to laugh.

"You should have stopped me sooner."

"But I didn't see . . ." Franck protests.

"Well, then," she answers, "you should keep your eye on the glass."

They look at each other without adding another word. Franck widens his smile, which wrinkles up the corners of his eyes. He opens his mouth as if he were going to say something. But he doesn't say anything. A . . .'s features, from a point three-quarters of the way behind her, reveal nothing.

After several minutes—or several seconds—both are still in the same position. Franck's face as well as his whole body are virtually petrified. He is wearing shorts and a short-sleeved khaki shirt, whose shoulder straps and buttoned pockets have a vaguely military look. Over his rough cotton knee socks he wears tennis-shoes coated with a thick layer of white shoe polish, cracked at the places where the canvas bends with the foot.

A . . . is about to pour the soda into the three glasses lined up on the low table. She distributes the first two, then, holding the third one in her hand, sits down in the empty chair beside Franck. He has already begun drinking.

"Is it cold enough?" A . . . asks him. "The bottles just came out of the refrigerator."

Franck nods and drinks another mouthful.

"There's ice if you want it," A . . . says. And without waiting for an answer she calls the boy.

There is a silence, during which the boy should appear on the veranda at the corner of the house. But no one comes.

Franck looks at A . . ., as if he expected her to call again, or stand up, or reach some decision. She makes a sudden face toward the balustrade.

"He doesn't hear," she says. "One of us had better go."

Neither she nor Franck moves. On A . . .'s face, turned

in profile toward the corner of the veranda, there is neither smile nor expectation now, nor a sign of encouragement. Franck stares at the tiny bubbles clinging to the sides of his glass, which he is holding in front of his eyes at very close range.

One mouthful is enough to tell that this drink is not cold enough. Franck has still not answered one way or the other, though he has taken two already. Besides, only one bottle comes from the refrigerator: the soda, whose greenish sides are coated with a faint film of dew where a hand with tapering fingers has left its print.

The cognac is always kept in the sideboard. A . . ., who brings out the ice bucket at the same time as the glasses every day, has not done so today.

"It's not worth bothering about," Franck says.

To get to the pantry, the easiest way is to cross the house. Once across the threshhold, a sensation of coolness accompanies the half darkness. To the right, the office door is ajar.

The light, rubber-soled shoes make no sound on the hallway tiles. The door turns on its hinges without squeaking. The office floor is tiled too. The three windows are closed and their blinds are only half-open, to keep the noonday heat out of the room.

Two of the windows overlook the central section of the veranda. The first, to the right, shows through its lowest chink, between the last two slats of wood, the black head of hair—at least the top part of it.

A . . . is sitting upright and motionless in her armchair. She is looking out over the valley in front of them. She is not speaking. Franck, invisible on her left, is also silent, or else speaking in a very low voice.

Although the office—like the bedrooms and the bathroom—opens onto the hallway, the hallway itself ends at the dining room, with no door between. The table is set for three. A . . . has probably just had the boy add Franck's place, since she was not supposed to be expecting any guest for lunch today.

The three plates are arranged as usual, each in the center of one of the sides of the square table. The fourth side, where there is no place set, is the one next to about six feet of the bare partition where the light paint still shows the traces of the squashed centipede.

In the pantry the boy is already taking the ice cubes out of their trays. A pitcher full of water, set on the floor, has been used to heat the backs of the metal trays. He looks up and smiles broadly.

He would scarcely have had time to go take A . . .'s orders on the veranda and return here (outside the house) with the necessary objects.

"Missus, she has said to bring the ice," he announces in the singsong voice of the Negroes, which detaches certain syllables by emphasizing them too much, sometimes in the middle of words.

To a vague question as to when he received this order, he answers: "Now," which furnishes no satisfactory indication. She might have asked him when she went to get the tray.

Only the boy could confirm this. But he sees in the awkwardly put question only a request to hurry.

"Right away I bring," he says.

He speaks well enough, but he does not always understand what is wanted of him. A . . ., however, manages to make herself understood without any difficulty.

From the pantry door, the dining-room wall seems to have no spot on it. No sound of conversation can be heard from the veranda at the other end of the hallway.

To the left, the office door has remained wide open this time. But the slats of the blind are too sharply slanted to permit what is outside to be seen from the doorway.

It is only at a distance of less than a yard that the elements of a discontinuous landscape appear in the successive intervals, parallel chinks separated by the wider slats

59

of gray wood: the turned wood balusters, the empty chair, the low table where a full glass is standing beside the tray holding the two bottles, and then the top part of the head of black hair, which at this moment turns toward the right, where above the table shows a bare forearm, dark brown in color, and its paler hand holding the ice bucket. A . . .'s voice thanks the boy. The brown hand disappears. The shiny metal bucket, immediately frosted over, remains where it has been set on the tray beside the two bottles.

The knot of A . . .'s hair, seen at such close range from behind, seems to be extremely complicated. It is difficult to follow the convolutions of different strands: several solutions seem possible at some places, and in others, none.

Instead of serving the ice, A . . . continues to look out over the valley. Of the garden earth, cut up into vertical slices by the balustrade, and into horizontal strips by the blinds, there remains only a series of little squares representing a very small part of the total surface—perhaps a ninth.

The knot of A . . .'s hair is at least as confusing when it appears in profile. She is sitting to Franck's left. (It is always that way: on Franck's right for coffee or cocktails, on his left during the meals in the dining room.) She still keeps her back to the windows, but it is now from these windows that the daylight comes. These windows are conventional ones with panes of glass: facing north, they never receive direct sunlight.

The windows are closed. No sound penetrates inside when a silhouette passes in front of one of them, walking alongside the house from the kitchen toward the sheds. Cut off below the knee, it was a Negro wearing shorts, undershirt, and an old soft hat, walking with a quick, loose gait, probably barefoot. His felt hat, shapeless and faded, is unforgettable and should make him immediately recognizable among all the workers on the plantation. He is not, however.

The second window is located farther back, in relation to the table; to see it requires a pivoting of the upper part of the body. But no one is outlined against it, either because the man in the hat has already passed it, or because he has just stopped, or has suddenly changed his direction. His disappearance is hardly astonishing, it merely makes his first appearance curious.

"It's all mental, things like that," Franck says.

The African novel again provides the subject of their conversation.

"People say it's the climate, but that doesn't mean anything."

"Malarial attacks . . ."

"There's quinine."

"And your head buzzing all day long."

The moment has come to inquire after Christiane's health. Franck replies by a gesture of the hand: a rise followed by a slower fall that becomes quite vague, while the fingers close over a piece of bread set down beside his plate. At the same time his lower lip is projected and the chin quickly turned toward A . . ., who must have asked the same question a little earlier.

The boy comes in through the open pantry door, holding a large, shallow bowl in both hands.

A . . . has not made the remarks which Franck's gesture was supposed to introduce. There remains one remedy: to ask after the child. The same gesture—or virtually the same —is made, which again concludes with A . . .'s silence.

"Still the same," Franck says.

Going in the opposite direction behind the panes, the felt hat passes by again. The quick, loose gait has not changed. But the opposite orientation of the face conceals the latter altogether.

Behind the thick glass, which is perfectly clean, there is only the gravel courtyard, then, rising toward the road and the edge of the plateau, the green mass of the banana trees. The flaws in the glass produce shifting circles in their unvarying foliage.

The light itself has a somewhat greenish cast as it falls on the dining room, the black hair with the improbable convolutions, the cloth on the table, and the bare partition where a dark stain, just opposite A . . ., stands out on the pale, dull, even paint.

The details of this stain have to be seen from quite close range, turning toward the pantry door, if its origin is to be distinguished. The image of the squashed centipede then appears not as a whole, but composed of fragments distinct enough to leave no doubt. Several pieces of the body or its appendages are outlined without any blurring, and remain reproduced with the fidelity of an anatomical drawing: one of the antennae, two curved mandibles, the head and the first joint, half of the second, three large legs. Then come the other parts, less precise: sections of legs and the partial form of a body convulsed into a question mark.

It is at this hour that the lighting in the dining room is the most favorable. From the other side of the square table where the places have not yet been set, one of the French windows, whose panes are darkened by no dust at all, is open on the courtyard which is also reflected in the glass.

Between the two window-leaves, as through the half-open right one, is framed the left side of the courtyard where the tarpaulin-covered truck is parked, its hood facing the northern sector of the banana plantation. Under the tarpaulin is a raw wood case, marked with large black letters painted in reverse through a stencil.

In the left window-leaf the reflection is brighter, though deeper in hue. But it is distorted by flaws in the glass, the circular or crescent-shaped spots of verdure, the same colors as the banana trees, occurring in the middle of the courtyard in front of the sheds.

Nicked by one of the moving rings of foliage, the big blue sedan nevertheless remains quite recognizable, as well as A . . .'s dress where she is standing next to the car.

She is leaning toward the door. If the window has been lowered—which is likely—A . . . may have put her face into the opening above the seat. In straightening up she runs the risk of disarranging her hair against the edge of the window, and seeing her hair spread out and fall over the driver still behind the wheel.

The latter is here again for dinner, affable and smiling. He drops into one of the leather chairs without anyone's telling him which, and utters his usual exclamation as to their comfort.

"That feels good!"

His white shirt makes a paler spot in the darkness, against the wall of the house.

In order not to risk spilling the contents in the darkness, A . . . has come as close as possible to Franck's armchair, carefully holding his glass in her right hand. She rests her other hand on the arm of his chair and leans toward him, so close that their heads touch. He murmurs a few words, probably thanking her. But the words are drowned out by the deafening racket of the crickets that rises on all sides.

At table, once the arrangement of the lamps has been shifted so that the guests are in less direct a light, the conversation continues on familiar subjects, with the same phrases.

Franck's truck has had engine trouble on the middle of the hill, between the 40-mile marker—where the road leaves the plain—and the first village. It was a police car which passed the truck and then stopped at the plantation to inform Franck. When the latter reached the spot two hours later, he did not find his truck at the place indicated, but much lower down, the driver having tried to start the motor in reverse, at the risk of crashing into a tree if he missed one of the turns.

Expecting any results at all from such a method was ridiculous anyway. The carburetor would have to be completely dismantled all over again. Luckily Franck had brought along a snack lunch, for he didn't get home until three-thirty. He has decided to replace the truck as soon as possible, and it's the last time—he says—that he will buy old military matériel.

"You think you're getting a bargain, but in the long run it costs much more."

He now expects to buy a new truck. He is going down to the port himself at the first opportunity and meet with the sales agents of the chief makes, so that he can find out the exact prices, the various advantages, delivery time, etc. . . .

If he had a little more experience, he would know that new machines should not be entrusted to Negro drivers, who wreck them just as fast, if not faster.

"When do you think you'll be going down?" A . . . asks.

"I don't know. . . ." They look at each other, their glances meeting above the platter Franck is holding in one hand six inches above the table top. "Maybe next week."

"I have to go to town too," A . . . says; "I have a lot of shopping to do."

"Well, I'll be glad to take you. If we leave early, we can be back the same night."

He sets the platter down on his left and begins helping himself. A . . . turns back so that she is looking straight ahead.

"A centipede!" she says in a more restrained voice, in the silence that has just fallen.

Franck looks up again. Following the direction of A . . .'s motionless gaze, he turns his head to the other side, toward his right.

On the light-colored paint of the partition opposite A . . ., a common Scutigera of average size (about as long as a finger) has appeared, easily seen despite the dim light. It is not moving, for the moment, but the orientation of its body indicates a path which cuts across the panel diagonally: coming from the baseboard on the hallway side and heading toward the corner of the ceiling. The creature is easy to identify thanks to the development of its legs, especially on the posterior portion. On closer examination the swaying movement of the antennae at the other end can be discerned.

A . . . has not moved since her discovery: sitting very straight in her chair, her hands resting flat on the cloth on either side of her plate. Her eyes are wide, staring at the wall. Her mouth is not quite closed, and may be quivering imperceptibly.

It is not unusual to encounter different kinds of centipedes after dark in this already old wooden house. And this kind is not one of the largest; it is far from being one of the most venomous. A . . . does her best, but does not manage to look away, nor to smile at the joke about her aversion to centipedes.

Franck, who has said nothing, is looking at A . . . again. Then he stands up, noiselessly, holding his napkin in his hand. He wads it into a ball and approaches the wall.

A . . . seems to be breathing a little faster, but this may be an illusion. Her left hand gradually closes over her knife. The delicate antennae accelerate their alternate swaying.

Suddenly the creature hunches its body and begins descending diagonally toward the ground as fast as its long legs can go, while the wadded napkin falls on it, faster still.

The hand with the tapering fingers has clenched around the knife handle; but the features of the face have lost none of their rigidity. Franck lifts the napkin away from the wall and with his foot continues to squash something on the tiles, against the baseboard.

About a yard higher, the paint is marked with a dark shape, a tiny arc twisted into a question mark, blurred on one side, in places surrounded by more tenuous signs, from which A . . . has still not taken her eyes.

The brush descends the length of the loose hair with a faint noise something between the sound of a breath and a crackle. No sooner has it reached the bottom than it quickly rises again toward the head, where the whole surface of its bristles sinks in before gliding down over the black mass again. The brush is a bone-colored oval whose short handle disappears almost entirely in the hand firmly gripping it.

Half of the hair hangs down the back, the other hand pulls the other half over one shoulder. The head leans to the right, offering the hair more readily to the brush. Each time the latter lands at the top of its cycle behind the nape of the neck, the head leans farther to the right and then rises again with an effort, while the right hand, holding the brush, moves away in the opposite direction. The left hand, which loosely confines the hair between the wrist, the palm and the fingers, releases it for a second and then closes on it again, gathering the strands together with a firm, mechanical gesture, while the brush continues its course to the extreme tips of the hair. The sound, which gradually varies from one end to the other, is at this point nothing more than a dry, faint crackling, whose last sputters occur once the brush, leaving the longest hair, is already moving up the ascending part of the cycle, describing a swift curve in the air which brings it above the neck, where the hair lies flat on the back of the head and reveals the white streak of a part.

To the left of this part, the other half of the black hair hangs loosely to the waist in supple waves. Still further to the left the face shows only a faint profile. But beyond is the surface of the mirror, which reflects the image of the whole face from the front, the eyes—doubtless unnecessary for brushing—directed straight ahead, as is natural.

Thus A . . .'s eyes should meet the wide-open window which overlooks the west gable-end. Facing in this direction she is brushing her hair in front of the dressing table provided especially with a vertical mirror which reflects her gaze behind her, toward the bedroom's third window, the central portion of the veranda and the slope of the valley.

The second window, which looks south like this third one, is nearer the southwest corner of the house; it too is wide open. Through it can be seen the side of the dressing-table, the edge of the mirror, the left profile of the face, the loose hair which hangs over the shoulder, and the left arm which is bent back to reach the right half of the hair.

Since the nape of the neck is bent diagonally to the right, the face is slightly turned toward the window. On the gray-streaked marble table-top are arranged jars and bottles of various sizes and shapes; nearer the front lies a large tortoise-shell comb and another brush, this one of wood with a longer handle, which is lying with its black bristles facing up.

A . . . must have just washed her hair, otherwise she would not be bothering to brush it in the middle of the day. She has interrupted her movements, having finished this side perhaps. Nevertheless she does not change the position of her arms or move the upper part of her body as she turns her face all the way around toward the window at her left to look out at the veranda, the open-work balustrade and the opposite slope of the valley.

The foreshortened shadow of the column supporting the corner of the roof falls across the veranda flagstones toward the first window, that of the gable-end; but it is far from reaching it, for the sun is still too high in the sky. The gable-end of the house is entirely in the shadow of the roof; as for the western part of the veranda running the length of this gable-end, an unbroken sunny strip scarcely a yard wide lies between the shadow of the roof and the shadow of the balustrade.

It is in front of this window, inside the bedroom, that the

varnished mahogany-and-marble dressing-table has been set; there is always a specimen of such pieces in these colonial-style houses.

The back of the mirror is a panel of rougher wood, also reddish, but dark, oval in shape and with a chalk inscription almost entirely erased. To the right, A . . .'s face, which is now bent toward her left so she can brush the other half of her hair, shows one eye staring straight ahead of her, as is natural, toward the open window and the green mass of the banana trees.

At the end of this western side of the veranda opens the outside door of the pantry; the pantry opens onto the dining room, where it stays cool all afternoon. On the bare wall between the pantry door and the hallway, the stain formed by the remains of the centipede is scarcely visible because of the oblique light. The table is set for three; three plates occupy three sides of the square table: the sideboard side, the window side, and the side toward the center of the long room. The other half of this room forms a living room on the other side of an imaginary central line between the hall doorway and the door opening onto the courtyard. From the courtyard it is easy to reach the sheds where the native overseer has his office.

But this living room—or the side of the shed through a window—can be seen only from Franck's place at the table: back to the sideboard.

At present, this place is empty. The chair is nevertheless put in the right spot, the plate and silver are in their places too; but there is nothing between the edge of the table and the back of the chair, which shows its trimming of thick straw bound in a cross; and the plate is clean and shiny, surrounded by the usual knives and forks, as at the beginning of the meal.

A . . ., who has finally decided to have the lunch served without waiting for the guest any longer, since he hasn't come, is sitting rigid and silent in her own place, in front of the windows. Though the discomfort of this location,

with the light behind her, seems flagrant, it has been chosen
by A . . . once and for all. She eats with an extreme
economy of gestures, not turning her head right or left, her
eyes squinting slightly, as if she were trying to discover a
stain on the bare wall in front of her, where the immaculate
paint offers not the slightest object to her gaze, however.

After clearing away the *hors-d'oeuvres* but not bothering
to change the unused plate of the absent guest, the boy
comes in again through the open pantry door, holding a
wide, shallow platter in both hands. A . . . doesn't even turn
to give it her usual "mistress of the house" glance. Without
a word, the boy sets the platter down on the white cloth to
her right. It contains a yellowish puree, probably of yams,
from which rises a thin trail of steam which suddenly
curves, flattens out, and vanishes without leaving a trace,
reappearing at once—long, delicate and vertical—high
above the table.

In the middle of the table there is already another untouched platter on which, against a background of brown
sauce, are arranged three small roasted birds, one next to
the other.

The boy has withdrawn, silent as ever. A . . . suddenly
decides to look away from the bare wall and now considers
the two platters, one on her right and one in front of her.
Having grasped the appropriate spoon, she helps herself
with careful and precise gestures: the smallest of the three
birds, then a little of the puree. Then she picks up the
platter at her right and sets it down on her left, the large
spoon has remained in it.

She begins meticulously cutting up the bird on her plate.
Despite the smallness of the object, she takes apart the
limbs, as if she were performing an anatomical demonstration, cuts up the body at the joints, detaches the flesh from
the skeleton with the point of her knife while holding the
pieces down with her fork, without forcing, without ever
having to repeat the same gesture, without even seeming to

be accomplishing a difficult or unaccustomed task. These birds, it is true, are served frequently.

When she has finished, she raises her head, looking straight ahead of her, and remains motionless again, while the boy takes out the plates covered with the tiny bones, then the two platters, one of which still contains a third roasted bird, the one meant for Franck.

The latter's place remains as it was until the end of the meal. He has probably been delayed, as is not infrequently the case, by some incident occurring on his plantation, since he would not have put off this lunch for any possible ailments of his wife or child.

Although it is unlikely that the guest should come now, perhaps A . . . is still expecting to hear the sound of a car coming down the slope from the highway. But through the dining-room windows, of which at least one is half open, no motor hum or any other noise can be heard at this hour of the day when all work is interrupted and even the animals fall silent in the heat.

The corner window has both leaves open—at least partly. The one on the right is only ajar, so that it still covers at least half of the window opening. The left leaf, on the other hand, is pushed back toward the wall, but not all the way either—it is scarcely more than perpendicular, in fact, to the window sash. The window therefore shows three panels of equal height which are of adjoining widths: in the center the opening and, on each side, a glass area comprising three panes. In all three are framed fragments of the same landscape: the gravel courtyard and the green mass of the banana trees.

The windows are perfectly clean and, in the right-hand leaf, the landscape is only slightly affected by the flaws in the glass, which give a few shifting nuances to the too uniform surfaces. But in the left leaf, the reflected image, darker although more brilliant, is plainly distorted, circular or crescent-shaped spots of verdure the same color as the banana trees occurring in the middle of the courtyard in front of the sheds.

Franck's big blue sedan, which has just appeared here, is also nicked by one of these shifting rings of foliage, as is A . . .'s white dress when she gets out of the car.

She leans toward the door. If the window has been lowered—which is likely—A . . . may have put her face into the opening above the seat. In straightening up she runs the risk of disarranging her hair against the edge of the window, causing it to spread out and fall—all the more readily mussed since it has recently been washed—over the driver still behind the wheel.

But she draws away unscathed from the blue car whose motor, which has been idling, now fills the courtyard with a louder hum, and after a last look behind her, heads alone, with her decisive gait, toward the center door of the house which opens directly into the living room.

Opposite this door opens the hallway, with no door between it and the living room–dining room. Doors occur one after another on each side; the last to the left, that of the office, is not completely closed. The door moves without creaking on its well-oiled hinges; it then returns to its initial position with the same discretion.

At the other end of the house, the entrance door, opened with less care, has closed again; then the faint distinct sound of high heels on tiles crosses the living room–dining room and approaches down the length of the hallway.

The steps stop in front of the office door, but it is the door opposite, to the bedroom, which is opened, then shut again.

Symmetrical to those of the bedroom, the three windows of the office have their blinds more than half lowered at this hour. Thus the office is plunged into a dimness which makes it difficult to judge distances. Lines are just as distinct, but the succession of planes gives no impression of depth, so that hands instinctively reach out in front of the body to measure the space more precisely.

71

The room is fortunately not very full of furniture: files and shelves against the walls, a few chairs, and then the huge desk which fills the entire area between the two windows facing south, one of which—on the right, nearer the hallway—reveals through the chinks between its wood slats, the silhouette in luminous parallel stripes of the table and chairs on the veranda.

On the corner of the dressing-table stands a little mother-of-pearl inlaid frame with a photograph taken by a sidewalk photographer during the first vacation in Europe, after the African trip.

In front of the façade of a large "modern" cafe, A . . . is sitting on a complicated wrought-iron chair whose arms and back, in bracketed spirals, seem less comfortable than spectacular. But A . . ., from her manner of sitting on the chair, looks as natural as ever, though without the slightest slackness.

She has turned slightly to smile at the photographer, as if to authorize him to take this candid shot. Her bare arm, at the same moment, has not changed the gesture it was making to set the glass down on the table beside her.

But it was not to put ice in it, for she does not reach for the ice bucket of shiny metal which is immediately frosted over.

Motionless, she stares at the valley in front of them. She says nothing. Franck, invisible to her left, also says nothing. Perhaps she had heard some abnormal sound behind her and is about to make some movement without discernible preparation, which would permit her to look toward the blind quite by chance.

The window facing east, on the other side of the office, is not merely a window opening, like the corresponding one in the bedroom, but a French door which permits direct access to the veranda without passing through the hallway.

This part of the veranda receives the morning sun, the only kind that need not be avoided by some protection or other. In the almost cool air after daybreak, the song of birds replaces that of the nocturnal crickets, and resembles it, although less regular and sometimes embellished with slightly more musical sounds. As for the birds themselves, they were no more in evidence than the crickets were, remaining in hiding under the clusters of wide green leaves on all sides of the house.

In the zone of naked earth which separates the house from the trees, where at regular intervals the young orange trees are planted—thin stems with occasional dark-colored foliage—the ground sparkles with innumerable dew-covered webs spun by tiny spiders between the clods of spaded earth.

To the right, this part of the veranda adjoins the end of the living room. But it is always out-of-doors, in front of the southern facade—with a view over the entire valley—that the morning meal is served. On the low table, near the single chair brought here by the boy, the coffee pot and the cup are already arranged. A . . . is not up yet, at this hour. The windows of her bedroom are still closed.

In the hollow of the valley, on the log bridge that crosses the little stream, there is a man crouching, facing the opposite hillside. He is a native, wearing blue trousers and a colorless undershirt that leaves his shoulders bare. He is leaning toward the liquid surface as if he were trying to see something in the muddy water.

In front of him, on the opposite bank, stretches a trapezoid-shaped patch, the side along the bank curved, all of whose banana trees have been harvested more or less recently. It is easy to count their stumps, the cut trunks leaving a short stub with a disc-shaped scar, white or yellowish depending upon its freshness. Counting by rows,

73

there are: from left to right twenty-three, twenty-two, twenty-two, twenty-one, twenty-one, twenty, twenty-one, twenty, twenty, etc. . . . .

Beside each white disc, but in various directions, has grown the replacing sprout. Depending on the precocity of the first stem, this new plant is now between a foot and a half and a yard in height.

A . . . has just brought out the glasses, the two bottles, and the ice bucket. She begins serving: the cognac in the three glasses, then the soda, and finally three transparent ice cubes, each of which imprisons a bundle of silver needles in its heart.

"We'll be leaving early," Franck says.

"What do you mean—early?"

"Six o'clock, if you can make it."

"Six! My goodness. . . ."

"Too early for you?"

"Oh no." She laughs. Then, after a pause, "In fact, it'll be fun."

They sip their drinks.

"If all goes well," Franck says, "we'll be in town by ten and have an hour or two before lunch."

"Yes, of course. I'd prefer that too," A . . . says.

They sip their drinks.

Then they change the subject. Now both of them have finished the book they have been reading for some time; their remarks can therefore refer to the book as a whole: that is, both to the outcome and to the earlier episodes (subjects of past conversations) to which this outcome gives a new significance, or to which it adds a complementary meaning.

They have never made the slightest judgment as to the novel's value, speaking instead of the scenes, events, and characters as if they were real: a place they might remember (located in Africa, moreover), people they might have known, or whose adventures someone might have told them. Their discussions have never touched on the verisimilitude, the coherence, or the quality of the narrative. On the other hand, they frequently blame the heroes for certain acts or characteristics, as they would in the case of mutual friends.

They also sometimes deplore the coincidences of the plot, saying that "things don't happen that way," and then they construct a different probable outcome starting from a new supposition, "if it weren't for that." Other possibilities are offered, during the course of the book, which lead to different endings. The variations are extremely numerous; the variations of these, still more so. They seem to enjoy multiplying these choices, exchanging smiles, carried away by their enthusiasm, probably a little intoxicated by this proliferation . . .

"But that's it, he was just unlucky enough to have come home earlier that day, and no one could have guessed he would."

Thus Franck sweeps away in a single gesture all the suppositions they had just constructed together. It's no use making up contrary possibilities, since things are the way they are: reality stays the same.

They sip their drinks. In the three glasses, the ice cubes have now altogether disappeared. Franck inspects the gold liquid remaining in the bottom of his glass. He turns it to one side, then the other, amusing himself by detaching the little bubbles clinging to the sides.

"Still," he says, "it started out well." He turns toward A . . . for her support: "We left on schedule and were driving along without any trouble. It wasn't even ten o'clock when we reached town."

Franck has stopped talking. A . . . continues, as if to encourage him to resume:

"And you didn't notice anything funny that whole day, did you?"

"No, nothing at all. In a way, it would have been better if we had had trouble with the engine right away, before lunch. Not on the trip but in town, before lunch. It would have made it harder for me to do some of my errands—the ones that weren't in the middle of town—but at least I would have had time to find a garage that could have made the repairs during the afternoon."

"Because it really wasn't a very big job," A . . . put in, questioningly.

"No, it was nothing."

Franck looks at his glass. After a rather long pause, and although this time no one has asked him anything, he continues explaining:

"The moment we started back, after dinner, the engine wouldn't start. It was too late to do anything, of course: every garage was closed. All we could do was wait until morning."

The sentences followed one another, each in its place, connecting logically. The measured, uniform pace was like that of a witness offering testimony, or a recitation.

"Even so," A . . . says, "you thought you could fix it yourself, at first. At least you tried. But you're not much of a mechanic are, you?"

She smiles as she says these last words. They look at each other. He smiles too. Then, slowly, his smile becomes a kind of grimace. She, on the other hand, keeps her look of amused serenity.

Yet Franck can't be unused to makeshift repairs, since his truck is always having engine trouble . . .

"Yes," he says, "I'm beginning to know *that* motor pretty well. But the car hasn't given me trouble very often."

As a matter of fact, there has never been another incident with the big blue sedan, which is almost new, moreover.

"There has to be a first time for everything," Franck answers. Then, after a pause: "It was just my unlucky day . . ."

A little gesture of his right hand—rising, then falling more slowly—has just come to an end on the strip of leather that constitutes the arm of the chair. Franck's face is drawn;

his smile has not reappeared since the grimace of a few minutes ago. His body seems to be stuck to the chair.

"Unlucky, maybe, but it wasn't a tragedy," A . . . replies, in a casual tone that contrasts with that of her companion. "If we had been able to telephone, the delay wouldn't have mattered at all; but with these plantations isolated in the jungle, what could we do? In any case, it's better than being stuck on the road in the middle of the night!"

It's better than having an accident too. It was only a piece of bad luck, without consequences, an incident of no seriousness, one of the minor inconveniences of colonial life.

"I think I'll be getting along," Franck says.

He has just stopped here to drop A . . . off on his way home. He doesn't want to waste any more time. Christiane must be wondering what's become of him, and Franck is eager to reassure her. He stands up with sudden energy and sets down on the low table the glass he has emptied at one gulp.

"Till next time," A . . . says, without leaving her own chair, "and thank you."

Franck makes a vague gesture with his arm, a conventional protest. A . . . insists:

"No, really! I've been on your neck for two days."

"Not at all. I'm terribly sorry to have given you a night like that in that miserable hotel."

He has taken two steps, he stops before turning down the hallway that crosses the house, he half turns around: "And please forgive me for being such a bad mechanic." The same grimace, faster now, slides across his face. He disappears into the house.

His steps echo over the tiles of the hallway. He had leather-soled shoes on today, and a white suit that has been wrinkled by the trip.

When the door at the other end of the house has opened and closed again, A . . . gets up too and leaves the veranda by the same door. But she goes to her bedroom at once, closing and locking the door behind her, making the latch

77

click loudly. In the courtyard, in front of the northern façade of the house, the sound of a motor starting up is immediately followed by the shrill protest of gears forced to make too fast a getaway. Franck has not said what kind of repairs his car had needed.

A . . . closes the windows of her bedroom which have stayed wide open all morning, lowering the blinds one after the other. She is going to change; and take a shower, probably, after the long dusty road.

The bathroom opens off the bedroom. A second door opens onto the hallway; the bolt is closed from inside, with a swift gesture that makes a loud click.

The next room, still on the same side of the hallway, is a bedroom, much smaller than A . . .'s, which contains a single bed. Six feet further, the hallway ends at the dining room.

The table is set for one person. A . . .'s place will have to be added.

On the bare wall, the traces of the squashed centipede are still perfectly visible. Nothing has been done to clean off the stain, for fear of spoiling the handsome, dull finish, probably not washable.

The table is set for three, according to the usual arrangement. . . . Franck and A . . ., sitting in their usual places, are talking about the trip to town they intend to make together during the following week, she for various shopping errands, he to find out about a new truck he wants to buy.

They have already settled the time for their departure, as well as for their return, calculated the approximate duration of the time on the road in each direction, estimated the time they will have for their affairs, including lunch and dinner, in town. They have not specified whether they will take their meals separately or if they will meet to have them together. But the question hardly comes up, since only one restaurant serves decent meals to travelers passing through town. It is only natural that they will meet there, especially for dinner, since they must start back immediately afterwards.

It is also natural that A . . . would want to take advantage of this present opportunity to get to town, which she prefers to the solution of a banana truck, virtually impracticable on such a long road, and that she should furthermore prefer Franck's company to that of some native driver, no matter how great the mechanical ability she attributes to the latter. As for the other occasions which permit her to make the trip under acceptable circumstances, they are incontestably rather infrequent, even exceptional, if not nonexistent, unless there are serious reasons to justify a categorical insistence on her part, which always more or less upsets the proper functioning of the plantation.

This time, she has asked for nothing, nor indicated the precise nature of the purchases which motivated her expedition. There was no special reason to give, once a friend's car was available to pick her up at home and bring her back the same night. The most surprising thing of all, upon consideration, is that such an arrangement should not already have been made, one day or another.

Franck has been eating without speaking for several minutes. It is A . . ., whose plate is empty, her fork and knife laid across it side by side, who resumes the conversation, asking after Christiane whom fatigue (due to the heat, she thinks) has kept from coming with her husband on several occasions recently.

"It's always the same," Franck answers. "I've asked her to come down to the port with us, for a change of scene. But she didn't want to, on account of the child."

"Not to mention," A . . . says, "that it's much hotter down on the coast."

"More humid, yes," Franck agrees.

Then five or six remarks are exchanged as to the respective doses of quinine necessary down on the coast and up here. Franck returns to the ill effects quinine produces on the heroine of the African novel they are reading. The conversation is thus led to the central events of the story in question.

On the other side of the closed window, in the dusty courtyard whose rough gravel gathers into heaps, the truck has its hood turned toward the house. With the exception of this detail, it is parked precisely in the spot intended for it: that is, it is framed between the lower and middle panes of the right-hand window-leaf, against the inner jamb, the little crosspiece cutting its outline horizontally into two masses of equal size.

Through the open pantry door, A . . . comes into the dining room toward the table where the meal has been served. She has come around by the veranda, in order to speak to the cook, whose voluble, singsong voice rose just a moment ago, in the kitchen.

A . . . has changed her clothes after taking a shower. She has put on the light-colored, close-fitting dress Christiane says is unsuitable for a tropical climate. She is going to sit down at her place, her back to the window, before the setting the boy has added for her. She unfolds her napkin on her knees and begins to help herself, her left hand raising the cover of the still warm platter that has already been served while she was in the bathroom but still remains in the middle of the table.

She says: "The trip made me hungry."

Then she asks about the incidents occurring on the plantation during her absence. The expression she uses ("What's new?") is spoken in a light tone whose animation indicates no particular attention. Besides, there is nothing new.

Yet A . . . seems to have an unusual desire to talk. She feels—she says—that a lot of things must have happened during this period of time which, for her part, was busily filled.

On the plantation too this time has been well employed; but only by the usual series of activities, which are always the same, for the most part.

She herself, questioned as to her news, limits her remarks to four or five pieces of information already known: the road is still being repaired for five or six miles after the first village, the "Cap Saint-Jean" was in the harbor waiting for its cargo, the work on the new post office has not advanced much in the last three months, the municipal road service is still unsatisfactory, etc. . . .

She helps herself again. It would be better to put the truck in the shed, since no one is to use it at the beginning of the afternoon. The thick glass of the window nicks the body of the truck with a deep, rounded scallop behind the front wheel. Somewhat farther down, isolated from the principal mass by a strip of gravel, a half-circle of painted metal is refracted more than a foot and a half from its real location. This aberrant piece can also be moved about as the observer pleases, changing its shape as well as its dimensions: it swells from right to left, shrinks in the opposite direction, becomes a crescent toward the bottom, a complete circle as it moves upward, or else acquires a fringe (but this is a very limited, almost instantaneous position) of two concentric aureoles. Finally, with larger shifts, it melts into the main surface or disappears, with a sudden contraction.

A . . . tries talking a little more. She nevertheless does not describe the room where she spent the night, an uninteresting subject, she says, turning away her head: everyone knows that hotel, its discomfort and its patched mosquito-netting.

It is at this moment that she notices the Scutigera on the bare wall in front of her. In an even tone of voice, as if in order not to frighten the creature, she says:

"A centipede!"

Franck looks up again. Following the direction of A . . .'s motionless gaze, he turns his head to the other side.

The animal is motionless in the center of the panel, easily seen against the light-colored paint, despite the dim light. Franck, who has said nothing, looks at A . . . again.

Then he stands up, noiselessly. A . . . moves no more than the centipede while Franck approaches the wall, his napkin wadded up in his hand.

The hand with tapering fingers has clenched into a fist on the white cloth.

Franck lifts the napkin away from the wall and with his foot continues to squash something on the tiles, against the baseboard. And he sits down in his place again, to the right of the lamp lit behind him, on the sideboard.

When he passes in front of the lamp, his shadow swept over the table top, which it covered entirely for an instant. Then the boy comes in through the open door; he begins to clear the table in silence. A . . . asks him to serve the coffee on the veranda, as usual.

She and Franck, sitting in their chairs, continue a desultory discussion of which day would be most convenient for this little trip to town they have been planning since the evening before.

The subject is soon exhausted. Its interest does not diminish, but they find no new element to nourish it. The sentences become shorter and limit themselves, for the most part, to repeating fragments of those spoken during these last two days, or even before.

After some final monosyllables, separated by increasingly longer pauses and ultimately no longer intelligible, they let the night triumph altogether.

Vague shapes indicated by the less intense obscurity of a light-colored dress or shirt, they are sitting side by side, leaning back in their chairs, arms resting on the elbow-rests, occasionally making vague movements of small extent, no sooner moving from these original positions than returning to them, or perhaps not moving at all.

The crickets too have fallen silent.

There is only the shrill cry of some nocturnal carnivore to be heard from time to time, and the sudden buzzing of a beetle, the clink of a little porcelain cup being set on the low table.

Now the voice of the second driver reaches this central section of the veranda, coming from the direction of the sheds; it is singing a native tune, with incomprehensible words, or even without words.

The sheds are located on the other side of the house, to the right of the large courtyard. The voice must therefore come around the corner occupied by the office and beneath the overhanging roof, which noticeably muffles it, though some sound can cross the room itself through the blinds (on the south façade and the east gable-end).

But it is a voice that carries well, full and strong, though in a rather low register. It is flexible too, flowing easily from one note to another, then suddenly breaking off.

Because of the peculiar nature of this kind of melody, it is difficult to determine if the song is interrupted for some fortuitous reason—in relation, for instance, to the manual work the singer is performing at the same time—or whether the tune has come to its natural conclusion.

Similarly, when it begins again, it is just as sudden, as abrupt, starting on notes which hardly seem to constitute a beginning, or a reprise.

At other places, however, something seems about to end; everything indicates this: a gradual cadence, tranquillity regained, the feeling that nothing remains to be said; but after the note which should be the last comes another one, without the least break in continuity, with the same ease, then another, and others following, and the hearer supposes himself transported into the heart of the poem . . . when at that point everything stops without warning.

A . . ., in the bedroom, again bends over the letter she is writing. The sheet of pale blue paper in front of her has only a few lines on it at this point; A . . . adds three or four more words, rather hastily, and holds her pen in the air above the paper. After a moment she raises her head again while the song resumes, from the direction of the sheds.

It is doubtless the same poem continuing. If the themes sometimes blur, they only recur somewhat later, all the more clearly, virtually identical. Yet these repetitions, these tiny variations, halts, regressions, can give rise to modifications—though barely perceptible—eventually moving quite far from the point of departure.

To hear better, A . . . has turned her head toward the open window next to her. In the hollow of the valley, work is under way to repair the log bridge over the little stream. The dirt revetment has been removed from about a quarter of its width. The men are going to replace the termite-infested wood with new logs that still have their bark on, cut to the proper lengths beforehand, now lying across the road, just in front of the bridge. Instead of piling them up in an orderly fashion, the porters have thrown them down and left them lying in all directions.

The first two logs are lying parallel to each other (and to the bank), the space between them equivalent to approximately twice their common diameter. A third cuts across them diagonally at about a third of the way across their length. The next, perpendicular to this latter, touches its end; its other end almost touches the last log which forms a loose V with it, its point not quite closed. But this fifth log is also parallel to the two first logs, and to the direction of the stream the little bridge is built over.

How much time has passed since the bridge underpinnings last had to be repaired? The logs, supposedly treated against termite action, must have received defective treatment. Sooner or later, of course, these earth-covered logs, periodically doused by the rising stream, are liable to be infested by insects. It is possible to protect over long periods of time only structures built far off the ground, as in the case of the house, for instance.

In the bedroom, A . . . has continued her letter in her delicate, close-set, regular handwriting. The page is now half full. But she slowly raises her head and begins to turn it gradually but steadily toward the open window.

There are five workmen at the bridge, and as many new logs. All the men are now crouching in the same position: forearms resting on their thighs, hands hanging between their knees. They are facing each other, two on the right bank, three on the left. They are probably discussing how they are going to complete their job, or else are resting a little before the effort, tired from having carried the logs this far. In any case, they are perfectly motionless.

In the banana plantation behind them, a trapeze-shaped patch stretches uphill, and since no stems have been harvested in it yet, the regularity of the trees' alternate arrangement is still absolute.

The five men, on each side of the little bridge, are also arranged symmetrically: in two parallel lines, the intervals being the same in each group, and the two men on the right bank—whose backs alone are visible—placed in the center of the intervals determined by their three companions on the left bank, who are facing the house, where A . . . appears behind the open window recess.

She is standing. In her hand she is holding a sheet of pale blue paper of ordinary letter-paper size, which shows the creases where it has been folded into quarters. But her arm is half-bent, and the sheet of paper is only at her waist; her eyes, which are looking far above it, wander toward the horizon, at the top of the opposite hillside. A . . . listens to the native chant, distant but still distinct, which reaches the veranda.

On the other side of the hallway door, under the symmetrical window of the office, Franck is sitting in his chair.

A . . ., who has gone to get the drinks herself, sets down the loaded tray on the low table. She uncorks the cognac and pours it into the three glasses lined up on the tray. Then she fills them with soda. Having distributed the first two, she sits down in her turn in the empty chair, holding the third glass in one hand.

This is when she asks if the usual ice cubes will be necessary, declaring that these bottles come out of the refrigerator, though only one of the two has frosted over upon contact with the air.

She calls the boy. No one answers.

"One of us had better go," she says.

But neither she nor Franck moves.

In the pantry, the boy is already taking the ice cubes out of their trays, according to the orders his mistress gave him, he declares. And he adds that he is going to bring them right away, instead of specifying when this order was given.

On the veranda, Franck and A . . . have remained in their chairs. She has not been in any hurry about serving the ice: she has still not touched the shiny metal bucket which the boy has just set down next to her, its luster already frosted over.

Like A . . . beside him, Franck looks straight ahead, toward the horizon, at the top of the hillside opposite. A sheet of pale blue paper, folded several times—probably in eighths—now sticks out of his right shirt pocket. The left pocket is still carefully buttoned, while the flap of the other one is now raised by the letter, which sticks above the edge of the khaki cloth by a good half inch.

A . . . notices the pale blue paper is attracting attention. She starts explaining about a misunderstanding between herself and the boy with regard to the ice. Then did she tell him not to bring it? In any case, this is the first time she has not succeeded in making herself understood by one of her servants.

"There has to be a first time for everything," she answers, with a calm smile. Her green eyes, which never blink, merely reflect the outline of a figure against the sky.

Down below, in the hollow of the valley, the arrangement of the workmen is no longer the same, at either end of the log bridge. Only one remains on the right bank, the other four being lined up opposite him. But their postures have not changed at all. Behind the single man, one of the new logs has disappeared: the one which was lying on top of two others. A log with earth-covered bark, however, has appeared on the left bank, quite a way behind the four workmen facing the house.

Franck stands up with sudden energy, and sets down on the low table the glass he has just emptied at one gulp. There is nothing left of the ice cube in the glass. Franck walks stiffly to the hallway door. He stops there. His head and the upper part of his body turn toward A . . ., who is still sitting in her chair.

"Forgive me, again, for being such a bad mechanic."

But A . . .'s face is not turned toward him and the grimace which accompanies Franck's words has remained far outside her field of vision, a grimace that is, moreover, immediately absorbed, at the same time as the wrinkled white suit, by the shadow of the hallway.

At the bottom of the glass he has set down on the table as he left, a tiny piece of ice is melting, rounded on one side, on the other formed into a bevelled edge. A little further away come the bottle of soda, the cognac, then the bridge crossing the little stream where the five crouching men are now arranged as follows: one on the right bank, two on the left, two others on the bridge itself, near its far end, all facing the same central point which they seem to be considering with the closest attention.

There remain only two more new logs to put in place.

Then Franck and his hostess are sitting in the same chairs, but they have exchanged places: A . . . is in Franck's chair and vice versa. So now it is Franck who is nearest the low table where the ice bucket and the bottles are.

A . . . calls the boy.

He appears at once on the veranda, at the corner of the house. He walks with mechanical steps toward the little table, picks it up without spilling anything on it, sets the whole thing down a little farther away, near his mistress. He then continues on his way, without saying a word, in the same direction, with the same mechanical gait, toward the other corner of the house and the eastern side of the veranda, where he disappears.

Franck and A . . ., still silent and motionless in their chairs, continue to stare at the horizon.

Franck tells a story about his car's engine trouble, laughing and gesturing with a disproportionate energy and enthusiasm. He picks up his glass from the table beside him and empties it in one gulp, as if he had no need to open his throat to swallow the liquid: everything runs down into his stomach at once. He sets the glass down on the table, between his plate and the place-mat. He begins eating again right away. His considerable appetite is made even more noticeable by the numerous, emphatic movements he makes: his right hand that picks up in turn the knife, the fork and the bread, the fork that passes alternately from the right hand to the left, the knife that cuts up the pieces of meat one by one and which is laid on the table after each use, so as to leave the fork free play as it changes hands, the comings and goings of the fork between plate and mouth, the rhythmic distortions of all the muscles of the face during a conscientious mastication which, even before being completed, is already accompanied by an accelerated repetition of the whole series.

The right hand picks up the bread and raises it to the mouth, the right hand sets the bread down on the white cloth and picks up the knife, the left hand picks up the fork, the fork sinks into the meat, the knife cuts off a piece of meat, the right hand sets down the knife on the cloth, the left hand puts the fork in the right hand, which sinks the fork into the piece of meat, which approaches the mouth, which begins to chew with movements of contraction and extension which are reflected all over the face, in the cheekbones, the eyes, the ears, while the right hand again picks up the fork and puts it in the left hand, then picks up the bread, then the knife, then the fork. . . .

The boy comes in through the open pantry door. He approaches the table. His steps are increasingly jerky, as are his gestures when he raises the plates one by one to put them on the sideboard and replace them by clean plates. He goes out immediately afterwards, moving arms and legs in cadence, like a crude mechanism.

This is the moment when the scene of the squashing of the centipede on the bare wall occurs: Franck stands up, picks up his napkin, approaches the wall, squashes the centipede against the wall, lifts his napkin, squashes the centipede on the floor.

The hand with tapering fingers has clenched into a fist on the white cloth. The five widespaced fingers have closed over the palm with such force that they have pulled the cloth with them. The cloth shows five convergent creases, much longer than the fingers which have produced them.

Only the first joint is still visible. On the ring finger gleams a thin ribbon of gold that barely rises above the flesh. Around the hand radiate the creases, looser and looser as they move out from the center, but also wider and wider, finally becoming a uniform white surface on which Franck's brown, muscular hand wearing a large flat ring of the same type comes to rest.

Just beside it, the knife blade has left on the cloth a tiny, dark, elongated, sinuous stain surrounded by more tenuous marks. The brown hand, after wavering in the vicinity a moment, suddenly rises to the shirt pocket where it again tries, with a mechanical movement, to push down the pale blue folded letter which sticks out by a good half inch.

The shirt is made of a stiff fabric, a twilled cotton whose khaki color has faded slightly after many washings. Under the upper edge of the pocket runs a line of horizontal stitching over a sewn bracket with the point downward. At the tip of this point is sewn the button normally intended to close the pocket. The button is made of a yellowish plastic material; the thread that attaches it forms a little cross at the center. The letter, above, is covered with a fine, close-set handwriting, perpendicular to the edge of the pocket.

To the right come, in order, the short sleeve of the khaki shirt, the bulging native terra-cotta pitcher which marks the middle of the sideboard, then, at the end of the latter, the two kerosene lamps, extinguished and set side by side against the wall; still further to the right, the corner of the room, immediately followed by the open leaf of the first window.

And Franck's car appears, brought into view through the window quite naturally by the conversation. It is a big blue sedan of American manufacture, whose body—though dusty—seems new. The motor too is in good condition: it never gives its owner any trouble.

The latter is still behind the wheel. Only his passenger has stepped out onto the gravel of the courtyard. She is wearing shoes with extremely high heels and must be careful to put her feet down in places that are level. But she is not at all awkward at this exercise, whose difficulty she does not even seem to notice. She stands motionless next to the front door of the car, leaning toward the gray imitation-leather upholstery, above the window which has been rolled down as far as it will go.

The white dress with the wide skirt almost disappears above the waist: the head, arms, and upper part of the body, filling the window opening, also obscure what is happening inside. A . . . is probably gathering up the purchases she has just made to carry them with her. But the left elbow reappears, soon followed by the forearm, the wrist, the hand, which holds onto the edge of the window-frame.

After another pause, the shoulders emerge into daylight too, then the neck, and the head with its heavy mass of black hair, whose loose curls are a little disarranged, and finally the right hand which holds by its string only an extremely tiny green cubical package.

Leaving the print of four parallel tapering fingers on the dusty enamel of the window-frame, the left hand hurriedly arranges the hair, while A . . . walks away from the blue car and, after a last look back, heads toward the door with her decisive gait. The uneven surface of the courtyard seems to level out in front of her, for A . . . never even glances at her feet.

Then she is standing in front of the door which she has closed behind her. From this point she sees the whole house down the middle: the main room (living room on the left and dining room on the right, where the table is already set for dinner), the central hallway (off which open five doors, all closed, three on the right and two on the left), the veranda, and beyond its openwork balustrade, the opposite slope of the valley.

Starting from the crest, the slope is divided horizontally into three parts: an irregular strip of brush and two culti- vated patches of different ages. The brush is reddish- colored, dotted here and there with green bushes. A clump of trees marks the highest point of cultivation in this sec- tor; it occupies the corner of a rectangular patch where the bare earth can still be distinguished in spots between the clusters of young leaves. Lower down, the second patch, in the shape of a trapezoid, is being harvested: the plate-sized white discs of the cut trunks are about as numerous as the adult trees still standing.

One side of this trapezoid is formed by the dirt road which ends at the little bridge over the stream. The five men are now arranged in a quincunx, two on each bank and one in the middle of the bridge, all facing upstream and watching the muddy water flowing between two vertical banks which have collapsed a little here and there.

On the right bank there still remain two new logs to be set in place. They form a kind of loose V with an open point across the road rising toward the house and the garden.

A . . . is just coming home. She has been visiting Chris- tiane, who has been kept from going out for several days by her child's poor health, as delicate as her mother's and just as badly adapted to colonial life. A . . ., whom Franck has driven home in his car, crosses the living room and walks down the hallway to her bedroom which opens onto the terrace.

The bedroom windows have remained wide open all morning long. A . . . approaches the first one and closes its right-hand leaf, while the hand resting on the left one interrupts her gesture. The face turns in profile toward the half-opening, the neck straight, the ear cocked.

The low voice of the second driver reaches her.

The man is singing a native tune, a wordless, seemingly endless phrase which suddenly stops for no apparent reason. A . . ., finishing her gesture, closes the second leaf of the window.

Then she closes the two other windows. But she lowers none of the blinds.

She sits down in front of the dressing-table and looks at herself in the oval mirror, motionless, her elbows on the marble top and her hands pressing on each side of her face, against the temples. Not one of her features moves, nor the long-lashed eyelids, nor even the pupils at the center of the green irises. Petrified by her own gaze, attentive and serene, she seems not to feel time passing.

Leaning to one side, her tortoise-shell comb in her hand, she fixes her hair again before coming to the table. A mass of the heavy black curls hangs over the nape of her neck. The free hand plunges its tapering fingers into it.

A . . . is lying fully dressed on the bed. One of her legs rests on the satin spread; the other, bent at the knee, hangs half over the edge. The arm on this side is bent toward the head lying on the bolster. Stretched across the wide bed, the other arm lies out from the body at approximately a forty-five degree angle. Her face is turned upward toward the ceiling. Her eyes are made still larger by the darkness.

Near the bed, against the same wall, is the heavy chest. A . . . is standing in front of the open top drawer, on which she is leaning in order to look for something, or else to arrange the contents. The operation takes a long time and requires no movement of the body.

She is sitting in the chair between the hallway door and the writing table. She is rereading a letter which shows the creases where it has been folded. Her longs legs are crossed. Her right hand is holding the sheet in front of her face; her left hand is gripping the end of the armrest.

A . . . is writing, sitting at the table near the first window. Actually, she is getting ready to write, unless she has just finished her letter. The pen remains suspended an inch or so above the paper. Her face is raised toward the calendar hanging on the wall.

Between this first window and the second, there is just room enough for the large wardrobe. A . . ., who is standing beside it, is therefore visible only from the third window, the one that overlooks the west gable-end. It is a mirrored wardrobe. A . . . is carefully examining her face at close range.

Now she has moved still further to the right, into the corner of the room which also comprises the southwest corner of the house. It should be easy to observe her from one of the two doors, that of the hallway or that of the bathroom; but the doors are of wood, without blinds that can be seen through. As for the blinds on the three windows, none of them is now arranged so that anything can be seen through them.

Now the house is empty.

A . . . has gone to town with Franck to make a few necessary purchases. She has not said what they were.

They left very early, so as to have enough time to run

their errands and still be able to return to the plantation the same night.

Having left the house at six-thirty this morning, they expect to be back a little after midnight, which means an absence of eighteen hours, at least eight of which will be spent on the road, if all goes well.

But delays are always likely on these bad roads. Even if they start back at the expected time, immediately after a quick dinner, the travellers might not get home until around one in the morning, or even much later.

Meanwhile, the house is empty. All the bedroom windows are open, as well as its two doors, opening onto the hallway and the bathroom. The door between the bathroom and the hallway is also wide open, as is that from the hallway to the central part of the veranda.

The veranda is empty too; none of the armchairs has been brought outside this morning, nor has the low table that is used for cocktails and coffee. But under the open office window, the flagstones show the trace of eight chair legs: two sets of four shiny points, smoother than the stone around them. The two left-hand corners of the right-hand square are scarcely two inches away from the two right-hand corners of the left-hand square.

These shiny points are clearly visible only from the balustrade. They disappear when the observer comes closer. Looking down from the window immediately above them, it becomes impossible to tell where they are.

The furnishings of this room are very simple: files and shelves against the walls, two chairs, the massive desk. On one corner of the latter stands a little mother-of-pearl inlaid frame with a photograph taken at the seaside, in Europe. A . . . is sitting on the terrace of a large cafe. Her chair is set at an angle to the table on which she is about to set down her glass.

The table is a metal disc pierced with innumerable holes, the largest of which form a complicated rosette: a series of S's all starting at the center, like double-curved spokes of a wheel, and each spiraling at the outer end, at the periphery of the disc.

The base supporting the table consists of a slender triple stem whose strands separate to converge again, coiling (in three vertical planes through the axis of the system) into three similar volutes whose lower whorls rest on the ground and are bound together by a ring placed a little higher on the curve.

The chair is similarly constructed, with perforated metal sheets and stems. It is harder to follow its convolutions, because of the person sitting on it, who largely conceals them from view.

On the table near a second glass, at the right edge of the picture, are a man's hand and the cuff of a jacket sleeve, cut off by the white vertical margin.

All the other portions of chairs evident in the photograph seem to belong to unoccupied seats. There is no one on the veranda, as elsewhere in the house.

In the dining room, a single place has been set for lunch, on the side of the table facing the pantry door and the long, low sideboard extending from this door to the window.

The window is closed. The courtyard is empty. The second driver must have parked the truck near the sheds, to wash it. In the place it usually occupies, all that remains is a large black spot contrasting with the dusty surface of the courtyard. This is a little oil which has dripped out of the motor, always in the same place.

It is easy to make this spot disappear, thanks to the flaws in the rough glass of the window: the blackened surface has merely to be brought into proximity with one of the flaws of the windowpane, by successive experiments.

The spot begins by growing larger, one of its sides bulging to form a rounded protuberance, itself larger than the initial object. But a few fractions of an inch farther, this bulge is transformed into a series of tiny concentric crescents which diminish until they are only lines, while the other side of the spot shrinks, leaving behind it a stalk-shaped appendage which bulges in its turn for a second; then suddenly everything disappears.

Behind the glass, now, in the angle determined by the central vertical frame and the horizontal cross-piece, there is only the grayish-beige color of the dusty gravel that constitutes the surface of the courtyard.

On the opposite wall, the centipede is there, in its tell-tale spot, right in the middle of the panel.

It has stopped, a tiny oblique line two inches long at eye level, halfway between the baseboard (at the hall doorway) and the corner of the ceiling. The creature is motionless. Only its antennae rise and fall one after the other in an alternating, slow, but continuous movement.

At its posterior extremity, the considerable development of the legs—of the last pair especially, which are longer than the antennae—identifies it unquestionably as the Scutigera, also known as the "spider-centipede" or "minute-centipede," so called because of a native belief as to the rapidity of the action of its bite, supposedly mortal. Actually this species is not very venomous; it is much less so, in any case, than many Scolopendra common in the region.

Suddenly the anterior part of the body begins to move, executing a rotation which curves the dark line toward the lower part of the wall. And immediately, without having time to go any further, the creature falls onto the tiles, still twisting and curling up its long legs while its mandibles rapidly open and close around its mouth in a quivering reflex.

Ten seconds later, it is nothing more than a reddish pulp in which are mingled the debris of unrecognizable sections.

But on the bare wall, on the contrary, the image of the squashed Scutigera is perfectly clear, incomplete but not blurred, reproduced with the faithfulness of an anatomical drawing in which only a portion of the elements are shown: an antenna, two curving mandibles, the head and the first joint, half of the second, a few large legs, etc. . . .

The outline seems indelible. It has no relief, none of the

thickness of a dried stain which would come off if scratched at with a fingernail. It looks more like brown ink impregnating the surface layer of the paint.

Besides, it is not practical to wash the wall. This dull-finish paint is much more fragile than the ordinary gloss paint with linseed oil in it which was previously used on the walls of this room. The best solution would be to use an eraser, a hard, fine-grained eraser which would gradually wear down the soiled surface—the typewriter eraser, for instance, which is in the top left desk drawer.

The slender traces of bits of legs or antennae come off right away, with the first strokes of the eraser. The larger part of the body, already quite pale, is curved into a question mark that becomes increasingly vague toward the tip of the curve, and soon disappears completely. But the head and the first joints require a more extensive rubbing: after losing its color, the remaining shape stays the same for quite a long time. The outlines have become only a little less sharp. The hard eraser passing back and forth over the same point does not have much effect now.

A complementary operation seems in order: to scratch the surface very lightly, with the corner of a razor blade. Some white dust rises from the wall. The precision of the tool permits the area exposed to its effect to be carefully determined. A new rubbing with the eraser now finishes off the work quite easily.

The stain has disappeared altogether. There now remains only a vaguely outlined paler area, without any apparent depression of the surface, which might pass for an insignificant defect in the finish, at worst.

The paper is much thinner nevertheless; it has become more translucid, uneven, a little downy. The same razor blade, bent between two fingers to raise the center of its cutting edge, also serves to shave off the fluff the eraser has made. The back of a fingernail finally smoothes down the last roughness.

In broad daylight, a closer inspection of the pale blue

sheet reveals that two short pen strokes have resisted every-thing, doubtless because they were made too heavily. Unless a new word, skillfully arranged to cover up these two unnecessary strokes, replaces the old one on the page, the traces of black ink will still be visible there. Unless the eraser is used once again.

It stands out clearly against the dark wood of the desk, as does the razor blade, and the foot of the mother-of-pearl inlaid frame where A . . . is about to set down her glass on the round table with its many perforations. The eraser is a thin pink disc whose central part is covered by a little white-metal circle. The razor blade is a flat, polished rectangle, its short sides rounded, and pierced with three holes in a line. The central hole is circular; the two others, one on each side, reproduce precisely—on a much smaller scale—the general shape of the blade, that is, a rectangle with its short sides rounded.

Instead of looking at the glass she is about to set down, A . . ., whose chair is set at an angle to the table, is turning in the opposite direction to smile at the photographer, as if encouraging him to take this candid shot.

The photographer has not lowered his camera to put it on a level with his model. In fact he seems to have climbed up onto something: a stone bench, a step, or a low wall. A . . . has to raise her head to turn her face toward the lens. The slender neck is erect, turned toward the right. On this side, the hand is resting easily on the far edge of the chair, against the thigh; the bare arm slightly bent at the elbow. The knees are apart, the legs half extended, ankles crossed.

The delicate waist is encircled by a wide belt with a triple clasp. The left arm, extended, holds the glass a few inches above the openwork table.

The lustrous black curls fall free to the shoulders. The flood of heavy locks with reddish highlights trembles at the slightest movement the head makes. The head must be shaken with tiny movements, imperceptible in themselves, but amplified by the mass of hair, creating gleaming, quickly vanishing eddies whose sudden intensity is reawakened in unlooked-for convulsions a little lower . . . lower still . . . and a last spasm much lower.

The face, hidden because of her position, is bending over the table where the invisible hands are busy with some long-drawn-out and laborious task: mending a stocking, polishing nails, a tiny pencil drawing, erasing a stain or a badly chosen word. From time to time she straightens up and leans back to judge her work from a distance. With a slow gesture, she pushes back a shorter strand of hair which has come loose from this unstable arrangement and is annoying her.

But the rebellious curl remains on the white silk of her shoulder, where it traces a wavy line ending in a hook. Under the moving mass of hair, the delicate waist is divided vertically, along the spine, by the narrow line of the metal zipper.

A . . . is standing on the veranda, at the corner of the house, near the square column that supports the southwest corner of the roof. She is leaning both hands on the railing, facing south, looking over the garden and the whole valley.

She is in full sunlight. The sun strikes her directly on the forehead. But she does not mind it, even at noon. Her fore-shortened shadow falls perpendicularly across the flagstones of which it covers, lengthwise, no more than one. A quarter of an inch behind it begins the roof shadow, parallel with the railing. The sun is almost at its zenith.

The two extended arms are an equal distance from either side of the hips. The hands are both holding the wooden hand-rail in the same way. Since A . . . is standing with half her weight on each of her high-heeled shoes, the symmetry of her whole body is perfect.

A . . . is standing in front of one of the closed windows of the living room, directly opposite the dirt road that comes down from the highway. Through the glass she looks straight ahead of her, toward the place where the road enters the dusty courtyard, which the shadow of the house darkens with a strip about three yards wide. The rest of the courtyard is white in the sunlight.

The large room, in comparison, seems dark. Her dress takes on a cold blue tinge from the shadows. A . . . does not move. She continues to stare at the courtyard and the road between the banana trees, straight ahead of her.

A . . . is in the bathroom, whose door to the hallway she has left ajar. She is not washing. She is standing against the white lacquer table in front of the square window that comes down to her breast. Beyond the open window-recess, above the veranda, the openwork balustrade, the garden down the slope, her eyes can see only the green mass of the banana trees, and farther on, passing above the highway going down to the plain, the rocky spur of the plateau, behind which the sun has just disappeared.

The night does not take long falling in these countries without twilight. The lacquered table suddenly turns deep blue, like her dress, the white floor, and the sides of the bathtub. The whole room is plunged into darkness.

Only the square of the window makes a spot of paler violet, against which A . . .'s black silhouette appears: the line of her shoulders and arms, the contour of her hair. It is impossible, in this light, to know if her head is turned toward the window or in the opposite direction.

In the office, the light suddenly fades. The sun has set. A . . . can no longer be seen. The photograph can be distinguished only by the mother-of-pearl edges of its frame, which gleam in the remaining light. In front of it shines the oblong of the razor blade and the metal ellipse in the center of the eraser. But this lasts only a moment. Now the eye can distinguish nothing any longer, despite the open windows.

The five workmen are still at their post, in the hollow of the valley, squatting in a quincunx on the little bridge. The running water of the stream still glitters in the last reflections of the daylight. And then, nothing more.

On the veranda, A . . . will have to close her book soon.

She has continued reading until the light has become too faint. Then she lifts her face, puts the book down on the low table within arm's reach, and remains motionless, her bare arms stretched out on the elbow-rests, leaning back in her chair, her eyes wide open, staring at the empty sky, the absent banana trees, the railing engulfed in its turn by the darkness.

And the deafening racket of the crickets already fills the night, as if it had never ceased to be there. The continuous grating, without progression or nuance, immediately reaches its full development, has been at its climax for some time already, minutes or hours, for no beginning can be perceived at any one moment.

Now the area is altogether dark. Although there is time for eyes to become accustomed to it, no object appears, even those closest.

But now once again there are balusters toward the corner of the house, half-balusters, more precisely, and a hand-rail on top; and the flagstones gradually appear at their feet. The corner of the wall reveals its vertical line. A warm glow appears behind it.

It is a lighted lamp, one of the big kerosene lamps that reveals two walking legs as far up as the bare knees and calves. The boy approaches, holding the lamp at arm's length. Shadows dance in all directions.

The boy has not yet reached the little table when A . . .'s voice can be heard, precise and low; she tells him to put the lamp in the dining room, after being careful to shut the windows, as every evening.

"You know you're not supposed to bring the lamp out here. It attracts mosquitoes."

The boy has said nothing and has not stopped for even a moment. Even the regularity of his gait has not been altered. Having reached a point opposite the door he makes a quarter-turn toward the hallway where he disappears, leaving behind him only a fading gleam: the doorway, a rectangle on the veranda flagstone, and six balusters at the other end. Then nothing more.

A . . . has not turned her head in speaking to the boy. Her face received the lamp's beams on the right side. This brightly illuminated profile still clings to the retina. In the darkness where no object can be seen, even those closest, the luminous spot shifts at will, without its intensity fading, keeping the outline of the forehead, the nose, the chin, the mouth. . . .

The spot is on the wall of the house, on the flagstones, against the empty sky. It is everywhere in the valley, from the garden to the stream and up the opposite slope. It is in the office too, in the bedroom, in the dining room, in the living room, in the courtyard, on the road up to the highway.

But A . . . has not moved an inch. She has not opened her mouth to speak, her voice has not interrupted the racket of the nocturnal crickets; the boy has not come out on the veranda, so he has not brought the lamp, knowing perfectly well that his mistress does not want it.

He has carried it into her bedroom, where his mistress is now preparing to leave.

The lamp is set on the dressing-table. A . . . is putting on the last of her discreet make-up: the lipstick which merely accentuates the natural color of her lips but which seems darker in this glaring light.

Dawn has not yet broken.

Franck will come soon to call for A . . . and take her down to the port. She is sitting in front of the oval mirror where her full face is reflected, lit from only one side, at a short distance from her own face seen in profile.

A . . . bends toward the mirror. The two faces come closer. They are no more than four inches from each other, but they keep their forms and their respective positions: a profile and a full face, parallel to each other.

The right hand and the hand in the mirror trace on the lips and on their reflection the exact image of the lips, somewhat brighter, clearer, slightly darker.

Two light knocks sound at the hallway door.

The bright lips and the lips in profile move in perfect synchronization:

"Yes, what is it?"

The voice is restrained, as in a sickroom, or like the voice of a thief talking to his accomplice.

"The gentleman, he is here," the boy's voice answers on the other side of the door.

No sound of a motor, however, has broken the silence (which has no silence, but the continuous hissing of the kerosene lamp).

A . . . says: "I'm coming."

She calmly finishes the curving rim above her chin with an assured gesture.

She stands up, crosses the room, walks around the big bed, picks up her handbag on the chest and the white wide-brimmed straw hat. She opens the door without making any noise (though without excessive precautions), goes out, closes the door behind her.

The sound of her steps fades down the hallway.

The entrance door opens and closes.

It is six-thirty.

The whole house is empty. It has been empty since morning.

It is now six-thirty. The sun has disappeared behind the rocky spur which bounds the main section of the plateau.

The night is black and heavy, without the least breath of air, full of the deafening noise of crickets which seems to have been going on forever.

A . . . is not returning for dinner, which she will take in town with Franck before starting back. She has said nothing

103

about preparing anything for her return. Because she will not need anything. It is useless to expect her. In any case it is useless to expect her at dinner.

On the dining room table the boy has set a single place, opposite the long, low sideboard which takes up almost the entire wall between the open pantry door and the closed window overlooking the courtyard. The curtains, which have not been drawn, reveal the six black panes of the window.

A single lamp illuminates the large room. It is placed on the southwest corner of the table (that is, toward the pantry), lighting up the white cloth. To the right of the lamp, a little spot of sauce marks Franck's place: an elongated, sinuous stain surrounded by more tenuous markings. On the other side, the lamp's beams strike perpendicularly against the nearby naked wall, showing quite clearly in the full light the image of the centipede Franck squashed.

If each of the Scutigera's legs consists of four joints of varying lengths, none of those which are outlined here, on the dull finish of the paint, is intact—except perhaps one, the first on the left. But it is stretched out, almost straight, so that its joints are not easy to determine with any certitude. The original leg may have been considerably longer. The antenna, too, has doubtless not been printed on the wall to its very tip.

On the white plate, a land crab spreads out its five pairs of clearly jointed, muscular legs. Around its mouth, many smaller appendages are arranged in pairs. The creature uses them to produce a kind of crackling sound, audible at close range, like that which the Scutigera makes in certain cases.

But the lamp prevents any such sound from being heard because of its constant hissing, of which the ear is aware only when it tries to hear any other sound.

On the veranda, where the boy has now carried the little table and one of the low chairs, the sound of the lamp fades whenever an animal cry interrupts it.

The crickets have fallen silent for some time now. The

night is already well-advanced. There is neither moon nor stars. There is not a breath of air. It is a black, calm, hot night, like all the rest, occasionally interrupted only by the short, shrill calls of tiny nocturnal carnivores, the sudden buzzing of a beetle, the rustle of a bat's wings.

Then a silence. But a fainter sound, something like a hum, makes the ear strain. . . . It stops at once. And again the lamp's hissing can be heard.

Besides, it was more like a growl than the sound of a car motor. A . . . has not yet returned. They are a little late, which is quite normal, on these bad roads.

There is no doubt the lamp draws mosquitoes; but it draws them toward its own light. So it is enough to put it at some distance in order not to be bothered by them or by other insects.

They all turn around the glass, accompanying the even hiss of the kerosene lamp with their circular flights. Their small size, their relative distance, their speed—all the greater the closer they fly to the source of light—keep the shapes of the bodies and wings from being recognized. It is not even possible to distinguish among the different species, not to mention naming them. They are merely particles in motion, describing more or less flattened ellipses in horizontal planes or at slight angles, cutting the elongated cylinder of the lamp at various levels.

But the orbits are rarely centered on the lamp; almost all fly further to one side, right or left, than the other—so far, sometimes, that the tiny body disappears in the darkness. It immediately returns to view—or another returns in its place—and soon retraces its orbit, so that it circles with others of its kind in a common, harshly illuminated zone about a yard and a half long.

At every moment, certain ellipses narrow until they become tangent to the lamp on each side (front and back). They are then reduced to their smallest dimensions in both directions, and attain their highest speeds. But they do not maintain this accelerated rhythm long: by a sudden withdrawal, the generating element resumes a calmer gravitation.

Besides, whether it is a question of amplitude, shape, or the more or less eccentric situation, the variations are probably incessant within the swarm. To follow them it would be necessary to differentiate individuals. Since this is impossible, a certain general unity is established within which the local crises, arrivals, departures and permutations no longer enter into account.

Shrill and short, an animal's cry sounds quite close, seeming to come from the garden, just at the foot of the veranda. Then the same cry, after three seconds, indicates its presence on the other side of the house. And again there is silence, which is not silence but a succession of identical, shriller, more remote cries in the mass of the banana trees near the stream, perhaps on the opposite slope, reaching from one end of the valley to the other.

Now there is a duller sound, less fugitive, that attracts the attention: a kind of growl, or rumble, or hum. . . .

But even before being sufficiently clear to be identified, the noise stops. The ear, which vainly tries to locate it again in the darkness, no longer hears anything in its place except the hiss of the kerosene lamp.

Its sound is plaintive, high-pitched, somewhat nasal. But its complexity permits it to have overtones at various levels. Of an absolute evenness, both muffled and shrill, it fills the night and the ears as if it came from nowhere.

Around the lamp, the circling of the insects is still the same. By examining it closely, however, the eye at last manages to make out some bodies that are larger than others. Yet this is not enough to determine their nature. Against the black background they form only bright points which become increasingly brilliant as they approach the light, turning black as soon as they pass in front of the lamp with the light behind them, then recovering all their brilliance whose intensity now decreases toward the tip of the orbit.

In the suddenness of its return toward the glass, the bright point violently plunges against it, producing a dry click. Fallen on the table, it has become a tiny reddish beetle with closed wing cases which slowly circles on the darker wood.

Other creatures similar to this one have already fallen on the table; they wander there, tracing uncertain paths with many detours and problematical goals. Suddenly raising its wing cases into a V with curved sides, one of them extends its filmy wings, takes off, and immediately returns to the swarm of flying bodies.

But it constitutes one of its heaviest, slowest elements, therefore less difficult for the eyes to follow. The whorls which it describes are also probably among the more capricious: they include loops, garlands, sudden ascents and brutal falls, changes of direction, abrupt retracings. . . .

The duller sound has already lasted several seconds, or even several minutes now: a kind of growling, or rumble, or hum of a motor, the motor of an automobile on the highway rising toward the plateau. It fades for a moment, only to resume all the more clearly. This time it is certainly the sound of a car on the road.

It rises in pitch as it draws nearer. It fills the whole valley with its regular, monotonous throbbing, much louder than it seems in daylight. Its importance quickly surpasses what would normally be expected of a mere sedan.

The sound has now reached the point where the dirt road turns off the highway toward the plantation. Instead of slowing down to turn to the right, it continues its uniform progress, now reaching the ears from behind the house, toward the east gable-end. It has gone past the turn-off.

Having reached the flat section of the road, just below the rocky rim where the plateau comes to an end, the truck shifts gears and continues with a fainter rumble. Then the sound gradually fades away, as the truck drives east, its powerful headlights lighting up the clumps of stiff-leaved trees that dot the brush on the way to the next plantation, Franck's.

His car might have had engine trouble again. They should have been back long since.

Around the kerosene lamps the ellipses continue to turn, lengthening, shortening, moving off to the right or left, rising, falling, or swaying first to one side then the other, mingling in an increasingly tangled skein in which no autonomous curve remains identifiable.

A . . . should have been back long since.

Nevertheless there is no lack of probable reasons for the delay. Apart from an accident—never impossible—there are the two successive punctures that oblige the driver to repair one of the tires himself: take off the wheel, remove the inner tube, find the hole in the light from the head-lights, etc. . . .; there is the severance of some electrical connection, due to a jolt that was too violent, which might cut the headlight wires, involving long investigations and a haphazard mending job by the poor light of a pocket flash-light. The road is in such bad condition that an important part of the car's engine might be damaged, if the car is going too fast: shock-absorber broken, axle bent, crank case split. . . . There is also the help that cannot be refused to another driver in difficulty. There are the various risks de-laying the departure itself: unforeseen prolongation of some errand, excessive slowness of the waiter, invitation to dinner accepted at the last minute with a friend met by chance, etc., etc. . . . There is, last of all, the driver's fatigue which has made him postpone his return to the next day.

The sound of a truck coming up the road along the near slope of the valley fills the air again. It is moving east from one end of the auditory field to the other, reaching its maximum volume as it passes behind the house. It is moving just as fast as the preceding one, which for a moment might cause it to be confused with a touring car; but the sound is much too loud. The truck is apparently empty. They are the banana trucks returning, empty, from the port after leaving their stems in the sheds on the docks, where the "Cap Saint-Jean" is moored.

This is the picture on the post-office calendar hanging on the bedroom wall. The brand-new white ship is moored beside the long pier which juts out into the sea from the lower margin. The structure of the pier cannot be clearly discerned: apparently there is a wood (or iron) framework supporting a tar-paved roadway. While the pier is virtually at water level, the ship's sides rise far above it. The ship is shown head on, revealing the vertical line of its stem and its two smooth sides, of which only one is in sunlight.

The ship and the pier take up the center of the picture, the former to the left, the latter on the right. Around it, the sea is covered with canoes and rowboats: eight are clearly visible and three others suggested in the background. A less fragile craft, provided with a square wind-filled sail, is about to pass the end of the pier. The latter is covered with a brightly dressed crowd near a pile of bales, in front of the ship.

A little to one side, but in the foreground, turning his back to this confusion and to the great white ship which provokes it, someone in European clothes is looking toward the right side of the picture at some sort of flotsam whose vague mass is floating a few yards away from him. The surface of the water is faintly rippled with a short, regular swell which advances toward the man. The flotsam, half raised by the tide, seems to be an old piece of clothing or an empty sack.

The largest of the canoes is quite near it, but is moving away from it; all the attention of the two natives maneuvering it is occupied by the concussion of a little wave against the prow, falling back in a plume of foam caught in mid-air by the camera.

To the left of the pier, the sea is calmer. It is also a deeper green. Large patches of oil form blue-green stains at the foot of the pier. It is on this side that the "Cap Saint-Jean" is moored; toward it converges the interest of all the other people comprising the scene. Because of the position the ship occupies, its superstructures are somewhat vague, save for the forecastle, the bridge, the top of the smoke-stack, and the first loading mast with its oblique arm, pullies, cables and ropes.

At the top of the mast is perched a bird, not a sea bird, but a vulture with a naked neck. A second such bird soars in the sky, above and to the right; its wings are stretched straight across, widespread and strongly raked toward the top of the mast; the bird is executing a banked turn. Still higher runs a horizontal white margin half an inch wide, then a red border narrower by half.

Above the calendar, which is hanging from a tack by a red thread in the shape of a circumflex accent, the wooden wall is painted pale gray. Other tack holes show nearby. A larger hole to the left marks the location of a missing screw, or of a heavy nail.

Aside from these perforations, the paint in the bedroom is in good condition. The four walls, like those of the whole house, are covered with vertical laths two inches wide separated by a double groove. The depth of these grooves shows a deep shadow under the glare of the kerosene lamp.

This striped effect is reproduced on all four sides of the square bedroom—actually cubical, since it is as high as it is wide or long. The ceiling, moreover, is also covered by the same gray laths. As for the floor, it too is similarly constructed, as is evidenced by the clearly marked longitudinal interstices, hollowed out by the frequent washings that discolor the wood laths, and parallel to the grooves of the ceiling.

Thus the six interior surfaces of the cube are distinctly outlined by thin laths of constant dimensions, vertical on the four vertical surfaces, running east and west on the two horizontal surfaces. When the lamp sways a little at the end of an extended arm, all these lines with their short, moving shadows seem animated with a general swirling movement.

The outside walls of the house are made of planks set

horizontally; they are also wider—about eight inches—and overlap each other on the outer edge. Their surface is therefore not contained within a single vertical plane, but in many parallel planes, inclined at several degrees' pitch and a plank's thickness from each other.

The windows are framed by a molding and topped by a pediment in the shape of a flattened triangle. The laths which compose these embellishments have been nailed above the imbricated boards constituting the walls, so that the two systems are in contact only at series of ridges (the inner edge of each board), between which exist considerable gaps.

Only the two horizontal moldings are fastened along their entire undersurface: the base of the pediment and the base of the frame beneath the window. From one corner of the window, a dark liquid has flowed down over the wood, crossing the boards one after another from ridge to ridge, then the concrete substructure, making an increasingly narrow streak which finally dwindles to a thread, and reaches the veranda floor in the middle of a flagstone, ending there in a little round spot.

The nearby flagstones are perfectly clean. They are frequently washed—as recently as this afternoon. The smooth stone has a dull, grayish surface, oily to the touch. The stones are large; starting from the round spot, following the wall, there are only five and a half until the doorstep into the hallway.

The door is also framed by a wooden molding and topped by a flattened triangular pediment. On the other side of the sill, the floor consists of tiles much smaller than the flagstones, half their size in each direction. Instead of being smooth like the veranda flagstones, they are crisscrossed in one or the other diagonal direction by shallow grooves; the grooved areas are as wide as the ribs, that is, a few fractions of an inch. Their arrangement alternates from one tile to the next, so that the floor is set in successive chevrons. This low relief, scarcely visible in daylight, is accentuated by artificial light, especially at a certain distance ahead of the lamp, and still more if the latter is set on the floor.

The slight swaying of the lamp advancing along the hallway animates the uninterrupted series of chevrons with a continual undulation like that of waves.

The same tiling continues, without any separation, in the living room-dining room. The area where the table and chairs are is covered with a fiber carpet; the shadow of their legs swirls quickly across it, counterclockwise.

Behind the table, in the center of the long sideboard, the native pitcher looks even larger: its bulging shape, made of unglazed red clay, casts a dense shadow which enlarges as the source of light draws nearer, a black disc surmounted by an isosceles trapezoid (whose base is at the top) and a thin curve which connects the circular side to one of the ends of the trapezoid.

The pantry door is closed. Between it and the doorway to the hall is the centipede. It is enormous: one of the largest to be found in this climate. With its long antennae and its huge legs spread on each side of its body, it covers the area of an ordinary dinner plate. The shadow of various appendages doubles their already considerable number on the light-colored paint.

The body is curved toward the bottom: its anterior part is twisted toward the baseboard, while the last joints keep their original orientation—that of a straight line cutting diagonally across the panel from the hall doorway to the corner of the ceiling above the closed pantry door.

The creature is motionless, alert, as if sensing danger. Only its antennae are alternately raised and lowered in a swaying movement, slow but continuous.

Suddenly the front part of the body begins moving, executing a rotation which turns the creature toward the bottom of the wall. And immediately, without having a chance to go any farther, the centipede falls on the tiles, half twisted and curling its long legs one after the other while its mandibles rapidly open and close in a reflex quiver. . . . It is possible for an ear close enough to hear the faint crackling they produce.

The sound is that of the comb in the long hair. The tortoise-shell teeth pass again and again from top to bottom of the thick black mass with its reddish highlights, electrifying the tips and making the soft, freshly washed hair crackle during the entire descent of the delicate hand —the delicate hand with tapering fingers that gradually closes on the strands of hair.

The two long antennae accelerate their alternating swaying. The creature has stopped in the center of the wall, at eye level. The considerable development of the posterior legs identifies it unmistakably as the Scutigera or "spider-centipede." In the silence, from time to time, the characteristic buzzing can be heard, probably made by the buccal appendages.

Franck, without saying a word, stands up, wads his napkin into a ball as he cautiously approaches, and squashes the creature against the wall. Then, with his foot, he squashes it against the bedroom floor.

Then he comes back toward the bed and in passing hangs the towel on its metal rack near the washbowl.

The hand with the tapering fingers has clenched into a fist on the white sheet. The five widespread fingers have closed over the palm with such force that they have drawn the cloth with them: the latter shows five convergent creases. . . . But the mosquito-netting falls back all around the bed, interposing the opaque veil of its innumerable meshes where rectangular patches reinforce the torn places.

In his haste to reach his goal, Franck increases his speed. The jolts become more violent. Nevertheless he continues to drive faster. In the darkness, he has not seen the hole running halfway across the road. The car makes a leap, skids. . . . On this bad road the driver cannot straighten out in time. The blue sedan goes crashing into a roadside tree whose rigid foliage scarcely shivers under the impact, despite its violence.

The car immediately bursts into flames. The whole brush is illuminated by the crackling, spreading fire. It is the sound the centipede makes, motionless again on the wall, in the center of the panel.

Listening to it more carefully, this sound is more like a breath than a crackling: the brush is now moving down the loosened hair. No sooner has it reached the bottom than it quickly enters the ascending phase of the cycle, describing a curve which brings it back to its point of departure on the smooth hair of the head, where it begins moving down once again.

On the opposite wall of the bedroom, the vulture is still at the same point in its banked turn. A little below it, on top of the ship's mast, the other bird has not moved either. Below, in the foreground, the piece of cloth is still half raised by the same undulation of the swell. And the two natives in the canoe have not stopped looking at the plume of foam still about to fall back on the prow of their fragile craft.

And down below, the table top offers a varnished surface where the leather writing-case is in its place parallel with the long side of the table. To the left, a circle of felt intended for this use receives the circular base of the kerosene lamp.

Inside the writing-case, the green blotter is covered with fragments of handwriting in black ink: tiny lines, arcs, crosses, loops, etc. . . .; no complete letter can be made out, even in a mirror. Eleven sheets of pale blue writing paper of ordinary commercial size have been slipped into the side pocket of the portfolio. The first of these shows the evident traces of a word scratched out—on the upper right—of which only two tiny lines remain, greatly lightened by the eraser. The paper at this point is thinner, more translucent, but its grain is almost smooth, ready for the new inscription. As for the old letters, those which were there before, it is not possible to reconstitute them. The leather writing-case contains nothing else.

In the drawer of the table, there are two pads of writing-paper; one is new, the second almost used up. The size of the sheets, their quality, and their pale blue color are identical with those of the preceding ones. Beside them are lying three packages of envelopes lined with dark blue, still surrounded by their white band. But one of the packages is missing a good half of its envelopes, and the band is loose around those that remain.

Except for two black pencils, a circular typewriter eraser, the novel that has been the object of many discussions, and an unused booklet of stamps, there is nothing else in the drawer.

The top drawer of the heavy chest requires a longer inventory. In its right half are several boxes full of old letters; almost all are still in their envelopes, with stamps from Europe or Africa: letters from A . . .'s family, letters from various friends. . . .

A series of faint slaps is audible from the west side of the veranda, on the other side of the bed, behind the window with its lowered blinds. This might be the sound of steps on the flagstones. Yet the boy and the cook must long since be in bed. Besides, their feet—either bare or in espadrilles—are completely silent.

The noise has stopped again. If it was actually a step, it was a quick, slight, furtive one. It did not sound like a man's step, but that of a four-footed creature: some wild dog that managed to get up onto the veranda.

It has disappeared too quickly to leave a precise recollection: the ear has not even had time to hear it. How many times was the faint impact repeated against the flagstones? Barely five or six, or even less. Not many for a passing dog. The fall of a big lizard from the eaves often produces a similar muffled "slap"; but then it would have taken five or six lizards falling one after another, which is unlikely. . . . Only three lizards? That would be too many

115

too. Perhaps, after all, the noise was repeated only twice.

As it fades in time, its likelihood diminishes. Now it is as if there had been nothing at all. Through the chinks of the blinds—a little later—it is, of course, impossible to see anything at all. All that can be done is to close the blinds by manipulating the cord at the side.

The bedroom is closed again. The chevrons of the floor tiles, the grooves of the walls, and those of the ceiling turn faster and faster. Standing on the pier, the person watching the floating debris begins to bend over, without losing any of his stiffness. He is wearing a well-cut white suit and has a colonial helmet on his head. The tips of his black mustache are waxed and point upward in an old-fashioned style.

No. His face, which is not illuminated by the sun, lets nothing be supposed, not even the color of his skin. It looks as if the little wave, continuing its advance will unfold the piece of material and reveal whether it is an article of clothing, a canvas sack, or something else, if there is still enough daylight to see.

At this moment the light suddenly goes out.

It has probably faded gradually, up to now; but this is not for sure. Was its range shortened? Was its color yellower?

Yet the pump valve was primed several times early in the evening. Has all the kerosene been burned already? Had the boy forgotten to fill the reservoir? Or does the suddenness of the phenomenon indicate the sudden obstruction of a tube, due to some impurity in the fuel?

In any case, relighting the lamp is too complicated to bother about. To cross the bedroom in darkness is not so difficult, nor to reach the big chest and its open drawer, the packages of unimportant letters, the boxes of buttons, the balls of yarn, a skein of fine silk threads like hair, nor to close the drawer again.

The absence of the hissing of the kerosene lamp makes it easier to understand the considerable volume it produced. The chain which was gradually playing out has suddenly been broken or unhooked, abandoning the cubical cage to its own fate: falling free. The animals too must have fallen silent, one by one, in the valley. The silence is such that the faintest movements become impracticable.

Like this shapeless darkness, the silky hair flows between the curving fingers. It falls free, thickens, pushes its tentacles in all directions, coiling over itself in an increasingly complex skein whose convolutions and apparent mazes continue to let the fingers pass through it with the same indifference, with the same facility.

With the same facility, the hair lets itself be unknotted, falls over the shoulder in a docile tide while the brush moves smoothly from top to bottom, from top to bottom, from top to bottom, guided now by the breathing alone, which in the complete darkness is enough to create a regular rhythm capable of measuring something, if something remains to measure, to limit, to describe in the total darkness, until the day breaks, now.

The day has broken long since. At the bottom of the two windows facing south, rays of light filter through the chinks of the closed blinds. For the sun to strike the facade at this angle, it must already be quite high in the sky. A . . . has not come back. The drawer of the chest to the left of the bed is still half open. Since it is quite heavy, it creaks as it slips back into place.

The bedroom door, on the contrary, turns silently on its hinges. The rubber-soled shoes make no sound on the hallway tiles.

To the left of the door to the veranda, the boy has arranged as usual the low table and the single chair and the single coffee-cup on the table. The boy himself appears at the corner of the house, carrying in both hands the tray with the coffee-pot on it.

Having set down his burden near the cup, he says: "Missy, she has not come back."

In the same tone he might have said, "The coffee, it is

117

served," "God bless you," or anything at all. His voice invariably chants the same notes, so that it is impossible to distinguish questions from other sentences. Besides, like all the native servants, this boy is accustomed never to expect an answer to his questions. He immediately leaves again, this time going into the house through the open hall door.

The morning sun rakes this central part of the veranda, as it does the whole valley. In the almost cool air that follows daybreak, the singing of birds has replaced that of the nocturnal crickets, and resembles it, though less even, embellished occasionally by a few somewhat more musical sounds. As for the birds, they are no more evident than the crickets—no more than usual—fluttering in concealment beneath the green clusters of the banana trees, all around the house.

In the zone of bare earth that separates the trees from the house, the ground sparkles with innumerable dew-covered webs which the tiny spiders have spun between the clumps of dirt. Further down, on the log bridge over the little stream, a crew of five workmen is preparing to replace the logs which the termites have eaten away inside.

On the veranda, at the corner of the house, the boy appears, following his usual route. Six steps behind him comes a second Negro, barefoot and wearing shorts and an undershirt, his head covered with an old, soft hat.

The gait of this second native is supple, lively and yet unconcerned. He advances behind his guide toward the low table without taking off his extraordinarily shapeless, faded felt hat. He stops when the boy stops, that is, five steps behind him, and remains standing there, his arms hanging at his sides.

"The other master, he has not come back," the boy says.

The messenger in the soft hat looks up toward the beams, under the roof, where the pinkish-gray lizards chase each other in short, quick runs, suddenly stopping in the middle of their trajectory, heads raised and cocked to one side, tails frozen in the middle of an interrupted undulation.

"The lady, she is angry," the boy says.

He uses this adjective to describe any kind of uncertainty, sadness, or disturbance. Probably he means "anxious" today; but it could just as well be "outraged," "jealous," or even "desperate." Besides he has asked no questions; he is about to leave. Yet an ordinary sentence without any precise meaning releases from him a flood of words in his own language, which abounds in vowels, particularly a's and e's.

He and the messenger are now facing each other. The latter listens, without showing the least sign of comprehension. The boy talks at top speed, as if his text had no punctuation, but in the same singsong tone as when he is not speaking his own language. Suddenly he stops. The other does not add a word, turns around and leaves by the same route he came in, with his swift, soft gait, swaying his head and hat, and his hips, and his arms beside his body, without having opened his mouth.

After having set the used cup on the tray beside the coffee-pot, the boy takes the tray away, entering the house by the open door into the hallway. The bedroom windows are closed. At this hour A . . . is not up yet.

She left very early this morning, in order to have enough time to do her shopping and be able to get back to the plantation the same night. She went to the port with Franck, to make some necessary purchases. She has not said what they were.

Once the bedroom is empty, there is no reason not to open the blinds, which fill all three windows instead of glass panes. The three windows are similar, each divided into four equal rectangles, that is, four series of slats, each window-frame comprising two sets hung one on top of another. The twelve series are identical: sixteen slats of wood manipulated by a cord attached at the side to the outer frame.

The sixteen slats of a series are continuously parallel. When the series is closed, they are pressed one against the other at the edge, overlapping by about half an inch. By pulling the cord down, the pitch of the slats is reduced, thus creating a series of openings whose width progressively increases.

When the blinds are open to the maximum, the slats are almost horizontal and show their edges. Then the opposite slope of the valley appears in successive, superimposed strips separated by slightly narrower strips. In the opening at eye level appears a clump of trees with motionless foliage at the edge of the plantation, where the yellowish brush begins. Many trunks are growing in a single cluster from which the oval fronds of dark green leaves branch out, so distinct they seem drawn one by one, despite their relative smallness and their great number. On the ground the converging trunks form a single stalk of colossal diameter, with projecting ribs that flare out as they near the ground.

The light quickly fades. The sun has disappeared behind the rocky spur that borders the main section of the plateau. It is six-thirty. The deafening racket of the crickets fills the whole valley—a constant grating with neither nuance nor progression. Behind, the whole house has been empty since daybreak.

A . . . is not coming home for dinner, which she is taking in town with Franck before starting back. They will be home by about midnight, probably.

The veranda is empty too. None of the armchairs has been carried outside this morning, nor the low table used for cocktails and coffee. Eight shiny points mark the place where the two chairs are set on the flagstones under the first window of the office.

Seen from outside, the open blinds show the unpainted edge of their parallel slats, where tiny scales are half detached here and there, which a fingernail could chip off without difficulty. Inside, in the bedroom, A . . . is stand-

ing in front of the window and looking through one of the
chinks toward the veranda, the openwork balustrade, and
the banana trees on the opposite hillside.

Between the remaining gray paint, faded by time, and
the wood grayed by the action of humidity, appear tiny
areas of reddish brown—the natural color of the wood—
where the wood has been left exposed by the recent flaking
off of new scales of paint. Inside her bedroom, A . . . is
standing in front of the window and looking out between
one of the chinks in the blinds.

The man is still motionless, leaning toward the muddy
water, on the earth-covered log bridge. He has not moved
an inch: crouching, head down, forearms resting on his
thighs, hands hanging between his knees. He seems to be
looking at something at the bottom of the little stream
—an animal, a reflection, a lost object.

In front of him, in the patch along the other bank, several stems look ripe for cutting, although the harvest has
not yet been started in this sector. The sound of a truck
shifting gears on the highway on the other side of the
house is answered here by the creak of a window-lock. The
first bedroom window opens.

The upper part of A . . .'s body is framed in it, as well
as her waist and hips. She says "Good morning" in the
playful tone of someone who, having slept well, wakes up
in a good mood—or of someone who prefers not to show
what she is thinking about, always flashing the same smile,
on principle.

She immediately steps back inside, to reappear a little
further on a few seconds afterwards—perhaps ten seconds,
but at a distance of at least two or three yards—in the next
window-opening where the blinds have just been opened.

121

Here she stays longer, her head turned toward the column at the corner of the terrace that supports the overhang of the roof.

From her post of observation, she can see only the green stretch of banana trees, the edge of the plateau and, between the two, a strip of uncultivated brush, high yellow weeds with a few scattered trees.

On the column itself there is nothing to see except the peeling paint and, occasionally, at unforeseeable intervals and at various levels, a grayish-pink lizard whose intermittent presence results from shifts of position so sudden that no one could say where it comes from or where it is going when it is no longer visible.

A . . . has stepped back again. To find her, the eye must be placed in the axis of the first window: she is in front of the big chest, against the rear wall of the bedroom. She opens the top drawer and leans over the right-hand side of the chest, where she spends a long time looking for something she cannot find, searching with both hands, shifting packages and boxes and constantly coming back to the same point, unless she is merely rearranging her effects.

In her present position, between the big bed and the hall door, other sight-lines can easily reach her from the veranda, passing through one or another of the three open window-recesses.

From a point on the balustrade located two steps from the corner, an oblique sight-line thus enters the bedroom through the second window and cuts diagonally across the foot of the bed to the chest. A . . ., who has straightened up, turns toward the light and immediately disappears behind the section of wall that separates the two windows and conceals the back of the large wardrobe.

She appears, an instant later, behind the left frame of the first window, in front of the writing table. She opens the leather writing-case and leans forward, the top of her thighs pressed against the table edge. Her body, wider at the hips, again makes it impossible to follow what her hands are doing, what they are holding, picking up, or putting down.

A . . . appears from a three-quarter view, as before, although from the opposite side. She is still in her dressing gown, but her hair, though loose, has already been carefully brushed; it gleams in the sunlight when her head, turning, shifts the soft, heavy curls whose black mass falls on the white silk of her shoulder, while the silhouette again steps back toward the rear of the room along the hallway wall.

The leather writing-case, parallel with the long side of the table, is closed, as usual. Above the varnished wood surface, instead of the hair, there is nothing but the post-office calendar where only the white boat stands out from the gray tint of the wall behind.

The room now looks as if it were empty. A . . . may have noiselessly opened the hall door and gone out; but it is more likely that she is still there, outside the field of vision, in the blank area between this door, the large wardrobe and the corner of the table where a felt circle constitutes the last visible object. Besides the wardrobe, there is only one piece of furniture (an armchair) in this area. Still, the concealed exit by which it communicates with the hall, the living room, the courtyard, and the highway multiplies to infinity her possibilities of escape.

The upper part of A . . .'s body appears in the window opening in receding perspective from the third window, overlooking the west gable-end of the house. At a given moment she must have passed in front of the exposed foot of the bed before entering the second blank area between the dressing-table and the bed.

She stays there, motionless, for some time as well. Her profile is distinctly outlined against the darker background. Her lips are very red; to say whether they have been made up or not would be difficult, since it is their natural color in any case. Her eyes are wide open, resting on the green mass of the banana trees, which they slowly move across as they approach the corner column with the gradual turning of the head and neck.

On the bare earth of the garden, the column's shadow now makes an angle of forty-five degrees with the perforated shadow of the balustrade, the western side of the veranda, and the gable-end of the house. A . . . is no longer at the window. Neither this window nor either of the two others reveals her presence in the room. And there is no longer any reason to suppose her in any one of the three blank areas rather than in any other. Two of them, moreover, present an easy egress: the first into the central hallway, the other into the bathroom, whose other door opens out onto the hallway, the courtyard, etc. . . . The bedroom again looks as if it were empty.

To the left, at the end of this western side of the veranda, the Negro cook is peeling yams over a tin basin. He is kneeling, sitting back on his heels, the basin between his thighs. The shiny pointed blade of the knife detaches an endless narrow peel from the long yellow tuber which revolves in his hand with a regular motion.

At the same distance but in the opposite direction, Franck and A . . . are drinking cocktails, sitting back in their usual armchairs, under the office window. "That feels good!" Franck is holding his glass in his right hand, which is resting on the elbow-rest of the chair. The three other arms are stretched out parallel on the parallel strips of leather, but the three hands are lying palms-down against the elbow-rests where the leather curves over the ridge before coming to a point just below three large nailheads which attach it to the red wood.

Two of the four hands are wearing, on the same finger, the same gold ring, wide and flat: the first on the left and the third, which is holding the cylindrical glass half-filled with a golden liquid, Franck's right hand. A . . .'s glass is beside her on the little table. They are talking desultorily of the trip to the port they plan to make together during

124

the following week, she for various purchases, he to find out about the new truck he intends to buy.

They have already settled the time of departure as well as that of the return, calculated the approximate duration of the ride and estimated the time in which they must settle their affairs. All that remains is to decide which day will best suit them both. It is only natural that A . . . should want to take advantage of such an occasion, which will permit her to make the trip under acceptable conditions without bothering anyone. The only surprising thing, really, is that such an arrangement has not already been made in similar circumstances previously, one day or another.

Now the tapering fingers of the second hand circle the large shiny nailheads: the ball of the last joint of the index finger, the middle finger, and the ring finger circle round and round the three smooth, bulging surfaces. The middle finger is stretched out vertically following the direction of the triangular point of the leather; the index and ring fingers are half bent to reach the two upper nailheads. Soon, twenty inches to the left, the same three delicate fingers of the other hand begin the same exercise. The furthest to the left of these six fingers is the one wearing the ring.

"Then Christiane doesn't want to come with us? That's too bad. . . ."

"No, she can't," Franck said, "because of the child."

"And of course it's much hotter on the coast."

"More humid, yes, that's right."

"Still, it would be a change for her. How is she feeling today?"

"It's always the same thing," Franck says.

The low voice of the second driver, who is singing a native lament of some kind, reaches the three armchairs grouped in the middle of the veranda. Although distant, this voice is perfectly recognizable. Coming around each gable-end at the same time, it reaches the ears simultaneously from right and left.

"It's always the same thing," Franck says.

125

A . . . presses the point, full of solicitude: "In town, though, she could see a doctor."

Franck raises his left hand from the leather armrest, but without lifting his elbow off, and then lets it fall back, more slowly, to where it was.

"She's already seen enough doctors as it is. With all those drugs she takes, it's as if she. . . ."

"Still, you have to try something."

"But she claims it's the climate!"

"You can talk all you want about the climate, but that doesn't mean a thing."

"The attacks of malaria."

"There's quinine. . . ."

Then five or six remarks are exchanged about the respective doses of quinine necessary in the various tropical regions, according to the altitude, the latitude, the proximity of the sea, the presence of swamps, etc. . . . Then Franck refers again to the disagreeable effects quinine produces on the heroine of the African novel A . . . is reading. Afterwards he makes an allusion—obscure for anyone who has not even leafed through the book—to the behavior of the husband, guilty of negligence at least in the opinion of the two readers. His sentence ends in "take apart" or "take a part" or "break apart," "break a heart," "heart of darkness," or something of the kind.

But Franck and A . . . are already far away. Now they are talking about a young white woman—is it the same one as before, or her rival, or some secondary character? —who gives herself to a native, perhaps to several. Franck seems to hold it against her:

"After all," he says, "sleeping with Negroes. . . ."

A . . . turns toward him, raises her chin, and asks smilingly: "Well, why not?"

Franck smiles in his turn, but answers nothing, as if he is embarrassed by the tone their dialogue is taking—before a third person. The movement of his mouth ends in a sort of grimace.

The driver's voice has shifted. It now comes only from the east side; it apparently emanates from the sheds, to the right of the main courtyard.

The singing is at moments so little like what is ordinarily called a song, a complaint, a refrain, that the western listener is justified in wondering if something quite different is involved. The sounds, despite apparent repetitions, do not seem related by any musical law. There is no tune, really, no melody, no rhythm. It is as if the man were content to utter unconnected fragments as an accompaniment to his work. According to the orders he has received this very morning, this work must have as its object the impregnation of the new logs with an insecticide solution, in order to safeguard them against the action of the termites before putting them in place.

"Always the same thing," Franck says.

"Mechanical troubles again?"

"This time it's the carburetor. . . . The whole engine has to be replaced."

On the hand-rail of the balustrade, a lizard is perched in absolute immobility: head raised and cocked toward the house, body and tail forming a flattened S. The animal looks as if it were stuffed.

"That boy has a lovely voice," A . . . says, after a rather long silence.

Franck continues: "We'll be leaving early."

A . . . asks him to be specific, and Franck gives details, asking if it is too early for his passenger.

"Not at all," she says. "It'll be fun."

They sip their drinks.

"If all goes well," Franck says, "we could be in town by ten and have a good bit of time before lunch."

"Of course I'd prefer that too," A . . . answers, her face serious again.

"I won't have too much time all afternoon finishing up my visits to the sales agents and asking the advice of my

127

regular garageman, Robin—you know, down on the waterfront. We'll start back right after dinner."

The details he furnishes as to his schedule for this day in town would be more natural if they were provided to satisfy an interlocutor's question, but no one has shown the slightest interest, today, in the purchase of his new truck. And he nearly furnishes aloud—very loud—the program of his movements and his interviews yard by yard, minute by minute, constantly emphasizing the necessity of his behavior in each case. A . . ., on the other hand, makes only the smallest reference to her own errands, whose total duration will be the same, however.

For lunch, Franck is here again, loquacious and affable. This time Christiane has not accompanied him. They had almost had an argument the day before about the cut of a dress.

After the customary exclamation as to the comfort of the armchair, Franck begins telling, with a great wealth of detail, a story about a car with engine trouble. It is the sedan he is referring to, and not the truck; since the sedan is still almost new, it does not often give its owner problems.

The latter should, at this moment, refer to an analogous incident which occurred in town during his trip with A . . ., an incident of no importance but which postponed their return to the plantation by a whole night. The comparison would be only normal. Franck refrains from making it.

A . . . has been looking at her neighbor with increased attention these last few seconds, as if she were expecting a remark he was on the point of making. But she says nothing either, and the remark is not made. Besides, they have never again referred to that day, that accident, that night—at least when they are not alone together.

Now Franck is recapitulating the list of parts to dismantle for the complete inspection of a carburetor. He performs this exhaustive inventory with a concern for exactitude which obliges him to mention a number of elements that are ordinarily understood without being referred to; he goes almost to the point of describing the removal of a screw turn by turn, and similarly, afterwards, for the converse operation.

"You seem to be up on your mechanics today," A . . . says.

Franck suddenly stops talking, in the middle of his account. He looks at the lips and the eyes on his right, upon which a calm smile, as though with no meaning behind it, seems to be fixed by a photographic exposure. His own mouth has remained half open, perhaps in the middle of a word.

"In theory, I mean," A . . . specifies, without abandoning her most amiable tone of voice.

Franck turns his eyes away toward the open-work balustrade, the last flakes of gray paint, the stuffed lizard, the motionless sky.

"I'm beginning to get used to it," he says, "with the truck. All engines are alike."

Which is obviously untrue. The engine of his big truck, in particular, offers few points in common with that of his American car.

"That's right," A . . . says, "like women."

But Franck seems not to have heard. He keeps his eyes fixed on the pinkish-gray lizard—opposite him—whose soft skin, under the lower jaw, throbs faintly.

A . . . finishes her glass of golden soda, sets it down empty on the table, and begins again to caress the three bulging nailheads on each leg of her chair with the tips of her six fingers.

Upon her closed lips floats a half-smile of serenity, revery, or abstraction. Since it is immutable and of too accomplished a regularity, it may also be false, entirely made up, polite, or even imaginary.

The lizard on the hand-rail is now in shadow; its colors have turned dark. The shadow cast by the roof coincides exactly with the outlines of the veranda: the sun is at its zenith.

Franck, who was passing by and stopped in, declares he doesn't want to stay any longer. He actually stands up and sets down on the low table the glass he has just emptied in one gulp. He stops before walking down the hallway that crosses the house; he turns back to wave goodbye to his hosts. The same grimace, but swifter now, passes over his lips again. He disappears inside the house.

A . . . has not left her chair. She remains leaning back, arms stretched out on the elbow-rests, eyes looking up at the empty sky. Beside her, near the tray with the two bottles and the ice bucket, is lying the novel Franck has lent her, which she has been reading since the evening before, a novel whose action takes place in Africa.

On the hand-rail of the balustrade, the lizard has disappeared, leaving in its place a flake of gray paint which seems to have the same shape: a body lying in the direction of the grain of the wood, a tail twisted into two curves, four rather short legs, and the head cocked toward the house.

In the dining room, the boy has laid only two places on the square table: one opposite the open pantry door and the long sideboard, the other on the window side. It is here that A . . . sits, her back to the light. She eats little, as usual. During almost the entire meal, she sits without moving, very straight on her chair, her hands with their tapering fingers framing a plate as white as the cloth, her gaze fixed on the brownish remains of the squashed centipede which stain the bare wall in front of her.

Her eyes are very large, brilliant, green in color, fringed with long curving lashes. They always seem to be seen from straight on, even when the face is seen in profile. She keeps them as wide as possible in all circumstances, without ever blinking.

After lunch, she returns to her chair in the middle of the veranda, to the left of Franck's empty chair. She picks up her book which the boy left on the table when he took away the tray; she looks for the place where her reading was interrupted by Franck's arrival, somewhere in the first part of the story. But having found the page again, she lays the open book face down on her knees and remains where she is without doing anything, leaning back in the leather chair.

From the other side of the house comes the sound of a heavy truck heading down the highway toward the bottom of the valley, the plain, and the port—where the white ship is moored alongside the pier.

The veranda is empty, the house too. The shadow cast by the roof coincides exactly with the outlines of the veranda: the sun is at its zenith. The house no longer casts the slightest black band over the freshly spaded earth of the garden. The trunks of the thin orange trees also show no shadows.

It is not the sound of the truck that can be heard, but that of a sedan coming down the dirt road from the highway, toward the house.

In the open left leaf of the first dining-room window, in the middle of the central pane of glass, the reflected image of the blue car has just stopped in the middle of the courtyard. A . . . and Franck get out of it together, he on one side, she on the other, by the two front doors. A . . . is holding a tiny package of indeterminate shape which immediately vanishes, absorbed by a flaw in the glass.

The two people immediately come closer together in front of the hood of the car. Franck's silhouette, larger than A . . .'s, conceals hers behind his. Franck's head is bent forward.

The irregularities of the glass obscure the details of their actions. The living-room windows would give a direct view of the same spectacle and from a more convenient angle: both people seen side by side.

But they have already separated, walking side by side toward the door of the house, across the gravel of the courtyard. The distance between them is at least a yard. Under the precise noonday sun, they cast no shadows.

They are smiling at the same time, the same smile, when the door opens. Yes, they are in good health. No, there was no accident, only a little difficulty with the car which obliged them to spend the night at the hotel, waiting for a garage to open in the morning.

After a quick drink, Franck, who is in a great hurry to get back to his wife, stands up and leaves. His steps echo down the hallway tiles.

A . . . immediately goes to her bedroom, takes a bath, changes her dress, eats lunch with a good appetite, and returns to the veranda where she sits down under the office window whose blinds, three-quarters lowered, permit only the top of her hair to be seen.

The evening finds her in the same position, in the same chair, in front of the same gray stone lizard. The only difference is that the boy has added the fourth chair, the one that is less comfortable, made of canvas stretched over a metal frame. The sun is hidden behind the rocky spur which comprises the western boundary of the chief section of the plateau.

The light rapidly fades. A . . ., who can no longer see clearly enough to continue reading, closes her novel and puts it down on the little table beside her (between the two groups of chairs: the pair with its backs against the wall beneath the window, and the two other dissimilar chairs placed at an angle nearer the balustrade). To mark her place, the outer edge of the shiny paper jacket protecting the cover has been inserted in the book, approximately a quarter of the way into it.

A . . . asks for today's news on the plantation. There is no news. There are only the trivial incidents of the work of cultivation which periodically recur in one patch or another, according to the cycle of operations. Since the patches are numerous, and the plantation managed so as to stagger the harvest through all twelve months of the year, all the elements of the cycle occur at the same time every day, and the periodical trivial incidents also repeat themselves simultaneously, here or there, daily.

A . . . hums a dance tune whose words remain unintelligible. It may be a popular song she has heard in town, to whose rhythm she may have danced.

The fourth chair was superfluous. It remains vacant all evening long, further isolating the third leather chair from the other two. Franck, as a matter of fact, has come alone. Christiane did not want to leave the child, who has a little fever. It is not unusual, nowadays, that her husband comes without her for dinner. Tonight, though, A . . . seemed to expect her; at least she has had four places set. She orders the one which is not to be used to be taken away at once.

Although it is quite dark now, she orders the boy not to bring out the lamps which—she says—attract mosquitoes. In the complete darkness, only the paler spots formed by a dress, a white shirt, a hand, two hands, soon four hands (the eyes getting used to the darkness) can be even guessed at.

No one speaks. Nothing moves. The four hands are lined up parallel to the wall of the house. On the other side of the balustrade, toward the hillside, there is only the starless sky and the deafening racket of the crickets.

During dinner, Franck and A . . . make a plan to go down to the port together, someday soon, for various reasons. Their conversation returns to this projected trip after the meal, while they are drinking their coffee on the veranda.

When the violent cry of a nocturnal animal indicates its proximity—in the garden itself, at the southwest corner of the house—Franck suddenly stands up and walks with long strides to this side of the veranda; his rubber soles make no noise on the flagstones. In a few seconds his white shirt has completely vanished into the darkness.

Since Franck says nothing and does not return, A . . .,

doubtless supposing he sees something, also stands up, supple and silent, and moves away in the same direction. Her dress is swallowed up in its turn by the opaque darkness.

After quite a long time, no word has yet been spoken loud enough to be heard at a distance of ten yards. It is also possible that there is no longer anyone in that direction.

Franck has left now. A . . . has gone into her bedroom. The interior of this room is lit, but the blinds are entirely closed: between the slats filter only a few tiny lines of light.

The violent cry of an animal, shrill and short, echoes again in the garden below, at the foot of the veranda. But this time it is from the opposite corner, facing the bedroom, that the signal seems to come.

It is, of course, impossible to see anything, even leaning as far out as possible, the body halfway over the balustrade, against the square column, the column which supports the southwest corner of the roof.

Now the shadow of the column falls across the flagstones over this central part of the veranda in front of the bedroom. The oblique direction of the dark line points, when it is extended to the wall itself, to the reddish streak which has run down the vertical wall from the right corner of the first window, the one nearest the hallway.

The shadow of the column, though it is already very long, would have to be nearly a yard longer to reach the little round spot on the flagstones. From the latter runs a thin vertical thread which increases in size as it rises from the concrete substructure. It then climbs up the wooden surface, from lath to lath, growing gradually larger until it reaches the window sill. But its progression is not constant: the imbricated arrangement of the boards intercepts its route by a series of equidistant projections where the liquid spreads out more widely before continuing its ascent. On the sill itself, the paint has largely flaked off after the streak occurred, eliminating about three-quarters of the red trace.

The spot has always been there, on the wall. For the moment there is no question of repainting anything but the blinds and the balustrade—the latter a bright yellow. That is what A . . . has decided. . . .

She is in her bedroom, whose two southern windows have been opened. The sun, very low in the sky now, is already much less warm; and when it strikes the façade directly, before disappearing, it will be only for a few seconds, at a raked angle, its beams entirely without strength.

A . . . is standing motionless in front of the writing table; she is facing the wall; she therefore appears in profile in the open window-recess. She is rereading the letter received in the last post from Europe. The opened envelope forms a white rhombus on the varnished table top, near the leather writing-case and the gold-capped fountain pen. The sheet of paper which she holds spread out in both hands still shows the creases where it has been folded.

Having read to the bottom of the page, A . . . puts the letter beside its envelope, sits down in the chair, and opens the writing case. Out of the pocket of this, she takes a leaf of the same size, but blank, which she puts on the green blotter provided for this purpose. She then takes the cap off the pen and bends forward to begin writing.

The shiny black curls tremble slightly on her shoulders as the pen advances. Although neither the arm nor the head seems disturbed by the slightest movement, the hair, more sensitive, captures the oscillations of the wrist, amplifies them, and translates them into unexpected eddies which awaken reddish highlights in its moving mass.

These propagations and interferences continue to multiply their interactions when the hand has stopped. But the head rises and begins to turn, slowly and steadily, toward the open window. The large eyes unblinkingly endure this transition to the direct light of the veranda.

Down below, in the hollow of the valley, in front of the patch shaped like a trapezoid, where the slanting rays of the sun outline each frond of the banana trees with extreme distinctness, the water of the little stream shows a ruffled surface which gives evidence of the swiftness of the current. It takes this last sunlight to reveal so clearly the successive chevrons and crisscrossings which the many interwoven ripples create. The wave moves on, but the surface remains as if petrified beneath these immutable lines.

Its brilliance is similarly fixed, and gives the liquid surface a more transparent quality. But there is no one to judge this on the spot; from the bridge, for instance. In fact, no one is in sight anywhere near. No crew is at work in this sector, for the moment. Besides, the workday is over.

On the veranda, the shadow of the column is still longer. It has turned. It has almost reached the door to the house now, which marks the middle of the façade. The door is open. The hallway tiles are covered with chevron-shaped grooves, like those of the stream, though more regular.

The hallway leads straight toward the other door, the one that opens onto the entrance courtyard. The big blue car is parked in the middle. The passenger gets out and heads at once toward the house, without being inconvenienced by the gravel, despite her high-heeled shoes. She has been visiting Christiane, and Franck has brought her back.

The latter is sitting in his armchair, beneath the first office window. The shadow of the column moves toward him; after having diagonally crossed more than half the veranda, moved along the bedroom for its entire length, and passed the hallway door, it now reaches to the low table where A . . . has just put down her book. Franck is staying only a minute before going home; his workday is over too.

It is almost time for cocktails, and A . . . has not waited any longer to call the boy, who appears at the corner of the house, carrying the tray with the two bottles, three large glasses and the ice bucket. The route he follows over the flagstones is apparently parallel to the wall and converges with the line of shadow when he reaches the low, round table where he carefully puts down the tray, near the novel with the shiny paper jacket.

It is the latter which provides the subject for the conversation. Psychological complications aside, it is a standard narrative of colonial life in Africa, with a description of a tornado, a native revolt, and incidents at the club. A . . . and Franck discuss it animatedly, while sipping the mixture of cognac and soda served by the mistress of the house in the three glasses.

The main character of the book is a customs official. This character is not an official but a high-ranking employee of an old commercial company. This company's business is going badly, rapidly turning shady. This company's business is going extremely well. The chief character—one learns—is dishonest. He is honest, he is trying to re-establish a situation compromised by his predecessor, who died in an automobile accident. But he had no predecessor, for the company was only recently formed; and it was not an accident. Besides, it happens to be a ship (a big white ship) and not a car at all.

Franck, at this point, begins to tell an anecdote about a truck of his with engine trouble. A . . ., as politeness demands, asks for details to prove the attention she is paying to her guest, who soon stands up and takes his leave, in order to return to his own plantation, a little farther east.

A . . . is leaning on the balustrade. On the other side of the valley, the sun rakes the isolated trees scattered over the brush above the cultivated zone. Their long shadows stripe the terrain with heavy parallel lines.

The stream in the hollow of the valley has grown dark. Already the northern slope receives no more light. The sun is hidden behind the rocky spur to the west. Outlined against the light, the silhouette of the rock wall appears distinctly for an instant against a violently illuminated sky: a sudden, barely swelling line which connects with the plateau by a sharp-pointed outcropping, followed by a less emphatic second projection.

Very quickly the luminous background becomes more somber. On the opposite hillside, the clumps of banana trees grow blurred in the twilight.

It is six-thirty.

Now the dark night and the deafening racket of the crickets again engulf the garden and the veranda, all around the house.

IN THE LABYRINTH

This narrative is not a true account, but fiction. It describes a reality not necessarily the same as the one the reader has experienced: for example, in the French army, infantrymen do not wear their serial numbers on their coat collars. Similarly, the recent history of Western Europe has not recorded an important battle at Reichenfels or in the vicinity. Yet the reality in question is a strictly material one; that is, it is subject to no allegorical interpretation. The reader is therefore requested to see in it only the objects, actions, words, and events which are described, without attempting to give them either more or less meaning than in his own life, or his own death.

A. R.-G.

I am alone here now, under cover. Outside it is raining, outside you walk through the rain with your head down, shielding your eyes with one hand while you stare ahead nevertheless, a few yards ahead, at a few yards of wet asphalt; outside it is cold, the wind blows between the bare black branches; the wind blows through the leaves, rocking whole boughs, rocking them, rocking, their shadows swaying across the white roughcast walls. Outside the sun is shining, there is no tree, no bush to cast a shadow, and you walk under the sun shielding your eyes with one hand while you stare ahead, only a few yards in front of you, at a few yards of dusty asphalt where the wind makes patterns of parallel lines, forks, and spirals.

The sun does not get in here, nor the wind, nor the rain, nor the dust. The fine dust which dulls the gloss of the horizontal surfaces, the varnished wood of the table, the waxed floor, the marble shelf over the fireplace, the marble top of the chest, the cracked marble on top of the chest, the only dust comes from the room itself: from the cracks in the floor maybe, or else from the bed, or from the curtains or from the ashes in the fireplace.

On the polished wood of the table, the dust has marked the places occupied for a while—for a few hours, several days, minutes, weeks—by small objects subsequently removed whose outlines are still distinct for some time, a circle, a square, a rectangle, other less simple shapes, some partly overlapping, already blurred or half obliterated as though by a rag.

When the outline is distinct enough to permit the shape to be identified with certainty, it is easy to find the original object again, nor far away. For example, the circular shape

141

has obviously been left by a glass ashtray which is lying beside it. Similarly, a little farther away, the square occupying the table's left rear corner corresponds to the base of the brass lamp that now stands in the right corner: a square pedestal about one inch high capped by a disk of the same height supporting a fluted column at its center.

The lampshade casts a circle of light on the ceiling, but this circle is not complete: it is intersected by the wall behind the table. This wall, instead of being papered like the other three, is concealed from floor to ceiling and for the greater part of its width by thick red curtains made of a heavy velvety material.

Outside it is snowing. Across the dark asphalt of the sidewalk the wind is driving the fine dry crystals which after each gust form white parallel lines, forks, spirals that are immediately broken up, seized by the eddies driven along the ground, then immobilized again, recomposing new spirals, scrolls, forked undulations, shifting arabesques immediately broken up. You walk with your head a little farther down, pressing the hand shielding your eyes closer, leaving only a few inches of ground visible in front of your feet, a few grayish inches where your feet appear one after the other and vanish behind you, one after the other, alternately.

But the staccato sound of hobnail boots on the asphalt, coming steadily closer down the straight street, sounding louder and louder in the calm of the frostbound night, the sound of boots cannot come in here, any more than other sounds from outside. The street is too long, the curtains too thick, the house too high. No noise, even muffled, ever penetrates the walls of the room, no vibration, no breath of air, and in the silence tiny particles descend slowly, scarcely visible in the lamplight, descend gently, vertically, always at the same speed, and the fine gray dust lies in a uniform layer on the floor, on the bedspread, on the furniture.

On the waxed floor, the felt slippers have made gleaming paths from the bed to the chest, from the chest to the fireplace, from the fireplace to the table. And on the table, the shifting of objects has also disturbed the continuity of the film of dust; the latter, more or less thick according to the length of time the surfaces have been exposed, is even occasionally interrupted altogether: as distinct as though drawn with a drafting-pen, a square of varnished wood thus occupies the left rear corner, not precisely at the corner of the table but parallel to its edges, set back about four inches. The square itself is about six inches on each side, and in it the reddish-brown wood gleams, virtually without any deposit.

To the right, a simple shape that is vaguer, already covered by several days' dust, can nevertheless still be recognized; from a certain angle it is even distinct enough so that its outlines can be followed without too much uncertainty. It is a kind of cross: an elongated main section about the size of a table knife but wider, pointed at one end and broadening slightly at the other, cut perpendicularly by a much shorter crosspiece; this latter is composed of two flaring appendages symmetrically arranged on each side of the axis at the base of its broadening portion— that is, about a third of the way from the wider end. It resembles a flower, the terminal widening representing a long closed corolla at the end of the stem with two small lateral leaves beneath. Or else it might be an approximately human statuette: an oval head, two very short arms, and the body terminating in a point toward the bottom. It might also be a dagger, with its handle separated by a guard from the wide, rounded, double-edged blade.

Still farther to the right, in the direction indicated by the tip of the flower, or by the point of the dagger, a slightly dusty circle is tangent to a second circle the same size, the latter not reduced to its mere outline on the table: the glass ashtray. Then come uncertain, overlapping shapes probably left by various papers whose successive changes of position have blurred their outlines, which in some places are quite distinct, in others obscured by dust, and in

143

still others more than half obliterated, as though by a rag.

Beyond stands the lamp, in the right corner of the table: a square base six inches on each side, a disk tangent with its sides, of the same diameter, a fluted column supporting a dark, slightly conical lampshade. A fly is moving slowly and steadily around the upper rim of the shade. It casts a distorted shadow on the ceiling in which no element of the original insect can be recognized: neither wings nor body nor feet; the creature has been transformed into a simple threadlike outline, not closed, a broken regular line resembling a hexagon with one side missing: the image of the incandescent filament of the electric bulb. This tiny open polygon lies tangent at one of its corners to the inner rim of the great circle of light cast by the lamp. It changes position slowly but steadily along the circumference. When it reaches the vertical wall it disappears into the folds of the heavy red curtain.

Outside it is snowing. Outside it has been snowing, it was snowing, outside it is snowing. The thick flakes descend gently in a steady, uninterrupted, vertical fall—for there is not a breath of air—in front of the high gray walls whose arrangement, the alignment of the roofs, the location of the doors and windows, cannot be distinguished clearly because of the snow. There must be identical rows of regular windows on each floor from one end of the straight street to the other.

A perpendicular crossroad reveals a second street just like the first: the same absence of traffic, the same high gray walls, the same blind windows, the same deserted sidewalks. At the corner of the sidewalk, a street light is on, although it is broad daylight. But it is a dull day which makes everything colorless and flat. Instead of the striking vistas these rows of houses should produce, there is only a crisscrossing of meaningless lines, the falling snow depriving the scene of all relief, as if this blurred view were merely badly painted on a bare wall.

Where the wall and ceiling meet, the fly's shadow, the

enlarged image of the filament of the electric bulb, reappears and continues its circuit around the rim of the white circle cast by the lamp. Its speed is always the same: slow and steady. In the dark area to the left a dot of light appears, corresponding to a small, round hole in the dark parchment of the lampshade; it is not actually a dot, but a thin broken line, a regular hexagon with one side missing: another enlarged image, this one stationary, of the same luminous source, the same incandescent thread.

It is the same filament again, that of a similar or slightly larger lamp, which glows so uselessly at the crossroads, enclosed in its glass cage on top of a cast-iron pedestal, a gas light with old-fashioned ornaments that has been converted into an electric street light.

Around the conical base of the cast-iron pedestal that widens toward the bottom and is ringed by several more or less prominent moldings, are embossed the slender stems of a stylized spray of ivy: curling tendrils; pointed, five-lobed, palmate leaves, their five veins very prominent where the scaling black paint reveals the rusted metal. Slightly higher a hip, an arm, a shoulder are leaning against the shaft of the lamppost. The man is wearing a faded military overcoat of no particular color, perhaps once green or khaki. His face is grayish; his features are drawn and give the impression of extreme fatigue, but perhaps a beard more than a day old is largely responsible for this impression. Prolonged waiting, prolonged immobility in the cold may also have drained the color from his cheeks, forehead, and lips.

The eyelids are gray, like the rest of the face; they are lowered. The head is bowed. The eyes are looking at the ground, that is, at the edge of the snow-covered sidewalk in front of the base of the street light and the two heavy marching boots with rounded toes whose coarse leather shows scratches and other signs of wear and tear, more or less covered by the black polish. The layer of snow is not thick enough to yield visibly underfoot, so that the soles of the boots are resting—or virtually resting—on the level of the white snow extending around them. At the edge of the sidewalk, this surface is completely unmarked, not shining but smooth, even, delicately stippled with its original granulation. A little snow has accumulated on the upper edge of the last projecting ring that encircles the widening base of the lamppost, forming a white circle above the black circle by which the latter rests on the ground. Higher up, some flakes have also stuck to other asperities of the cone, accenting the successive rings and the upper edges of the ivy leaves with a white line, as well as all the fragments of stems and veins that are horizontal or only slightly inclined.

But the bottom of the overcoat has swept away several of these tiny agglomerations, just as the boots, changing position several times, have trampled the snow in their immediate vicinity, leaving in places yellower areas, hardened, half-raised pieces and the deep marks of hobnails arranged in alternate rows. In front of the chest, the felt slippers have cleared a large gleaming area in the dust, and another one in front of the table at the place that must be occupied by a desk chair or an armchair, a stool or some kind of seat. A narrow path of gleaming floor has been made from one to the other; a second path goes from the table to the bed. Parallel to the housefronts, a little closer to the walls than to the gutter, a yellowish-gray straight path also indicates the snow-covered sidewalk. Produced by the footsteps of people now gone, the path passes between the lighted street light and the door of the last apartment house, then turns at right angles and disappears in the perpendicular cross street, still following the line of the housefronts about a third of the way across the sidewalk, from one end of its length to the other.

Another path then leads from the bed to the chest. From here, the narrow strip of gleaming floor which leads from the chest to the table, joining the two large areas cleared of dust, swerves slightly in order to pass closer to the fireplace whose grate contains a heap of ashes, without andirons. The black marble of the mantlepiece, like everything else, is covered with gray dust. But the layer is not so thick as on the table or on the floor, and it is uniform on the entire surface of the shelf; now no object encumbers the shelf, and only one has left its outlines, clear and black, in the exact center of the rectangle. This is the same four-branched cross: one branch elongated and pointed, one shorter and oval, the continuation of the first, and two small flaring appendages set perpendicularly on each side.

A similar design also embellishes the wallpaper. The wallpaper is pale gray with slightly darker vertical stripes; between the dark stripes, in the middle of each lighter stripe, runs a line of small dark-gray identical designs: a rosette, some kind of clove, or a tiny torch whose handle consists of what was just now the blade of a dagger, the dagger handle now representing the flame, and the two lateral flaring appendages which were the dagger's guard now representing the little cup which keeps the burning substance from running down the handle.

But it might be a kind of electric torch instead, for the tip of what is supposed to produce the light is clearly rounded like an oblong bulb instead of being pointed like a flame. The design, reproduced thousands of times up and down the walls all around the room, is a simple silhouette about the size of a large insect, of a uniform color so that it is difficult to make it out: it reveals no greater relief than the incandescent filament which must be inside the bulb. Besides, the bulb is hidden by the lampshade. Only the image of the filament is visible on the ceiling: a small, open hexagon appearing as a luminous line against the dim background, and farther to the right an identical small hexagon, but in motion, silhouetted against the circle of light cast by the lamp, advancing slowly, steadily, along the inner rim until it reaches the vertical wall and disappears.

The soldier is carrying a package under his left arm. His right arm, from shoulder to elbow, is leaning against the lamppost. His head is turned toward the street, show-ing his growth of beard and the serial number on the collar of his overcoat, five or six black figures in a red diamond. Behind him the double door of the corner apartment house is not completely closed—not ajar either, but one leaf simply pushed against the fixed one, which is narrower, leaving perhaps an inch or two of space between them, a vertical stripe of darkness. To the right is the row of ground floor windows interrupted only by the doors of the build-ings, identical windows and identical doors, the latter similar to the windows in shape and size. There is not a single shop in sight from one end of the street to the other.

To the left of the door that is not closed tight, there are only two windows, then the corner of the building, then, at right angles, another row of identical windows and doors which look like the reflection of the first, as if a mirror had been set there, making an obtuse angle (a right angle in-creased by half a right angle) with the plane of the house-fronts; and the same series is repeated: two windows, a door, four windows, a door, etc. . . . The first door is ajar on a dark hallway, leaving between its two unequal leaves a dark interval wide enough for a man, or at least a child, to slip through.

In front of the door, at the edge of the sidewalk, a street light is on, although it is still daylight. But the dim and diffuse light of this snowy landscape makes the light from the electric bulb apparent at first glance: somewhat brighter, a little yellower, a little more localized. Against the base of the street light a bareheaded soldier is leaning, his head lowered, his hands hidden in his overcoat pockets. Under his right arm is a package wrapped in brown paper that looks something like a shoe box, with a white string doubtless tied in a cross; but only that part of this string around the length of the box is visible, the other part, if it exists, being hidden by the overcoat sleeve. On this sleeve at elbow level are several dark stains that may be the re-mains of fresh mud, or paint, or grease.

The box wrapped in brown paper is now on the chest. It no longer has its white string, and the wrapping paper, carefully folded back along the shorter side of the parallelepiped, gapes a little in a sharp fold narrowing toward the bottom. At this point the marble top of the chest shows a long, almost straight crack passing diagonally under the corner of the box and reaching the wall toward the middle of the chest. Just over it is hung the picture.

The picture framed in varnished wood, the striped wallpaper, the fireplace with its heap of ashes, the table with its lamp and its glass ashtray, the heavy red curtains, the large day bed covered with the same red velvety material, and finally the chest with its three drawers and its cracked marble top, the brown package on top of it, and above that the picture, and the vertical lines of little gray insects rising to the ceiling.

Outside, the sky remains the same dull white. It is still daylight. The street is empty: there is no traffic, and there are no pedestrians on the sidewalks. It has been snowing; and the snow has not yet melted. It forms a rather thin layer —an inch or so—which is quite regular, however, and covers all the horizontal surfaces with the same dull, neutral whitish color. The only interruptions visible are the straight paths parallel to the housefronts and the gutters (made even more distinct by their vertical curbs which have remained black) separating the sidewalks into two unequal strips for their entire length. At the crossroads, at the base of the street light, a small circle of trampled snow has the same yellowish color as the narrow paths that run alongside the buildings. The doors are closed. The windows show no figure either pressed against the panes or even looming farther back in the rooms. The flatness of this entire setting, moreover, suggests that there is nothing behind these panes, behind these doors, behind these housefronts. And the entire scene remains empty: without a man, a woman, or even a child.

The picture, in its varnished wood frame, represents a tavern scene. It is a nineteenth-century etching, or a good reproduction of one. A large number of people fill the room, a crowd of drinkers sitting or standing, and, on the far left, the bartender standing on a slightly raised platform behind his bar.

The bartender is a fat, bald man wearing an apron. He leans forward, both hands resting on the edge of the bar, over several half-full glasses that have been set there, his massive shoulders turned toward a small group of middle-class citizens in frock coats who appear to be engaged in an animated discussion; standing in various attitudes, many are making expansive gestures that sometimes involve the whole body, and are doubtless quite expressive.

To their right, that is, in the center of the scene, several groups of drinkers are sitting at tables that are irregularly arranged—or rather, crammed—in a space too small to hold them all comfortably. These men are also making extravagant gestures and their faces are violently contorted, but their movements, like their expressions, are frozen by the drawing, suspended, stopped short, which also makes their meaning uncertain; particularly since the words being shouted on all sides seem to have been absorbed by a thick layer of glass. Some of them, carried away by their excitement, have half risen from their chairs or their benches and are pointing over the heads of the others toward a more distant interlocutor. Everywhere hands rise, mouths open, heads turn; fists are clenched, pounded on tables, or brandished in mid-air.

At the far right a group of men, almost all workers judging from their clothes, like those sitting at the tables, have their backs to the latter and are crowding around some poster or picture tacked on the wall. A little in front of them, between their backs and the first row of drinkers facing in the other direction, a boy is sitting on the floor among all these legs with their shapeless trousers, all these clumsy boots stamping about and trying to move toward his left; on the other side he is partially protected by the bench. The child is shown facing straight ahead. He is sitting with his legs folded under him, his arms clasped around a large box something like a shoe box. No one is paying any attention to him. Perhaps he was knocked down in the confusion. As a matter of fact, in the foreground, not far from where he is sitting, a chair has been overturned and is still lying on the floor.

Somewhat apart, as though separated from the crowd surrounding them by an unoccupied zone—narrow, of course, but nevertheless wide enough for their isolation to be noticeable, in any case wide enough to call attention to them though they are in the background—three soldiers are sitting around a smaller table, the second from the rear on the right, their motionlessness and rigidity in marked contrast to the civilians who fill the room. The soldiers are looking straight ahead, their hands resting on the checkered oilcloth; there are no glasses in front of them. They are the only men whose heads are not bare, for they are wearing low-peaked fatigue caps. Behind them, at the extreme rear, the last seated drinkers are mingled with others who are standing, forming a confused mass; besides, the drawing here is vaguer too. Under the print, in the white margin, someone has written a title: "The Defeat of Reichenfels."

On closer examination, the isolation of the three soldiers seems to result less from the narrow space between them and the crowd than from the direction of the glances around them. All the figures in the background look as if they are passing—or trying to pass, for the space is cramped—behind the soldiers to reach the left side of the picture, where there is probably a door (though this hypothetical exit cannot be seen in the picture because of a row of coat racks covered with hats and coats); every head is looking straight ahead (that is, toward the coat racks), except for one here and there who turns to speak to someone who has remained in the rear. Everyone in the crowd gathered on the right is looking toward the right wall. The drinkers at the tables are represented in natural poses, turning toward the center of each group or else toward one neighbor or another. As for the middle-class citizens in front of the bar, they too are completely absorbed in their own conversation, and the bartender leans toward them without paying any attention to the rest of his customers. Among the various groups circulate a number of persons not yet settled, but obviously about to adopt one of several probable attitudes: either walking over to examine the bulletin board, sitting down at one of the tables, or else going out behind the coat racks; a moment's scrutiny is enough to reveal that each man has already determined what he is going to do next; here, as among the groups, no face, no movement betrays hesitation, perplexity, inner vacillation, or contradiction. The three soldiers, on the contrary, seem forsaken. They are not talking to each other; they are not looking at anything in particular: neither glasses, nor bulletins, nor their neighbors. They have nothing to do. No one looks at them and they themselves have nothing to look at. The position of their faces—one full face, the other in profile, the last in a three-quarters view —indicates no common subject of attention. Besides, the first man—the only one whose features are completely visible—betrays no expression whatever, merely a fixed, vacant stare.

The contrast between the three soldiers and the crowd is further accentuated by a precision of line, a clarity in rendering, much more evident in their case than in that of other individuals the same distance from the viewer. The artist has shown them with as much concern for detail and almost as much sharpness of outline as if they were sitting in the foreground. But the composition is so involved that this is not apparent at first glance. Particularly the soldier shown full face has been portrayed with a wealth of detail that seems quite out of proportion to the indifference it expresses. No specific thought can be discerned. It is merely a tired face, rather thin, and narrowed still further by several days' growth of beard. This thinness, these shadows that accentuate the features without, on the other hand, indicating the slightest individual characteristic, nevertheless emphasize the brilliance of the wide-open eyes.

The military overcoat is buttoned up to the neck, where the regimental number is embroidered on a diamond-shaped tab of material. The cap is set straight on the head, covering the hair, which is cut extremely short, judging from its appearance at the temples. The man is sitting stiffly, his hands lying flat on the table which is covered with a red-and-white checked oilcloth.

He has finished his drink some time ago. He does not look as if he were thinking of leaving. Yet, around him, the café has emptied. The light is dim now, the bartender having turned out most of the lamps before leaving the room himself.

The soldier, his eyes wide open, continues to stare into the half-darkness a few yards in front of him, where the child is standing, also motionless and stiff, his arms at his side. But it is as if the soldier did not see the child—or anything else. He looks as if he has fallen asleep from exhaustion, sitting close to the table, his eyes wide open.

It is the child who speaks first. He says: "Are you asleep?" He has spoken almost in a whisper, as if he were afraid to awaken the sleeper. The latter has not stirred. After a few seconds the child repeats his question a trifle louder: "Are you asleep?" and he adds, in the same expressionless, slightly singsong tone of voice: "You can't sleep here, you know."

The soldier has not stirred. The child might suppose he

153

is alone in the room, merely pretending to have a conversation with someone who does not exist, or else with a doll, a toy unable to answer. Under these conditions there was certainly no need to speak louder; the voice was actually that of a child telling himself a story.

But the voice has stopped, as if unable to struggle further against the silence which has prevailed again. The child, too, may have fallen asleep.

"No . . . Yes . . . I know," the soldier says.

Neither one has moved. The child is still standing in the half-darkness, his arms at his sides. He has not even seen the man's lips moving as he sits at the table under the one light bulb that is still on in the room; his head has not moved at all, his eyes have not even blinked, and his mouth is still closed.

"Your father . . ." the soldier begins. Then he stops. But this time the lips have stirred a little.

"He's not my father," the child says.

And he turns his head toward the door with its black rectangle of window glass in the upper half.

Outside it is snowing. The fine flakes have begun falling thickly again on the already white road. The wind has risen and is blowing them horizontally, so that the soldier has to keep his head down, a little farther down, as he walks, pressing the hand shielding his eyes still closer against his forehead, leaving visible only a few square inches of thin, crunching snow that is already trampled hard. Reaching a crossroad, the soldier hesitates and looks around for the plaques that should indicate the name of that cross street. But it is useless, for there are no blue enamel plaques here, or else they are set too high and the night is too dark; besides, the fine, close flakes quickly blind him when he tries to look up. Then too, a street name would hardly furnish him much in the way of helpful information: he does not know this city anyway.

He hesitates for another moment, looks ahead again, then back at the road he has just taken, with its rows of

street lights whose circles of light, closer and closer together and increasingly dim, soon disappear in the darkness.
Then he turns right, into the cross street which is also deserted, lined with the same kind of apartment houses and
the same row of street lights, set fairly far apart but at
regular intervals, their dim circles of light revealing as he
passes the oblique fall of the snow.

The white flakes, falling thick and fast, suddenly change
direction; vertical for a few seconds, they suddenly become
almost horizontal. Then they stop suddenly and, with a sudden gust of wind, begin to blow at virtually the same angle
in the opposite direction, which they abandon after two or
three seconds just as abruptly as before, to return to their
original orientation, making new, almost horizontal parallel
lines that cross the circle of light from left to right toward
the unlighted windows.

In the window recesses the snow has formed an uneven
layer, very shallow on the sill but deeper toward the back,
making an already considerable drift that fills the right
corner and reaches as high as the pane. All the ground floor
windows, one after the other, show exactly the same
amount of snow which has drifted toward the right in the
same way.

At the next crossroad, under the corner street light, a
child is standing. He is partially hidden by the cast-iron
shaft whose broader base conceals the lower part of his
body altogether. He is watching the soldier approach. He
does not seem bothered by the storm, or by the snow that
whitens some of his black cape and his beret. He is a boy of
about ten, his expression serious and alert. He turns his
head as the soldier approaches him, watching him as he
reaches the lamppost, then passes it. Since the soldier is
not walking fast, the child has time to examine him carefully from head to foot: the unshaven cheeks, the apparent
fatigue, the dirty ragged overcoat, the sleeves without
chevrons, the wet package under his left arm, both hands
thrust deep in his pockets, the hurriedly wrapped, irregular

leggings, the wide gash down the back of the right boot, at least four inches long and so deep it looks as if it pierces the leather; yet the boot is not split and the damaged area has merely been smeared with black polish, which now gives it the same dark-gray color as the adjoining surfaces that are still intact.

The man has stopped. Without moving the rest of his body, he has turned his head around toward the child looking at him, already three steps away, already crisscrossed by many white lines.

A moment later, the soldier slowly pivots and takes a step toward the street light. The boy steps back, against the cast-iron shaft; at the same time he pulls the bottom of his cape around his legs, holding it from the inside without showing his hands. The man has stopped. Now that the gusts of snow are no longer striking him directly in the face, he can raise his head without too much trouble.

"Don't be afraid," he says.

He takes a step toward the child and repeats a little louder: "Don't be afraid."

The child does not answer. Without seeming to feel the thickly falling flakes that make him squint slightly, he continues to stare at the soldier directly in front of him. The latter begins:

"Do you know where . . ."

But he goes no further. The question he was going to ask is not the right one. A gust of wind blows the snow into his face again. He takes his right hand out of his overcoat pocket and shields his eyes with it. He has no glove, his fingers are red and dirty. When the gust is over he puts his hand back in his pocket.

"Where does this road go?"

The boy still says nothing. His eyes have left the soldier to look toward the end of the street in the direction the man has nodded toward; he sees only the succession of street lights, closer and closer together, dimmer and dimmer, which vanish into the darkness.

"What's the matter, are you afraid I'll eat you?"

"No," the child says. "I'm not afraid."

"Well then, tell me where this road goes."

"I don't know," the child says.

And he looks again at this badly dressed, unshaven soldier who does not even know where he is going. Then, without warning, he makes a sudden turn, skillfully avoids the base of the lamppost, and begins to run as fast as he can along the row of apartment houses, in the opposite direction from the way the soldier came. In a few seconds, he has disappeared.

At the next street light, he appears again for several seconds; he is still running just as fast; his cape billows out behind him. He reappears at each lamppost, once, twice, then no more.

The soldier turns back and continues on his way. Again the snow strikes him directly in the face.

He puts the package under his right arm to try to shield his face with his left hand, for the wind is blowing more continuously from this side. But he soon gives this up and puts his hand, numb with cold, back in his overcoat pocket. Now he merely turns his head away to get less snow in his eyes, tilting it toward the unlighted windows where the white drift continues to accumulate in the right-hand corner of the recess.

Yet it is this same boy with the serious expression who led him to the café run by the man who is not his father. And there was a similar scene under the same kind of lamppost, at an identical crossroads. Perhaps it was snowing a little less heavily. The flakes were thicker, heavier, slower. But the boy answered with just as much reticence, holding his black cape tight around his knees. He had the same alert expression and seemed to be just as untroubled by the snow. He hesitated just as long at each question before giving an answer which furnished his interlocutor no information. Where did the street go? A long silent stare toward the presumed end of the street, then the calm voice:

157

"To the boulevard."

"And this one?"

The boy slowly turns his eyes in the direction the man has just nodded toward. His features reveal no difficulty remembering, no uncertainty, when he repeats in the same expressionless tone:

"To the boulevard."

"The same one?"

Again there is silence, and the snow falling, slower and heavier.

"Yes," the boy says. Then, after a pause: "No," and finally, with a sudden violence: "It's the boulevard!"

"And is it far?" the soldier asks again.

The child is still looking at the series of street lights, closer and closer together, dimmer and dimmer, which here too vanish into the darkness.

"Yes," he says, his voice calm again and sounding as if it came from far away.

The soldier waits another minute to make sure there will not be another "no." But the boy is already running along the row of apartment houses, down the trampled snow path the soldier followed in the opposite direction a few minutes earlier. When the running boy crosses a circle of light, his black cape billowing out behind him can be seen for a few seconds, once, twice, three times, smaller and vaguer at each reappearance, until there is nothing but a confused whirl of snow.

Yet it is certainly the same boy who walks ahead of the soldier when the latter comes to the café. Before crossing the threshold, the child shakes his black cape and takes off his beret, which he knocks twice against the door jamb in order to brush off the bits of ice which have formed in the folds of the cloth. Then the soldier must have met him several times, while walking in circles through the maze of identical streets. He has never come to any boulevard, any broader avenue planted with trees or differing in any way at all from the other streets he has taken. Finally the

child had mentioned a few names, the few street names he
knew, which were obviously of no use at all.

Now he is knocking his beret sharply against the door
jamb in front of which they have both stopped. The interior
is brightly lit. A pleated curtain of white, translucent material covers the lower part of the window that is set in the
upper half of the door. But it is easy for a man of normal
height to see the entire room: the bar to the left, the tables
in the middle, a wall on the right covered with posters of
various sizes. There are few drinkers at this late hour: two
workers sitting at one of the tables and a better-dressed
man standing near the zinc-topped bar over which the bartender is leaning. The latter is a thickset man whose size
is even more marked in relation to his customer because of
the sightly raised platform he is standing on. Both men
have simultaneously turned their heads toward the door
where the boy has just knocked his beret against the
jamb.

But they see only the soldier's face above the curtain.
And the child, turning the doorknob with one hand, again
knocks his beret, this time against the door itself, which is
already some distance from the jamb. The bartender's eyes
have already left the soldier's pale face that is still silhouetted against the darkness, cut off at the level of the
chin by the curtain, and are fixed on the widening gap between door and jamb where the child is about to come in.

As soon as he is inside, the latter turns around and gestures to the soldier to follow him. This time everyone stares
at the newcomer: the bartender behind his bar, the man
dressed in middle-class clothes standing in front of it, the
two workers sitting at a table. One of the two, whose back
was to the door, has pivoted on his chair without letting
go of his glass that is half full of red wine and set in the
middle of the checkered oilcloth. The other glass, just beside the first, is also encircled by a large hand which completely conceals the probable contents. To the left, a ring

of reddish liquid indicates another place previously occupied by one of these glasses, or by a third.

Afterwards, it is the soldier himself who is sitting at a table in front of a similar glass, half full of the same dark-colored wine. The glass has left several circular marks on the red-and-white checked oilcloth, but almost all are incomplete, showing a series of more or less closed arcs, occasionally overlapping, almost dry in some places, in others still shiny with the last drops of liquid leaving a film over the blacker deposit already formed, while elsewhere the rings are blurred by being set too close together or even half obliterated by sliding, or else, perhaps, by a quick wipe of a rag.

The soldier, motionless at the foot of his lamppost, is still waiting, his hands in his overcoat pockets, the same package under his left arm. It is daylight again, the same pale, colorless daylight. But the street light is out now. These are the same apartment houses, the same empty streets, the same gray and white hues, the same cold.

It has stopped snowing. The layer of snow on the ground is scarcely any deeper, perhaps only a little more solidly packed. And the yellowish paths hurrying pedestrians have made along the sidewalks are just the same. On each side of these narrow paths, the white surface has remained virtually intact; tiny changes have nevertheless occurred here and there, for instance the circular area which the soldier's heavy boots have trampled near the lamppost.

It is the child who approaches him this time. At first he is only a vague silhouette, an irregular black spot approaching fairly fast along the outer edge of the sidewalk. Each time this spot passes a street light it makes a sudden movement toward it and immediately continues forward in its original direction. Soon it is easy to make out the agile legs in their narrow black trousers, the black cape billowing out over the shoulders, the beret pulled down over the boy's eyes. Each time the child passes a street light he stretches out his arm toward the cast-iron shaft which his gloved hand grasps while his whole body, with the momentum of its accumulated speed, makes a complete turn around this pivot, his feet scarcely touching the ground until the child is back in his original position on the outer edge of the sidewalk where he continues running forward toward the soldier.

He may not have noticed the latter immediately, for the soldier is partly concealed by the cast-iron shaft his hip and right arm are leaning against. But to get a better look at the boy whose movement is interrupted by pivots and gusts of wind which make his cape billow out each time, the man has stepped forward a little, and the child suddenly stops halfway between the last two lampposts, his feet together, his hands pulling the cape around his rigid body, his alert face with its wide eyes raised toward the soldier.

"Hello," the soldier says.

The child looks at him without surprise, but also without the slightest indication of friendliness, as if he found it both natural and annoying to meet the soldier again.

"Where did you sleep?" he says at last.

The soldier makes a vague gesture with his chin, without bothering to take a hand out of his pocket. "Back there."

"In the barracks?"

"That's right, in the barracks."

The child examines his uniform from head to foot. The greenish overcoat is neither more nor less ragged, the leggings are just as carelessly wrapped, the boots have virtually the same mud stains. But the beard may be a little darker.

"Where is your barracks?"

"Back there," the soldier says. And he repeats the same

161

gesture with his chin, pointing vaguely behind him, or over his right shoulder.

"You don't know how to wrap your leggings," the child says.

The man bends forward slightly and looks down at his boots. "It doesn't matter any more now, you know."

As he straightens up again he notices that the boy is much closer than he expected him to be: only three or four yards away. He did not think the child had come so close to him, nor does he remember having seen him come nearer afterwards. Still, it is hardly likely that the child has changed position without the soldier's knowing it, while the latter's head was down: in so short an interval of time he would scarcely have been able to take a step. Besides, he is standing in exactly the same position as when they first met: stiff in the black cape held shut—even tight, around the body—by his invisible hands, his eyes raised.

"Twelve thousand three hundred forty-five," the child says, reading the regimental number on the overcoat collar.

"Yes," the soldier says. "But that isn't my number."

"Yes it is. It's written on you."

"But now, you know . . ."

"It's even written twice." And the child sticks one arm out from under his cape and points his forefinger toward the two red diamond shapes. He is wearing a navy blue sweater and a knitted wool glove the same color.

"All right . . ." the soldier says.

The child puts his arm back under the cape, which he carefully closes again, holding it tight from inside.

"What's in your package?"

"I've already told you."

Suddenly the child turns his head toward the door of the apartment building. Thinking he has seen something unusual there, the soldier turns to look too, but sees only the same vertical dark opening, a hand's width across, separating the door from the jamb. Since the boy is still looking attentively in this direction, the man tries to discern some figure in the shadowy doorway, but without success.

Finally he asks: "What are you looking at?"

"What's in your package?" the child repeats instead of answering, still not looking away from the open door.

"I've already told you: things."

"What things?"

"My things!"

The boy looks at his interlocutor again:

"You have a knapsack to keep your things in. Every soldier has a knapsack."

He has become increasingly self-assured during the conversation. His voice is now not at all remote, but firm, almost peremptory. The man, on the other hand, speaks lower and lower:

"It's all over now, you know. The war's over . . ."

Again he feels how tired he is. He no longer wants to answer these questions that lead nowhere. He was almost ready to give the boy the package. He looks at the box in its brown wrapping paper under his arm; in drying, the snow has left dark rings on it, their edges fringed with tiny scallops; the string has stretched and slipped toward one of the corners.

The soldier then looks past the still motionless boy down the empty street. Having turned toward the opposite end, he sees the same shallow vista.

"Do you know what time it is?" he asks, resuming his initial position against the cast-iron shaft.

The boy shakes his head several times, from left to right, from right to left.

"Does your father serve meals?"

"He's not my father," the child says; and without giving the man time to ask his question again, he turns on his heel and walks stiffly toward the half-open door. He stops on the doorstep, pushes the door a little farther open, slips into the opening, and closes the door behind him without slamming it but so that the click of the latch falling back into place can nevertheless be clearly heard.

The soldier no longer sees anything in front of him now but the snow-covered sidewalk with its yellowish path on the right side and, to the left, a smooth surface broken by a single, regular set of tracks: two small, widely spaced footprints running parallel to the gutter, then, about four yards from the lamppost, coming together to form an irregular circle before turning at right angles to join the narrower path leading to the apartment house door.

The soldier raises his face toward the gray façade with its rows of uniform windows, a white streak along the bottom of each recess, thinking perhaps he will see the boy appear at one of the windows. But he knows that the child in the cape does not live in this house, for he has already gone with him to where he lives. Besides, judging from the look of the windows, the whole apartment building seems unoccupied.

The heavy red curtains extend across the entire wall from floor to ceiling. The wall opposite them has the chest against it and above that, the picture. The child is where he was, sitting on the floor with his legs folded under him; it looks as if he wants to slide all the way under the bench. But he continues to stare straight ahead, his attention indicated, for want of anything else, by his wide-open eyes.

This sign, of course, is not infallible; if the artist has meant the child to be looking at nothing in particular, if he has imagined no specific feature for the fourth wall of this rectangular room where only three are shown, it could be said that the child is merely staring into space. But in that case, it was not logical to represent him staring at the only one of the four walls that apparently looks out onto something. The three walls shown in the print have, as a matter of fact, no visible opening in them. Even if there is an exit at the left, behind the coat racks, it is certainly not the main entrance to the tavern, whose interior arrangement would then be too out of the ordinary. The main entrance, with white enamel letters spelling out the word "café" and the proprietor's name in two curved lines pasted on the glass in an oval, and below this a pleated curtain of thin, translucent material, obliging anyone who wants to look over it to stand close against the door—this main entrance can be nowhere else but in the wall not shown in the print, the rest of this wall being occupied by a large window, also with a long curtain covering its lower half, and decorated in the middle by three spheres attached to the glass—one red one above two white ones—certainly suggesting that the exit behind the coat racks leads to a poolroom.

The child holding the box in his arms would therefore be looking toward the door. But he is sitting almost at floor level and obviously cannot see the street over the curtain. He is not looking up to see some pale face pressed against the glass, cut off at the level of the neck by the curtain. His gaze is virtually horizontal. Has the door just opened to let in a newcomer who would attract the boy's attention by his unusual attire: a soldier, for instance? This solution seems unlikely, for ordinarily the main entrance is placed next to the bar, that is, in this case, on the far left, where there is a small cleared space in front of the men standing dressed in middle-class clothes. The child, though, is sitting on the right-hand side of the picture, where no passage among the jumble of benches and tables would permit access to the rest of the room.

The soldier, moreover, came in a long time ago. He is sitting at a table, far behind the child, who does not seem at all interested in his uniform. The soldier is also staring straight ahead, his eyes fixed slightly higher; but since he is much farther away from the window than the boy, he need only raise his eyes a few degrees to look through the window above the curtain at the heavily falling snow which again obliterates the footprints, the single set of tracks, the intersecting yellowish paths that run parallel to the high façades.

At the corner of the last apartment house, standing in the L-shaped strip of snow between the latter and the path, his body cut vertically by the angle of the stone, one foot, one leg, one shoulder, and half the black cape out of sight, the boy is on the lookout, his eyes fixed on the cast-iron lamppost. Has he come out of the apartment by another door opening on the cross street? Or has he stepped through a ground floor window? In either case, the soldier pretends not to have noticed his reappearance. Leaning against his street light, he is absorbed in examining the other end of the empty street.

"What are you waiting for?" Then, in the same tone of voice, after about ten seconds: "What are you waiting for there?"

The voice is certainly the boy's, the tone deliberate, calm, and not friendly, a little too deep for a boy of ten or twelve. But it sounds quite close, scarcely two or three yards away, whereas the corner of the building is at least eight yards off. The man feels like turning around to verify this distance and see if the child has not come closer again. Or else, without looking at him, he might answer his question with the first thing that comes into his head: "The streetcar," or "Christmas," to make the child understand what a bother he is. The soldier continues to stare down the street.

When he finally turns to look at the boy, the latter has completely disappeared. The soldier waits another minute, thinking the boy has only stepped behind the corner of the apartment house and will soon peek out from behind his hiding place. But no such thing happens.

The man looks down at the fresh snow, where the newly made footprints turn at a right angle just in front of him. In the section parallel to the sidewalk the footprints are wide apart and smudged by running, a tiny heap of snow having been thrown up behind each one by the movement of the shoe; on the other hand, the few footprints leading to the path show the pattern of the soles very clearly: a series of chevrons across the width of the sole and, beneath the heel, a cross inscribed in a circle—that is, on the heel itself, a cross inscribed in a circular depression in the rubber (a second round hole, much shallower and of extremely small diameter, perhaps indicating the center of the cross, with the shoe size shown by figures in relief: thirty-two, perhaps, thirty-three or thirty-four).

The soldier, who had bent over slightly to examine the details of the footprints, then walks to the path. As he does so, he tries to push open the apartment house door, but the door resists: it is shut tight. It is a wooden door with ornamental moldings and extremely narrow jambs on either side. The man continues walking toward the corner of the building and turns down the cross street, which is as empty as the one he has just left.

This new route leads him, like the other, to a right-angle crossroad with a last street light set some ten yards before the end of the sidewalk and identical façades on each side. The base of the cast-iron lamppost is a truncated cone embossed with a strand of ivy, with the same curves, the same leaves growing at the same places on the same stems, the same faults in the casting. The entire design is accentuated by the snow borders. Perhaps the meeting was supposed to be at this crossroads.

The soldier raises his eyes to look for the enamel plaques which should show the names of these streets. There is nothing visible on one of the stone walls at the corner. On the other, about three yards from the ground, is attached the usual blue plaque, from which the enamel has chipped off in large flakes, as if some boys had relentlessly aimed at it with pebbles; only the word "Rue" is still legible, and, further on, the two letters: ". . . na . . ." followed by a downstroke interrupted by the concentric rings of the next chip. Besides, the original name must have been an extremely short one. The depredations are quite old, for the exposed metal is already badly rusted.

As he is about to cross the street, still following the thin yellow path, to see if he cannot find other street signs in better condition, the man hears a voice quite close by, speaking three or four syllables whose meaning he has not time to grasp. He immediately turns around; but there is no one in sight. In this solitude, the snow probably conducts sound peculiarly.

The voice was low and yet it did not sound like a man's voice . . . A young woman with an extremely low voice—that may have been what it was, but the recollection is too fleeting: already nothing remains but a neutral timbre, without any particular tone; it could belong to anyone, and might not even be a human voice at all. At this moment the soldier notices that the corner apartment house door is not closed. Automatically, he takes a few steps toward it. The interior is so dark that it is impossible to see anything through the gap. To the right, to the left, up above, all the windows are closed, their dirty black panes with neither curtains nor shades suggesting no trace of life in the unlighted rooms, as if the entire building was deserted.

The wooden door has ornamental moldings and is painted dark brown; on either side of the open leaf are the narrow jambs. The soldier pushes the door wide open as he steps up onto the snowy stoop, already covered with footprints, and steps inside.

He is standing at the end of a dark hallway with several doors opening off it. At the other end can be seen the beginning of a staircase that soon vanishes in the darkness. The end of this long narrow hallway opens onto another hallway perpendicular to it, indicated by even darker shadows on each side of the staircase. The hallway is empty, without any of those household objects that generally suggest the existence of life: door mats in front of the doors, toys left at the foot of the stairs, a bucket and mop in a corner. Here there is nothing, except the floor and the walls; and even the walls are bare, all painted some very dark color; immediately to the left of the entrance is tacked the small white civil defense bulletin instructing the residents what to do in case of fire. The floor is made of wood blackened by mud and slops, as are the first steps—the only ones clearly visible—of the staircase. After five or six steps the staircase seems to turn to the right. The soldier can now make out the wall behind the stairs. Here, flattened against the wall, her arms held stiffly at her side, there is a woman in a full skirt with a long apron tied around her waist; she is staring at the open door and the figure standing in it, silhouetted against the light.

Before the man has had time to speak to her, a door on the left side of the hallway suddenly opens, and another woman in an apron, heavier-set than the first and perhaps older too, steps out. Looking up, she stops short, opens her mouth wide—too wide—and as she steps back into her doorway begins to scream, the shrill sound rising until it comes to an end with the violent slamming of her door. At the same moment comes the sound of hurried footsteps going up the staircase; it is the other woman running away, vanishing at once, the pounding of her clogs continuing without slowing down, but fading from floor to floor as she climbs, her full skirt, billowing around her legs, perhaps held down with one hand, not even stopping on the landings to catch her breath, the only clue as to her position being suggested by a different resonance at the beginning and the end of each flight: one floor, two floors, three or four floors, or even more.

Afterwards there is complete silence again. But, on the right side of the hallway this time, another door has opened. Or was it already open before? It is more likely that the sudden uproar has just attracted this new figure, which resembles the preceding two, or at least the first: a woman, also young, apparently, and wearing a long dark-gray apron tied around her waist and hanging full around her hips. Her eyes having met the soldier's, she asks:

"What's going on?"

Her voice is low, deep, but without any intonation; there is a premeditated quality about it, as if she wanted to sound as impersonal as possible. This might also be the voice heard in the street a moment ago.

"They got scared," the soldier says.

"Yes," the woman says, "it's from seeing you standing there like that . . . with the light behind you . . . they can't see . . . they thought you were a . . ."

She does not finish her sentence. She stands still, staring at him. She opens her door no wider, probably feeling safer inside, one hand resting on the jamb, the other holding the door, ready to close it again. She asks:

"What do you want?"

"I'm looking for a street . . ." the soldier says, "A street I have to go to."

"What street?"

"That's just it. I can't remember the name. It was something like Galavier, or Matadier. But I'm not sure. Could it be Montoret?"

The woman seems to be thinking.

"This is a big city, you know," she says at last.

"But it's around here somewhere, that's what they told me."

The young woman turns her head toward the interior of the apartment and in a louder voice questions someone who remains invisible: "Did you ever hear of a Rue Montoret? Somewhere near here? Or something that sounds like that?"

She waits for the answer, revealing her regular profile as she turns toward the open door. Everything behind her is dark: there must be a hallway without any windows. The heavy-set woman also came out of complete darkness. After a moment a faint voice answers a few indistinct words, and the young woman turns back toward the soldier:

"Wait here a minute. I'll go see."

She begins to close the door, then changes her mind: "Close the street door," she says, "the whole house is getting cold."

The soldier walks back to the door and pushes it shut, the latch making a faint click as it falls back into place. He is in the dark again. The woman's door must be closed too. It is not even possible to walk toward it, for there is no means of recognizing anything, not even a gleam of light. Complete darkness. Nor can the slightest sound be heard: neither steps nor murmurs nor the clatter of kitchen utensils. The whole house seems uninhabited. The soldier closes his eyes and again sees the white flakes falling slowly, the row of street lights at regular intervals from one end of the snow-covered sidewalk to the other, and the boy running away as fast as he can, appearing and disappearing, visible each time for a few seconds in the successive circles of light at equal intervals of time, though the space is increasingly foreshortened by the distance, so that the boy seems to be running slower and slower as he grows smaller and smaller.

It is six steps from the chest to the table: three steps to the fireplace and three more after that. It is five steps from the table to the corner of the bed; four steps from the bed to the chest. The path from the chest to the table is not quite straight: it swerves slightly in order to pass closer to the fireplace. Above the fireplace is a mirror, a large rectangular mirror fastened to the wall. The foot of the bed is directly opposite.

Suddenly the light reappears in the hallway. It is not the same light, and it does not directly illuminate the place where the soldier is standing, which remains in darkness. At the other end of the hallway, a pale yellow artificial light comes from the right side of the transverse hallway. A luminous rectangle thus appears against the far right wall just in front of the staircase, and the illuminated area begins to widen from there, tracing two oblique lines across the floor: one of which crosses the blackened flooring of the hallway, the other rising diagonally up the first three steps;

beyond the latter, as on this side of the former, the darkness remains, though slightly reduced.

Also on the right, in the area which cannot be seen, where the light is coming from, a door closes gently and a key turns in a lock. Then the lights go out and it is dark again. But footsteps, probably guided by long familiarity with the premises, are advancing down the transverse hallway. They are regular, distinct footsteps which do not hesitate. They advance down the hallway in front of the staircase opposite the soldier who, in order to avoid the collision of two bodies in the darkness, gropes blindly around him, looking for a wall against which he can flatten himself. But the footsteps are not heading toward him: instead of turning into the hallway at the end of which he is standing, they have continued straight ahead, into the left branch of the transverse hallway. A bolt is drawn and a harsher light, from outside, appears in this left section of the hallway, its intensity increasing until it becomes a kind of dim gray twilight. There must be another outside door here, opening onto the other street. It is through this door that the boy would have gone out again. Soon the light disappears as it had come, gradually, and the door closes at the same time that complete darkness is re-established.

Darkness. Click. Yellow light. Click. Darkness. Click. Gray light. Click. Darkness. And the footsteps echoing across the hallway floor. And the footsteps echoing across the pavement, in the snow-covered street. And the snow beginning to fall. And the boy's intermittent figure growing smaller and smaller in the distance, from street light to street light.

If the last person had not left by the same door as the boy, but from this side of the building, he would have let daylight into this part of the hallway as he opened the door, and discovered the soldier pressed against the wall, suddenly appearing in broad daylight a few inches away. As in the case of a collision in the darkness, new screams might then have aroused the whole house a second time, sending shadows scampering toward the staircase and bringing terrified faces to half-open doors, necks craning, eyes anxious, mouths already opening to shout . . .

"There is no Rue Montalet around here, nothing like that," the low voice announces; and immediately afterwards: "You're standing in the dark! You should have turned on the light." At these words the light comes on in the hallway, yellow light from a naked bulb on a wire from the ceiling, illuminating the young woman in a gray apron whose arm is still extended outside her doorway; her hand resting on the white porcelain switch moves downward while her pale eyes are fixed on the man, shifting from his hollow cheeks where the beard is almost a quarter of an inch long to the box wrapped in brown paper and the clumsily wrapped leggings, then moving back to the drawn features of his face. "You're tired," she says.

It is not a question. The voice has again become neutral, low, without intonation, cautious perhaps. The soldier makes a vague gesture with his free hand; a half-smile twists one corner of his mouth.

"You're not wounded, are you?"

His free hand rises a little higher: "No, no," the man says. "I'm not wounded." And his hand falls back slowly. Then they stand there for a while looking at each other without speaking.

"What are you going to do," the woman finally asks, "since you can't find the name of that street?"

"I don't know," the soldier says.

"Was it for something important?"

"Yes . . . No . . . Probably."

After another silence, the young woman asks again: "What was it?"

"I don't know," the soldier says. He is tired, he wants to sit down, anywhere, here, against the wall. Mechanically he repeats: "I don't know."

"You don't know what you were going to do there?"

"I have to go there to find out."

"Oh! . . ."

"I was supposed to meet someone. Now it's too late."

During this dialogue, the woman has opened her door wide and stepped forward in the opening. She is wearing a long black dress with a full skirt, the latter three-quarters hidden by a gray pleated apron tied around her waist. The bottom of the apron is extremely full, like the skirt, while the top is merely a simple square of material protecting the front of her dress. Her face has regular, strongly marked features. Her hair is black. But her eyes are pale, a color between blue-green and gray-blue. She does not avoid the soldier's eyes, but instead stares at him for a long time, though without permitting the soldier to determine what her attitude toward him is.

"You haven't eaten," she says. And a fleeting nuance, as though of pity or fear or surprise, can be detected in her words this time.

But as soon as she has spoken her sentence and silence has fallen again, it becomes impossible to recapture the intonation which seemed just now to have a meaning—fear, boredom, doubt, solicitude, some sort of interest—and all that remains is the declaration: "You haven't eaten," pronounced in a neutral tone of voice. The man repeats his evasive gesture.

"Come in for a minute," she says, perhaps reluctantly—or perhaps not.

Click. Darkness. Click. Yellow light, now illuminating a tiny vestibule where there is a coat rack covered with hats and coats. Click. Darkness.

Now a door opens into a square room furnished with a day bed, a rectangular table, and a marble-topped chest. The table is covered with a red-and-white checked oilcloth. A fireplace with cold ashes in an open grate but without andirons on the hearth occupies the center of one wall. To the right of this fireplace is another door, ajar, opening into a dark room or closet.

"Here," the young woman says, pointing to a wicker

chair beside the table, "sit down." The soldier shifts the chair slightly, grasping it at the top of its back, and sits down. He rests his right forearm and hand on the oilcloth. His left hand has remained in his overcoat pocket, the left arm still holding the box wrapped in brown paper at his side.

In the opening of the door, but one or two feet away, the figure of a child stands motionless, turned toward the man in uniform whom his mother (is it his mother?) has just brought into the apartment and who is sitting obliquely at the table, half-leaning on the red oilcloth, his shoulders hunched, his head bent forward.

The woman returns through the door to the vestibule. In one hand she is holding at her waist a piece of bread and a glass. Her other arm hangs at her side and in that hand she is holding a bottle by the neck. She sets everything down on the table in front of the soldier.

Without speaking she fills the glass to the brim. Then she leaves the room again. The bottle is an ordinary liter of colorless glass, half full of dark-red wine; the glass, which is in front of it, near the man's hand, is of coarse manufacture, the shape of a cylindrical goblet, fluted for half its height. The bread is to the left: the heel of a large black loaf whose cross-section is a half-circle with rounded corners; the loaf has a close texture with extremely small, evenly spaced holes. The man's hand is red, injured by rough work and the cold; the outer surface of the fingers, which are folded toward the palm, reveals many tiny crevices at the joints; they are, moreover, stained black, as though by grease, which might have adhered to the chapped areas of the skin so that a perfunctory washing would not have made them clean. Hence the bony protuberance at the base of the forefinger is crisscrossed with short black lines, mostly parallel or only slightly divergent, the others variously oriented, surrounding the first lines or cutting across them.

Above the fireplace a large rectangular mirror is fastened

to the wall; the wall reflected in it is the one with the large chest against the base of it. In the middle of this wall is the full-length photograph of a soldier in battle dress—perhaps the husband of the young woman with the low voice and the pale eyes, and perhaps the father of the child. Overcoat with front flaps folded back, leggings, heavy boots: the uniform is that of the infantry, as is the chin-strapped helmet and the full equipment of knapsack, canteen, belt, cartridge belt, etc. The man's hands are closed, one a little above his belt, over the two leather straps that cross each other over his chest; he has a carefully trimmed moustache; the figure as a whole, moreover, has a neat, almost lacquered quality, doubtless due to the skillful retouching of the specialist who has made this enlargement; the face itself, wearing the usual smile, has been so smoothed, scratched out, and rearranged that it no longer has any character at all, resembling all those faces of soldiers or sailors about to go into battle displayed in photographers' windows. Yet the original snapshot seems to have been taken by an amateur—probably the young woman or some friend in the regiment—for the setting is not that of a fake middle-class living room nor of a false terrace lined with potted palms in front of a park painted in *trompe-l'oeil* on canvas, but the street itself in front of the apartment house door near the street light with the conical shaft around which curls a spray of stylized ivy.

The man's equipment is brand new. The photograph must date from the beginning of the war, the period of general mobilization, or from the first draft of reservists, perhaps even from a date previous to this: during military service or a brief training period. Yet the full paraphernalia of the soldier in battle dress seems rather to indicate that the photograph dates from the beginning of the war itself, for the infantryman on leave in peacetime does not come home in such uncomfortable garb. Hence the most likely occasion would be an exceptional leave of a few hours, granted to the draftee to say goodbye to his family before starting for the front. No friend in the regiment came with him, for the young woman would then be in the photograph beside the soldier; she must have taken the photograph with her own camera; she has even probably devoted a whole roll of film to the occasion, and she has later had the best picture enlarged.

The man is standing outside, in full sunlight, because there is not enough light inside the apartment; he has simply stepped outside his door and decided to stand near the lamppost. In order to be facing the source of light, he has turned in the direction of the street, having behind him on the right (that is, on his left) the stone corner of the building; the street light on his other side is brushed by the bottom of his overcoat. The soldier glances at his feet and for the first time notices the spray of ivy embossed on the cast iron. The five-lobed, pointed palmate leaves with their five projecting veins are growing on a rather long stem; at the point where each of them joins it, this stem changes direction, but the alternating curves it thus describes are scarely evident on one side, and on the other are quite pronounced, which gives the entire stem a generally concave movement, preventing the spray from reaching very high and allowing it to curl around the cone; then it divides in two, and the upper branch, which is shorter and has only three leaves growing on it (of which the one at the tip is extremely small), rises in a blunted sine-curve; the other branch disappears toward the opposite side of the cone and the edge of the sidewalk. Once the roll of film is used up the soldier returns to the apartment house.

The hallway is dark, as usual. The apartment door has remained ajar; he pushes it open, crosses the unlighted vestibule, and sits down at the table where his wife pours him some wine. He drinks without saying anything, taking small mouthfuls, each time setting down the glass on the checkered oilcloth. After many repetitions of this action, the area in front of him is entirely covered with circular stains, though almost all of them are incomplete, showing a series of more or less closed arcs, occasionally overlapping, almost dry in some places, in others still shiny with the last drops of liquid. Between mouthfuls of wine, the soldier keeps his eyes fixed on this confused network which becomes increasingly complicated from moment to moment. He does not know what to say. He should be going now. But when he has finished his glass, the woman pours him another; and he drinks it too, in small mouthfuls, while slowly eating the rest of the bread. The child's silhouette he had noticed in the half-open door to the next room has disappeared in the darkness.

When the soldier decides to look up at the young woman, she is sitting opposite him: not at the table, but on a chair placed (has she just put it there?) in front of the chest, under the black frame of the portrait fastened to the wall. She is examining her visitor's faded uniform; her gray eyes move up as far as his neck where the two pieces of red felt marked with his serial number are sewn.

"What regiment is that?" she asks finally with an upward movement of her chin to indicate the two bright-red diamonds.

"I don't know," the soldier says.

This time the woman shows a certain amount of surprise. "You've forgotten the name of your regiment too?"

"No, that's not it . . . But this overcoat isn't mine." The young woman remains where she is for a moment without speaking. Yet she seems to have a question on her mind which she doesn't know how to formulate or which she hesitates to ask directly. Then, after a whole minute's silence, or even more, she asks: "Whose was it?"

"I don't know," the soldier says.

Besides, if he had known he could probably also have said what regiment the bright-red diamonds represented. Again he looks at the photographic enlargement hanging on the wall above the woman's black hair. The picture is oval-shaped, blurred around the edges; the mat around it has remained creamy-white all the way to the rectangular frame of dark wood. At this distance, the distinguishing insignia are not visible on the overcoat collar. In any case the uniform is that of the infantry. The man must have been billeted in the city or in its immediate environs while waiting to be sent to the front; otherwise he could not have come to say goodbye to his wife before leaving. But where are the barracks in this city? Are there a lot of them? What units are billeted there in peacetime?

The soldier decides he ought to show an interest in these matters: they would provide a normal and harmless subject of conversation. But he has scarcely opened his mouth when he notices a change in the woman's attitude. She is squinting slightly as she looks at him, seeming to wait for the rest of his words with exaggeratedly strained attention, considering the importance he himself attaches to them. He pulls up short in the middle of a vague sentence hurriedly concluded in a direction its inception did not suggest; its interrogative character is so faint that the woman has every opportunity to refrain from answering. And in fact this is the solution she adopts. But her features remain tense. Such questions are obviously the very ones a clumsy spy would ask, and suspicion is natural under such circumstances . . . although it is rather late, now, to conceal the location of military objectives from the enemy.

The soldier has finished his bread and his wine. He has no further reason to linger in this apartment, in spite of his desire to enjoy a few moments more of this relative warmth, this uncomfortable chair, and this guarded presence facing him. He should think up some way of leaving gracefully which would reduce the impression left by the recent misunderstanding. In any case, trying to justify himself would be the worst mistake of all; and how explain convincingly his ignorance about . . . The soldier now tries to remember the exact words he has just used. There was the word "barracks," but he cannot recall the strange sentence he has spoken; he is not even certain he has actually referred to the location of the buildings and still less whether he has definitely indicated that he was not familiar with it.

Without realizing it, he may have passed in front of a barracks during his peregrinations. However he has not noticed any structure in the usual barracks style: a low building (only two floors, with identical windows framed in red brick) about a hundred yards long with a low-pitched slate roof surmounted by high rectangular chimneys also made of brick. The structure rises at the far end of a large, bare, gravel courtyard separated from the boulevard and its luxuriant trees by a high iron fence supported by abutments and bristling with pickets on the inside as well as toward the street. Sentry boxes, placed at intervals, shelter armed guards; these sentry boxes are made of wood, with zinc roofs, and each side is painted with large black and red chevrons.

The soldier has seen nothing of the kind. He has passed along no fence; he has not noticed any large gravel courtyard; he has encountered neither luxuriant foliage nor sentry boxes, nor of course any armed guards. He has not even walked down any tree-lined boulevards. He has always followed only the same straight streets between two high rows of flat housefronts; but a barracks might also look like these. The sentry boxes have been removed, of course, as well as anything that might distinguish the building from those on either side; there remain only the iron bars protecting the first-floor windows for most of their height. These are square vertical bars a hand's breadth apart, connected by two horizontal bars placed not far from each end. The upper ends of these vertical bars are free, terminating in points about eight inches from the top of the window recess; the bases of the bars must be set in the stone sill, but this detail is not visible because of the snow which has drifted there, forming an irregular layer across the entire horizontal surface, particularly thick on the right side.

But this might just as well be a fire house, or a convent, or a school, or an office building, or merely an apartment house whose first-floor windows are protected by iron bars. Having reached the next crossroad, the soldier turns at right angles into the adjoining street.

And the snow continues falling—slow, vertical, uniform—and the white layer thickens imperceptibly on the windowsills, on the doorsteps, on the projecting parts of the black lampposts, on the street without traffic, on the deserted sidewalks where the paths made by pedestrians during the course of the day have already disappeared. And it is night once again.

The regular flakes, all the same size, equally spaced, fall at the same rate of speed, maintaining the same distance between themselves and the same arrangements, as if they belonged to the same rigid system which shifts position from top to bottom with a continuous, vertical, uniform, and slow movement.

The footprints of the straggling pedestrian walking head down in front of the houses, from one end of the straight street to the other, appear one by one in the smooth, fresh snow into which they already sink at least a half an inch. And behind him, the snow immediately begins covering up the prints of his hobnail boots, gradually reconstituting the original whiteness of the trampled area, soon restoring its granular, velvety, fragile appearance, blurring the sharp crests of its edges, making its outlines more and more fluid, and at last entirely filling the depression, so that the difference in level becomes indistinguishable from that of the adjoining areas, continuity then being re-established so that the entire surface is again smooth, intact, untouched.

181

Hence the soldier cannot know if someone else has passed along here, in front of the houses with their unlighted windows, some time before him. And when he reaches the next crossroad, no tracks appear along the sidewalks of the cross street, and this means nothing either.

However the boy's footprints take longer to disappear. In fact he leaves humps behind him as he runs: his sole, shifting sharply, accumulates a tiny heap of snow which then remains in the middle of the footprint (at the place where its outline is narrowest) whose more or less accentuated protuberance must take longer to efface than the rest; and the holes made on each side of the shoe's toe and heel are all the deeper since the boy does not follow the old paths made during the day, but prefers to walk near the edge of the sidewalk in the deeper snow (though no difference in depth is apparent to the eye), where he sinks in farther. Since, in addition, he proceeds very rapidly, from the point where he is to the last irregularity still discernible under the new layer of snow, the length of his course is much greater than that the soldier leaves behind him, particularly if the loops which punctuate the child's progress around each lamppost are included.

These loops, it is true, are not indicated with absolute clarity, for the child scarcely sets foot on the ground during the revolution he makes as he catches hold of the cast-iron shaft. As for the pattern of his rubber-soled shoes, it is already blurred: neither the chevrons nor the cross in the center of its circle are identifiable, even before the falling snow has begun to blur the image. The distortions produced by running, added to the uncertainty concerning the latter's characteristics, make it impossible, all in all, to differentiate these footprints from those left by another child of the same age—who would also be wearing, moreover, shoes with identical soles (the same shoes, perhaps, coming from the same store) and who would be making similar loops around the lampposts.

In any case, there are no tracks at all in the snow, no

footprints, and the snow continues falling over the empty street, uniform, vertical, and slow. It must be entirely dark now, and the flakes are no longer visible except when they fall through the zone of light around a street light. Hence the street is punctuated at regular intervals (though these seem to grow increasingly shorter in proportion to their distance to the right or the left), punctuated with lighter zones where the darkness is stippled with innumerable tiny white particles animated with a common falling movement. Since the window is located on the top floor, all these circles of light must look pale and distant at the bottom of the long trench formed by the two parallel planes of the housefronts; so distant, in fact, so quivering, that it is naturally impossible to tell the flakes apart: seen from so high up they form at intervals only a vague whitish halo, itself dim because the light from the street lamps is extremely weak and made still more uncertain by the diffused reflection which all these pale surfaces spread around them —the earth, the sky, the curtain of close flakes falling slowly but without interruption in front of the windows, so thick that it now completely conceals the building opposite, the cast-iron street lights, the last straggling pedestrian, the entire street.

Perhaps even the street lights have not been turned on this evening, tonight, that night. As for the sound of possible footsteps, muffled by the fresh snow, it could not reach such an altitude, penetrate the iron shutters, the windowpanes, the thick velvet curtains.

The shadow of the fly on the ceiling has stopped near the place where the circle cast by the lampshade meets the top of the red curtain. Once it is motionless, the shape becomes more complex. It is indeed the enlarged reproduction of the bent filament of the electric bulb, but the primary image is repeated nearby by two other paler, vaguer images framing the first. Perhaps, too, still other less distinct images are further multiplied on each side of the latter; they are not perceptible, for the whole of the tiny figure the fly projects is not situated in the most brightly illuminated area of the ceiling, but in a fringe of half-light about a quarter of an inch wide bordering the entire periphery of the circle, at the edge of the shadow.

All the rest of the room, lighted by only this one lamp on the corner of the table, seems to be in relative darkness compared to the brilliant circle of light cast on the white ceiling. Eyes which have stared too long at the latter no longer make out, when they turn away, any detail on the room's other walls. The picture hanging on the rear wall is nothing more than a gray rectangle framed in black; the chest beneath it is nothing more than a dark square as flat as the picture, pasted there like a piece of wallpaper; and the same is true for the fireplace in the center of the perpendicular wall. As for the wallpaper itself, the innumerable tiny spots which constitute its pattern look no more like a torch than a flower, a human figure, a dagger, a street light, or anything. The wallpaper merely looks as if silent feathers were falling in regular lines at a uniform rate, so slowly that their movement is scarcely noticeable, and it is difficult to decide whether their direction is up or down, like particles suspended in motionless water, tiny bubbles in a gaseous liquid, snowflakes, dust. And on the floor, which is also in semi-darkness, the gleaming paths have disappeared.

Only the table top under the conical lampshade is illuminated, as is the bayonet lying in the center. Its short heavy blade with two symmetrical edges reveals, on either side of the central axis, two symmetrically sloping planes of polished steel, one of which reflects the lamplight toward the middle of the room.

On the other side of the room, in the middle of the wall, the picture obscured by the darkness is nothing more than a gray oval within a vertical white rectangle, the latter framed in black.

At this moment a faint voice is heard, quite close, indistinct. The soldier lowers his gaze from the picture of the soldier fastened to the wall to the young woman sitting on her chair in front of the chest. But the voice heard just now is not hers; as low perhaps and not so young, it was certainly a man's voice this time. Besides, it is repeating a sentence of approximately the same sound, still just as incomprehensible, while the young woman remains bolt upright in her chair, her mouth closed, her eyes turned toward the corner of the room where the open door is, on the other side of the table. The dark area separating the open door from its jamb reveals nothing in the next room.

The young woman is now standing in front of this door which she has pushed farther open, wide enough to slip through it; then the door is pushed back without closing altogether, keeping the same open space as before. In the dark area which remains, the child then reappears.

At least a vertical strip of the child then reappears, consisting of an eye, the nose, three-quarters of the mouth and the chin, an elongated rectangle of blue smock, half a bare knee, a sock, a black felt slipper, remaining rigid while the man's voice repeats its same sentence for the third time, not so loud, which again keeps any sound from being recognized except the tentative noises that have no meaning. The woman's low voice answers, still more softly, almost in a whisper. The child's eye is on a level with the doorknob, a white porcelain oval. On the other side, an electric light switch also made out of porcelain is set in the wall near the jamb. An argument is going on; the young woman speaks more rapidly, giving long explanations in which the same groups of words with the same intonations seem to recur several times. The man's voice intervenes only in short sentences, or even in monosyllables, if not in snarls and grunts. The child, growing bolder, opens the door a little wider.

No, it is not the child, instead the child disappears, replaced by the young woman whose head appears a little higher in the widened opening: "It wasn't Boulard, was it?" And since the soldier looks at her questioningly, she repeats, "Rue Boulard? That isn't what you were looking for?"

"No . . . I don't think so . . ." the soldier says in an uncertain tone of voice. Then, after a moment's thought, with a little more assurance, he shakes his head several times from right to left: "I don't think so. No." But his interlocutor is already no longer there; and now the door has been shut tight.

The white oval knob shows several shining points; the brightest point is located at the very top; another much larger but less brilliant, makes a kind of curvilinear four-sided polygon on the right side. Bright lines of various widths, lengths, and intensities follow the general contour of the rounded surface at varying distances like those customarily represented in drawings to simulate relief.

But these concentric lines, instead of according the object a third dimension, seem to make it revolve: by staring at it continuously, the soldier can see the porcelain knob move, first scarcely perceptibly, then with increasing amplitude, the axis of the oval alternately tilting ten or twenty degrees to either side of the vertical. Nevertheless the door does not open. But perhaps the child, on the other side, is playing with the handle, with the other white porcelain handle identical with this one and symmetrically placed in relation to the plane of the door.

When the door opens again, it admits neither the timid and curious child nor the young woman with pale eyes, but someone new: doubtless the person who was speaking in the next room just now; it is, in fact, a voice of similar timbre and volume which is now assuring the soldier that there is no Rue Boucharet in either this neighborhood or the whole city for that matter. It must have been "Boulard" that he heard; and the man offers to explain where this street is. "It's not very near!" he adds, examining the soldier sitting in his chair, his hands lying flat on his thighs, his back a little hunched, the battered package still tucked under his arm, scrutinizing him with an insistence which seems to be calculating the number of miles he is still capable of covering before collapsing for good.

The man himself is well within draft age, but he is lame, which explains his presence among civilians. His left leg seems unusable; he walks with the help of a wooden crutch under one armpit, using it skillfully, judging by the swift maneuver he has just made in order to come into the room and approach the table, on the edge of which his right hand is now resting, on the red-and-white checked oil-cloth. Perhaps he is a war casualty: he might have been wounded at the beginning of hostilities and been sent home on foot despite his condition, before the retreat of the defeated armies and the evacuation of the military hospitals. He has a thin, carefully trimmed moustache, like the soldier in the photograph. As a matter of fact, he might resemble the latter quite closely, at least as much as a picture of that kind, after so much retouching, can resemble its model. But a picture of that kind, in fact, proves nothing. The soldier shakes his head several times to indicate his disagreement: "No," he answers, "it didn't sound like Bouchard."

"I said Bouvard."

"I don't think so. No, it was something else."

"There is nothing else."

"Besides it was around here."

"Then you know the city?"

"No . . . but it's . . ."

"Well if you don't know your way, how can you tell? I know this city. My leg hasn't always been like this . . ." With his chin he indicates his crutch. "Your Rue Bouvard is at the other end of town!"

The soldier is prepared to explain his reasons for being sure of the contrary, or, more exactly, for thinking that the street he is looking for is not the Rue Bouvard, but without going into complicated details it will be difficult for him to convince the invalid who, on his part, shows so much assurance. Besides, on reflection, his own reasons already seem less convincing to him. And he is about to resign himself to listening to the information the other man is so insistent on giving him, when the young woman also returns through the door which has remained ajar. She seems displeased. She comes in hurriedly, as if she had been delayed by a sudden, urgent task which has prevented her from accompanying the man a few moments before, or even from keeping him out of the visitor's sight.

The lame man has begun his topographical explanations in which a number of street names figure: Vanizier, Vantardier, Bazaman, Davidson, Tamani, Duroussel, Dirbonne, etc. The young woman interrupts him in the middle of his itinerary: "But he already told you it wasn't Broulard."

"Not Broulard: Bouvard! I know just where it is." And, turning toward the soldier as if he were in no doubt of the answer: "You're going to the warehouse?"

"The warehouse?"

"Yes: the military warehouse, the one they've been using as an auxiliary barracks."

"No," the soldier says, "it's not a barracks I'm looking for, and not a warehouse either."

"Well, barracks or not, that doesn't change where the street is." Suddenly getting an idea, he drums his fingertips on the table and speaks to the woman: "Let the boy take him there, that would be easiest."

Without changing her adamant expression, she shrugs her shoulders as she answers: "You know I don't want him to go out."

A new argument begins between them, if it was the same man the first time. Contrary, in any case, to the dialogue which took place in the next room, it is now the man who does most of the talking, asking for precise reasons why the child should be shut up, scarcely listening to the answers, repeating peremptorily that no one runs any danger crossing the city, especially a child, that it will not take him long anyway, that it will not even be dark by the time he gets back. The woman answers him with short, irritated, insistent sentences: "You just said it was far away."

"Far away for someone who doesn't know where it is. But not for the boy, he'll get there by the shortest route and come back again right away."

"I'd rather he didn't go out," the young woman says.

This time the man calls the visitor to witness: what danger would there be in going out today? Aren't the streets absolutely calm? Could anything happen before nightfall? . . . etc.

The soldier answers that he doesn't know. As for the streets being calm, for the moment it is certainly incontestable.

"But they might come any minute," the woman says.

The lame man does not agree with her: "Not before tomorrow night," he declares, "or even the day after. Otherwise do you think he'd just be standing here waiting for them?" He is referring to the soldier now, with a broad, vague gesture in his direction, across the table; but the latter personally does not find the argument very convincing, for he should not be here in any case. When the man appeals to him again, he can only make an evasive gesture with his hand which he barely lifts from his knee:

"I don't know," he says.

Besides, he is not at all eager to be taken to the other side of town, although he no longer knows now what else he could do. Far from feeling rested by this pause, an even greater lassitude has now come over him. He looks at the young woman with her pale eyes, her set face, her black hair, her wide apron tied around her waist; he looks at the lame man whose infirmity does not seem to tire him, since he remains standing, supported by his crutch, although there is an empty chair nearby; the soldier wonders whether his useless leg is resting on the floor, but he cannot tell, for the man, leaning on the other end of the table, is visible only above the thighs: he would therefore have to lean forward, raise the edge of the oilcloth, and look under the table, between the four square legs that taper toward the bottom—or else, tapering toward the bottom, but made out of turned, fluted wood, becoming cylindrical and smooth at the upper end, terminating at the top in four cubes with a carved rose on two of their sides —or else . . . ; the soldier looks again at the portrait on the rear wall: at this distance, the features of the face are quite indistinct; as for the details of the uniform, they would have to be already familiar in order to be visible: the two straps crossing each other over the chest, the dagger-bayonet with its black leather sheath attached to the belt, the overcoat with its front flaps folded back, the leggings . . . unless the latter are puttees, or even boots . . .

But now the child is coming in to the left of the chest, through the vestibule door. He is being pushed forward toward the soldier who is still sitting at the table. It is the lame man who pushes him from behind with his free hand while the crutch makes tiny quick movements in virtually the same place, for the boy does not move forward. The wounded leg is slightly shorter than the other one, or else slightly bent, so that the foot hangs about an inch or so above the floor.

The child has changed clothes, probably to go outside: he is now wearing long narrow trousers, out of which appear his high shoes, and a heavy wool turtleneck sweater that comes down to the hips; a cape, not closed, hangs from his shoulders to his knees; his head is covered with a beret pulled down on each side over his ears. Everything is of the same navy blue color, or, more exactly, of the various shades associated with this color.

The lame man having exerted a firmer pressure on the child's back, the latter advances a step towards the soldier; at the same time he draws tight the two flaps of his cape, holding the edges with both hands from the inside. Then the man speaks a sentence already heard a few seconds before: "He'll find your Rue Bouvard for you, he'll find it." The child stubbornly looks down at his heavy shoes whose rubber soles are a yellow line on the floor.

Has the woman finally given in? Yet the soldier has not noticed that she has given her consent, in his presence, for the child to go out. Had this scene taken place out of his sight? But where and when? Or was her consent not being considered? She is standing a little to one side, in the shadowy frame of the wide-open door. She is motionless, her arms hanging stiffly at her sides. She says nothing, but she has probably just said something, which might have attracted the soldier's attention in this direction. Her clothes too have been changed: she no longer wears an apron over her full gray skirt. Her face retains the same hostile expression, though perhaps it is gentler, more remote now. Her eyes are larger in the darkness; she looks across the table, where the empty glass is set, at the child, himself motionless in the dark cape which completely conceals him from neck to knees; the location of his invisible hands inside the cape is indicated at two different levels near the neck and toward the middle of the cape by a gathering of the edge of the material. Behind the child, the man with the crutch has also stopped moving entirely; he is leaning forward, his back bent, his balance, which seems precarious, made possible by the crutch held obliquely to support his body and firmly grasped in his hand, his arm extended, his shoulder high, his other free arm moving forward toward the boy's back, his hand partly open, his forefinger and middle finger almost straight while the other two are closed over the palm which is turned upward. The expression on his face has frozen into a kind of smile, a "kind smile" perhaps, that the stiffness of the features transforms, however, into a grimace: one corner of the mouth twisted, one eye more nearly closed than the other, and the cheek half contracted.

"He'll find your Rue Bouvard for you, he'll find it."

No one says anything. The child looks at his shoes. The lame man's body is still leaning forward as though about to fall, his right arm half extended, his mouth distorted by what was a smile. The woman seems to have stepped back still farther into the shadow of the next room, and her eyes look still larger, fixed now, perhaps, on the soldier.

And afterwards there is the street, the night, the falling snow. The soldier, hugging his package under his arm, his hands thrust into his overcoat pockets, laboriously follows the boy who is three or four yards ahead of him. The tiny dense flakes are driven horizontally by the wind, and the soldier, in order not to receive them full in the face, bends his head down farther; he also squints as much as he can without closing his eyes completely. He can scarcely see, vanishing and reappearing at the bottom of the overcoat, the two black shoes which alternately advance and retreat over the snow.

When he passes through the light of a street light, he sees the tiny white specks rushing toward him, quite distinct against the dark leather of his shoes, and, higher up, clinging to the material of his overcoat. Since he is then illuminated himself, he tries to raise his head at that moment in order to catch a glimpse of the boy in front of him. But the latter, of course, has already vanished into the darkness; and the many white flakes interposed between them are, on the contrary, illuminated by the street light, which prevents anything outside the zone of light from being distinguished. Soon blinded by the tiny crystals which whip against his face, the soldier must lower his eyes again to the overcoat, which is gradually being covered with snow, the badly tied package, and the heavy boots which continue their alternating movement like two pendulums making parallel, identical oscillations side by side but in the opposite directions.

It is only a few steps farther on, once out of the circle of light, that he can again ascertain the boy's presence, a wavering shadow, the cape fluttering in the wind against the bright background of the next street lamp, five or six yards ahead.

And the child has disappeared for good. The soldier is alone, standing stock still. This is a street like the others. The child has brought him here and left him alone, in front of a house like the others, and has told him: "It's here." The soldier has looked at the house, the street, from one side and then from the other, and the door. It was a door like the others. The street was long and black with only the series of lighted areas beneath the same cast-iron lamp-posts with their old-fashioned ornaments.

The boy has left again; but instead of turning back, he has continued straight ahead in the same direction. He has covered about a dozen yards and then, suddenly, has begun running. His cape was fluttering behind him. He has continued straight ahead, soon vanishing, appearing again under each street light, disappearing, and again, smaller and smaller, shapeless, blurred by the night and the snow . . .

The soldier is alone, he looks at the door in front of which he is standing. Why has the child shown him this house rather than any other, since he was told only to take him to this street? Which street is this anyway? Is it really the one they were talking about just now? The soldier can no longer remember the name the lame man insisted on so much: it was something like Mallart or Malibar, Malardier, Montoire, Moutardier . . . No, it didn't sound like that.

Against the part of the doorway perpendicular to the wall of the building, on the side receiving a little light from the nearest street light, a small plaque is attached at eye level: some identification concerning the tenant of the building, or at least one of the tenants. There is not enough light for the soldier to read. He puts his hand on it, having stepped onto the stoop, where he balances as well as he can, hampered by its narrowness. The letters are stamped on a cold polished substance, but they are too small and the soldier cannot make out a single word. He notices at this moment that the door is ajar: door, hallway, door, vestibule, door, then finally a lighted room, and a table with an empty glass with a circle of dark-red liquid still at the bottom, and a lame man leaning on his crutch, bending forward in a precarious balance. No. Door ajar. Hallway. Staircase. Woman running from floor to floor up the spiral staircase, her gray apron billowing about her. Door. And finally a lighted room: bed, chest, fireplace, table with a lamp on its left corner, and the lampshade casting a white circle on the ceiling. No. Above the chest is a print framed in black wood . . . No. No. No.

The door is not ajar. The soldier moves his finger across the polished plaque, but his hand is already numb with cold and he no longer feels anything at all. Then the door suddenly opens wide. The hallway is still the same, but this time it is lighted. There is the naked bulb at the end of its wire, the civil defense bulletin against the brown wall near the door, the closed doors to the right and left, and the staircase at the end rising in a spiral towards successive walls and dark corners.

"What do you . . ."

It is another soldier, or rather half a soldier, for he is wearing a field cap and military jacket, but black trousers and gray suede shoes. Arms and legs spread slightly, eyes squinting, mouth half open, the figure has frozen, startled, threatening, terrified, it retreats down the hallway, gradually at first, then more and more quickly but without the feet moving in relation to each other, the limbs and the whole body remaining rigid as if the whole figure were set on a rail and drawn backward by a thread. No.

While the soldier, having stepped onto the narrow stoop where he balances as well as he can, half leaning against the closed leaf of the door which restricts his movements and compels him to twist his body, his left hand still thrust into the overcoat pocket and his left arm still hugging the package wrapped in brown paper against the hollow of his hip, the other hand raised to the polished plaque attached to the left jamb—while the soldier vainly tries to make out the letters with the tips of his forefinger, middle finger, and ring finger, the door opens so suddenly that he has to grasp the jamb in order not to fall, in order not to be swallowed up by this yawning hallway in the middle of which, just inside the door, stands a man wearing a field cap and military jacket, but civilian trousers and low sport shoes; they probably have rubber soles, for there has been no sound of steps down the hallway. On the collar of the jacket, the two colored diamonds showing the serial number have been removed. In one hand the man is still holding the edge of the door which he has just pivoted on its hinges. His free right hand rises to shoulder height in an uncompleted gesture of welcome, then falls back.

"Come in," he says, "this is the place."

The soldier crosses the threshold, takes three steps down the hallway lit by a naked bulb at the end of a long twisted wire. The soldier stops. The other man has closed the door again. The gust of air has made the lamp move and it now continues to sway at the end of its wire.

The man in the military jacket is again standing motionless in front of the closed door, his arms and legs spread slightly, his hands dangling, in an attitude that is both irresolute and stiff. All the identifying insignia on his clothes have been removed: not only those on the collar, but also the stripes on the sleeves and on the cap, revealing, where they had been, small areas of new material softer and brighter than the faded surrounding areas dirtied by long wear. The difference is so evident that there can be no doubt about the shape of the missing insignia: the infantry diamond, the two parallel, slender, oblique rectangles indicating the rank of corporal; only the colors are missing (bright red, garnet, purple, blue, green, yellow, black . . .) which would furnish precise information as to regiment, duty, etc. The face, in full light now, seems tired, drawn, shrunken, the cheekbones too prominent, the cheeks grayish, the eyes deep in their sockets. The man's shadow is cast against the door to the right, then to the left, then to the right, to the left, to the right, according to the position of the electric bulb swaying at the end of its long wire perpendicular to the direction of the hallway. (The draft from the open door must have moved the lamp longitudinally, but the plane of the oscillations has gradually turned without their amplitude diminishing perceptibly, and the man's foreshortened shadow appears and disappears, now on the right, now on the left, alternately.)

"Are you wounded?" he asks at last.

The soldier shakes his head.

"Sick?"

"No . . . only tired."

"All right, come on up."

But neither one moves, and the man's shadow continues to sway. Then he says: "What do you have in your package?"

The soldier, after a moment's hesitation, looks down toward the brown spotted paper and the distended string.

"Some things."

"What kind of things?"

"My things." He raises his head. The man is still looking at him with the same weary, almost vacant expression.

"Do you have your identification papers?"

"No . . ." The soldier makes a half smile or a fleeting grimace which momentarily distorts his mouth; then his eyebrows rise to indicate his astonishment at this foolish request.

"No, of course not," the other man repeats, and after a few seconds: "All right, come on up."

At this moment the light goes out. Complete darkness replaces the pale, thin face, the dangling hands, and the swaying shadow. At the same time, the ticking, which had been regularly audible without the soldier's being aware of it since the beginning of the scene, has stopped.

And the scene is silent when the light comes on again. The setting is apparently the same: a narrow hallway painted dark brown halfway up the walls, the rest of the walls and the high ceiling being pale beige. But the doors, on the left as on the right, are more numerous. They are, as before, painted dark brown and are of identical dimensions: quite high for their width. The hallway is doubtless longer. The electric bulb is the same: round, quite weak, and hanging at the end of a twisted wire. The light switch, made of white porcelain, is placed just above the stairs at the corner of the wall. The two men are walking slowly, without speaking, one behind the other. The first, the one wearing what was once a corporal's jacket, has just pressed the light switch in passing (was there no switch on the first floor, since they climbed the stairs in darkness?); but the fact that the system is functioning is revealed only by a simple click; the ticking is too faint to be heard over the noise of heavy hobnail boots on the last steps, which the soldier climbs with less difficulty now that he sees clearly. His guide, in front of him, is wearing rubber-soled gray suede shoes; the whisper of his steps is scarcely audible. One behind the other, the two men pass in front of the high, narrow, closed doors on the right and left, one after the other, with their shiny white porcelain knobs that stand out against the dark paint, an egg-shaped object in which the image of the electric bulb makes a luminous speck repeated on the right and the left, in each doorknob, one after the other.

At the very end of the hallway is a last door that resembles the others. The soldier sees the man stop in front of him, his hand on the porcelain knob. When the soldier reaches him, the man quickly opens the door to let the soldier in first, walks in after him and closes the door behind them.

197

They are standing in a small room, its only illlmination a bluish gleam which comes from outside through the six panes of a window that has neither shutters nor curtain. The soldier walks over to the bare panes. He sees the empty street, uniformly white with snow. His hand is resting on the porcelain window fastening which is smooth and cold under his palm. The fastening is not closed, the two leaves of the French window are only pushed shut. They open of their own accord without any effort, by the mere weight of the arm pressing against them. The soldier leans out. It is no longer snowing. The wind has fallen. The night is calm. The soldier leans out a little farther. He sees the sidewalk, much farther down than he expected. Clinging to the sill, he sees beneath him the vertical series of successive windows, and at the bottom the doorway to the building, and the white stoop lighted by the nearby street lamp. The door itself, slightly recessed, is not visible. There are footsteps in the fresh snow, tracks of heavy boots which, coming from the left along the buildings, lead to the doorway and end there just beneath his eyes. A vague mass moves in the doorway. It looks like a man in a cloak or a military overcoat. He has stepped onto the stoop and his body is pressed against the door. But the part of his body outside the doorway clearly reveals a shoulder with a buttoned tab, a bent arm holding under the elbow a rectangular package the size of a shoe box.

"You don't look as if you were feeling very well," the man says as he comes toward him. The soldier has sat down on the first chair his hand encountered behind him. The man, who had gone to look for something at the back of the room, has returned holding in his arms a rather large bundle difficult to identify in this lunar half-light: cloth . . .

"You don't look as if you were feeling very well."

"I don't know . . . ," the soldier answers passing his hand across his face, "no . . . it's nothing." His other hand has remained in his overcoat pocket. He readjusts the package in the crook of his elbow. He sees the vertical series of successive windows, each one with a white line at the bottom of the snowy window recess, the vertical series of parallel rungs descending to the stoop—like a falling stone. He stands up and walks mechanically behind the man who is heading for the door. He is holding bedclothes under his arm. In the hallway, the light has gone out again.

They are standing in a long room lighted with blue electric bulbs. There are beds lined up on each side against both walls: on the left, a bare partition and on the right a series of equidistant windows whose six panes are covered with paper. The windows seem to be level with the wall, without the slightest inside recess; only their dark color distinguishes them; since the wall around them and the paper neatly covering each pane are of the same pale shade, in this blue light they look like imitation windows: a heavily drawn rectangle divided into six equal squares by thinner lines: a vertical central axis and two horizontals which cut it into thirds. Coming from the total darkness of the hallway, the soldier advances without difficulty between the two neat rows of metal beds; this dim lighting is enough for him to distinguish clearly the outline of things.

Men are lying on almost all the beds, covered with dark blankets. The man with the unsewn chevrons has led the soldier to the middle of the row on the side of the wall without windows, and has indicated an empty mattress by setting the bedclothes down on it; then he has left again without further explanations, and he has closed the door behind him.

The folded bedclothes form two dark rectangles against the lighter background of the mattress, two rectangles which overlap at one corner. The beds to the right and left are both occupied: two bodies lying on their backs, wrapped in their blankets; the heads are supported by bolsters of the same light shade as the mattresses; the man on the right has also put his hands under his neck, the

folded elbows pointing diagonally on each side. The man
is not sleeping: his eyes are wide open. The man on the
left, whose arms are hidden alongside his body, is also not
sleeping. Others farther away, lying on their sides, have
their bodies slightly raised on one elbow. One man is even
half sitting up: in the dim light he stares at the newcomer
who is standing in front of his bed, one hand resting its
fingertips on the horizontal iron bar which comprises its
foot, the other in the overcoat pocket, a shoe box under
the arm. Everyone is perfectly motionless and silent.
Doubtless they are not sleepy: it is still too early; and the
lack of adequate light prevents them from doing anything
but lying here, eyes wide open, staring at the motionless
newcomer with his shoe box or at the imitation windows
in front of them, or at the bare wall, or the ceiling, or into
space.

The soldier finally approaches the head of the bed while
he takes in his right hand the package he was holding
under his left arm. And again he stands perfectly still. This
room, as he now notices, differs in one important detail
from the dormitories of a military barracks: there is no
kit shelf running along the wall over the beds. The soldier
stands with his box in his hands, wondering where he can
put it for the night, hesitating to let it out of his sight or to
draw more attention to it. After considerable indecision,
he pulls the bolster away from the painted iron grill that
forms the head of the bed, sets the box down on the end of
the mattress, and pushes the bolster back against it in order
to secure it firmly. He decides that this way, when his head
is on the bolster, any attempt to take the box will awaken
him no matter how heavily he is sleeping. Then, sitting on
the bed and leaning forward, he slowly begins removing
his leggings, coiling up the strip of material as he unwraps
it from around his leg.

"You don't even know how to wrap your leggings." At
the foot of the lamppost, on the edge of the sidewalk, the
boy stares at the soldier's ankles. Then, raising his eyes, he

examines his entire outfit from his feet to his head, his gaze finally coming to rest on the hollow cheeks black with their growth of beard: "Where did you sleep last night?"

The soldier replies with a vague gesture. Still bending forward, he unties one shoe lace. The child begins to move away slowly, disappearing toward the rear of the scene but without turning around, without moving, his serious eyes still staring at the soldier beneath the navy blue beret pulled down on each side over his ears, holding the edges of his cape together from the inside, while his whole body seems to glide backwards across the snow-covered sidewalk along the flat housefronts, passing the ground floor windows one after the other: four identical windows followed by a door only slightly larger, then four more windows, a door, a window, a window, a window, a window, a door, a window, a window, faster and faster as he moves farther away, becoming smaller and smaller, vaguer and vaguer, fainter and fainter in the twilight, suddenly swallowed up toward the horizon and then disappearing in the wink of an eye, like a falling stone.

The soldier is lying on his mattress fully dressed, having merely taken off his heavy boots which he has put under the bed beside his leggings. He has wrapped himself up in the two blankets, over the overcoat which he has simply unbuttoned at the collar, too tired to make one more gesture. Besides, the room is not heated save by the bodies of the men lying there. There is no large square porcelain stove near the rear door at the end of the counter with its pipe bent at right angles and joining the wall above the shelves full of bottles. But the main thing is to be sheltered from the falling snow and the wind.

His eyes wide open, the soldier continues to stare into the darkness in front of him, a few yards in front of him, where the child stands, motionless and rigid too, his arms at his sides. But it is as if the soldier did not see the child—neither the child nor anything else.

He has long since emptied his glass. He does not seem

to be planning to leave. Yet around him, the room has been emptied of its last customers, and the bartender has gone out through the rear door after having turned out most of the lamps.

"You can't sleep here, you know."

Behind the table and the empty glass, behind the child, behind the large window with its pleated curtain which covers it halfway up, its three spheres arranged in a triangle and its inscription in reverse, the white flakes are still falling just as slowly, their descent vertical and regular. It is doubtless this continuous, uniform, immutable movement that the soldier is staring at, motionless at his table between his two companions. The child sitting on the floor in the foreground is also looking in this direction, although without raising his head he cannot see the bare panes above the pleated curtain. As for the other people, they do not seem to be concerned with what is happening over here: the group of seated drinkers talking heatedly and gesticulating, the crowd at the rear moving toward the left of the picture, where the overloaded coat racks are, the group standing at the right facing the wall, reading the bulletin which has been tacked there, and the bartender behind the bar, leaning forward toward the six men in middle-class clothes forming a small circle with emphatic postures, caught motionless like all the others in the middle of gestures which this arbitrary pause has deprived of any naturalness, like people at a party whom a photographer has tried to catch in candid movement, but whom technical necessities have kept too long in one position: "Don't move now! . . ." An arm remains half raised, a mouth gapes, a head is tipped back; but tension has replaced movement, the features are contorted, the limbs stiffened, the smile has become a grimace, the impulse has lost its intention and its meaning. There no longer remains, in their place, anything but excess, and strangeness, and death.

The six men in long frock coats who are standing in front of the bar, under the eye of the bartender whose thickset body, leaning toward them, is supported on his hands that grip the inner edge of the bar, on top of which are set the six glasses, still full, belonging to the customers momentarily distracted from their thirst by a discussion doubtless full of excitement and noise—a fist raised in anger, a head thrown back to shout the swearwords which the mouth shapes with violence, and the other men in the group approving, punctuating the remark with other solemn gestures, all talking or exclaiming at the same time— the six characters grouped in the left foreground are the ones who first catch the eye.

But the most noticeable man of the group is perhaps not the short fat man declaiming in the center, nor the four others around him (two seen full face, one in profile, one from behind) who are echoing his words, but the last man, situated behind them and slightly to one side, almost a head taller than his companions. His dress is apparently similar, as far as can be judged, since his body is almost completely hidden by his neighbors, except for the open collar above a wide white cravat and a well-fitted shoulder, and the opposite arm, which reappears behind one of the heads, stretched out to rest forearm and hand on the rounded edge of the counter in front of a glass shaped like a truncated cone mounted on a circular foot.

This last man seems uninterested in what his friends are saying and doing right in front of him. He is staring over the seated drinkers at the one female figure in the entire scene: a slender waitress standing in the middle of the room, carrying a tray with only one bottle on it among the benches, the tables, the chairs, and the bodies of the workers facing in different directions. She is wearing a simple long-sleeved dress with a full-pleated skirt gathered at the waist. She has thick black hair in a bun and a regular face with sharp but delicate features. Her movements give the impression of a certain grace. It is difficult to know which way she is going because of the pronounced torsion of her waist and her entire body; her profile does not indicate the same direction as her hips, so that she seems to be glancing at all the tables around the room to see if anyone is calling for her, while she raises the tray over her head in both hands. The tray, moreover, is tilting alarmingly, as is the liter bottle balanced on top of it. Instead of keeping her eye on this precarious burden, the woman is looking in the opposite direction, her head turned more than ninety degrees away from the tray toward the right side of the scene and the round table where the three soldiers are sitting.

It is not certain that she is looking only at them: other customers are also within her field of vision beyond this particular table, some civilians at another table, less apparent because drawn in vaguer outline, but still just as noticeable to the waitress herself. And in fact one of the latter seems to be holding up a hand to attract her attention.

But the look which the eye (seen in profile) of the young woman with black hair would direct toward this extended arm in the background would in any case cross the raised face of the soldier who is sitting facing her, a companion on either side (whose faces are not visible in the picture), an impassive face with features lined by fatigue, contrasting by its calm with the contortions and grimaces prevalent everywhere else. His hands, similarly, are lying flat on the table which is covered with a red-and-white checked oilcloth, where glasses, set down several times, have left a number of circular marks, some incomplete, some dry, some quite distinct, others completely obliterated by the sliding of a glass, or by an overcoat sleeve, or by a wipe of a rag.

And now the woman is sitting on a chair facing the soldier on the other side of the table with its red-and-white oilcloth which hangs in stiff folds over the edges. While the soldier is slowly chewing the bread which she has gone to get for him, along with the glass and the bottle, he stares at the half-closed door which reveals a child's figure in its opening. The young woman with black hair and pale eyes has just asked her questions about the regiment to which her visitor belongs—to which at least the latter's uniform and military insignia belong.

In the ensuing silence, when the soldier has raised his eyes to his hostess, the latter's head shifts slightly with a counter-clockwise movement toward the portrait fastened to the wall over the chest. It is a full length photograph of her husband, taken the morning he left for the front during the first days of the offensive, during the period when everyone behind the lines was convinced of an easy and rapid victory. Since then she has had no word from him. All she knows is that the unit he was fighting in was in the Reichenfels area at the time of the enemy breakthrough.

The soldier asks her which unit this was. Although her answer is not very exact, and although she has no idea of army organization, it seems that the position the woman gives is mistaken: the battalion she is talking about was never under fire, it was surrounded and disarmed much farther west. However, the soldier has no desire to begin a discussion on this subject, particularly since the young woman might feel he had insulting intentions concerning her husband's military career. He therefore confines himself to making a general remark: there were many less troops in Reichenfels than was subsequently claimed.

"Then you think he's a prisoner?"

"Yes," he says, "probably," which does not commit him to much, for unless he is dead the husband will soon be a prisoner in any case.

It is at this moment that the lame man has come into the room, through the half-open door to the next room, advancing without any evident awkwardness among the various obstacles, maneuvering his wooden crutch with agility. And the boy has soon reappeared at the other door.

It is this boy who afterwards leads the soldier through the empty streets as night falls, along the housefronts with their unlighted windows. Yet there are still inhabitants in the city; a large part of the civilian population must not have left it when there was still time. Does no one, then, dare turn on a light in rooms overlooking the street? Why do these people still obey the outdated civil defense instructions? Probably out of habit; or else because there is no administration to repeal the old regulations which of course would no longer apply. Besides, the city lighting system is functioning just as in peacetime; there are even street lights that have remained on all day long.

But the windows succeeding each other along the flat housefronts, on the ground floor as on every floor of the high uniform houses, do not reveal the least gleam of light, yet no shutter nor curtain has been drawn in front of or behind the panes, which are as black and bare as if all these apartments were uninhabited, gleaming only occasionally, at certain fleeting angles, with the brief reflection of a street light.

The boy seems to be going faster and faster, and the soldier, too exhausted, no longer manages to follow him. The slender figure, wrapped in its black cape, beneath which appear the two narrow black trouser legs, gets farther and farther ahead. The soldier is constantly afraid he has lost it. Then he catches a glimpse of it far ahead, much farther than he expected, suddenly illuminated as it passes under a street light, then immediately disappearing in the darkness again, invisible once more.

Hence the child may at any moment turn into a side street without being seen, for the route he has taken from the start is far from being straight. Luckily the fresh snow on the sidewalk shows his footprints, the only ones on the entire smooth surface between the housefronts and the parallel edge of the gutter, clear tracks despite the boy's rapidity, shallowly printed in the thin layer of new snow which has just fallen on the paths trampled hard during the day, footprints of chevroned rubber soles with a cross inscribed in a circle on the heel.

Now the tracks stop suddenly in front of a door just like the others, but not completely closed. The stoop is very narrow and can be crossed in one stride without setting foot on it. The light at the other end of the hallway is on; the ticking sounds like an alarm clock. At the far end of the hallway is a rather narrow staircase rising in short flights, separated by small square landings, turning at right angles. The floor landings, despite the many doors which open off them, are scarcely any larger. At the top is the closed room where the gray film of dust gradually settles on the table and on the small objects on top of it, on the mantelpiece, on the marble top of the chest, on the day bed, on the waxed floor where the felt slippers . . .

The tracks continue, regular and straight, across the fresh snow. They continue for hours, a right foot, a left foot, a right foot, for hours. And the soldier is still walking, mechanically, numb with cold and fatigue, mechanically setting one foot in front of the other without even being sure he is making any progress, for the same regular footprints are always there in the same places under his own feet. Since the spacing of the chevroned soles corresponds to his own stride (that of a man at the end of his strength), he has naturally begun putting his feet in the footprints already made. His boot is a little larger, but this is scarcely noticeable in the snow. Suddenly he has the feeling he has already been here, ahead of himself.

But the snow was still falling, at this moment, in close flakes, and no sooner were the guide's footprints made than they immediately began to lose their clarity and quickly filled up, becoming more and more unrecognizable as the distance increased between him and the soldier, their mere presence soon becoming a matter of doubt, a scarcely noticeable depression in the uniformity of the snow's surface, finally disappearing altogether for several yards . . .

The soldier thinks he has definitely lost the track when he sees the boy waiting for him a few feet away, under a street light, huddled in his black cape already white with snow.

"Here it is," he says, pointing to a door just like the others.

Then there is the electric bulb swaying at the end of its long wire and the man's shadow swaying across the closed door like a slow metronome.

During the night the soldier awakens with a start. The blue bulbs are still on, hanging from the ceiling, a row of three down the center of the room. In a single movement the soldier has thrown back his covers and sat up on the edge of his bed, his feet on the floor. He was dreaming that the alarm signal had sounded. He was in a winding trench whose top reached as high as his forehead; in his hand he was holding some kind of grenade, elongated in shape, with a delayed-action explosion device which he had just set going. Without a second to lose he had to throw it out of the trench. He heard it ticking steadily like an alarm clock. But he stood there with the grenade in his hand, his arm extended as if to throw it, inexplicably paralyzed, increasingly rigid, less and less able to move even a finger as the moment of the explosion approached. He must have shouted in his sleep to escape the nightmare.

Yet the other sleepers seem perfectly calm. Probably he has not really cried out. Looking more carefully, he discovers that his neighbor's eyes are wide open: both hands under his neck, he continues to stare straight ahead into the darkness.

Half intending to find some water to drink, half to look as if he knew what he were doing, the soldier stands up and, without putting on his shoes in order to avoid making noise, leaves the row of beds and heads for the door through which he first came. He is thirsty. Not only his throat feels dry, but his whole body is burning despite the cold. He reaches the door and tries to turn the handle, but the lock resists. He dare not shake it too hard for fear of waking everyone. Besides, the door seems to be locked.

Having turned around, panic-stricken, he realizes that the windows, the imitation windows drawn in black on the wall, are now on his left although they were on his right when he came into this room the first time. He then notices a second, identical door at the other end of the long passage between the two rows of beds. Realizing that he must have turned the wrong way, he crosses the entire length of the room between the two rows of prone bodies. All the eyes are wide open and watch him pass, in complete silence.

As a matter of fact, the other door opens easily. The latrines are located at the other end of the hall. The soldier noticed this as he came upstairs, before lying down. Intending to shift the package wrapped in brown paper under his arm, he suddenly remenbers having left it unguarded beneath the bolster. He immediately closes the door again and quickly returns to his bed. At first glance he sees that the bolster is now lying flat against the vertical iron bars; he approaches and discovers that the box is no longer there; he turns the bolster over as if it were necessary to convince himself further of the fact, turns the bolster over twice more; finally he straightens up, no longer knowing what to do, but there are no longer blankets on the mattress either. And three beds farther along the soldier recognizes some blankets bundled into a ball on an empty mattress. He has simply gone to the wrong bed.

On his bed, everything is where it was: blankets, bolster, and package. And, under the bed, the boots and the coiled-up leggings are also there. The soldier lies down again without having had anything to drink. Despite his burning throat, he no longer has the strength to make another attempt to walk through the labyrinth of unlighted hallways

209

until he reaches this infinitely distant and problematical water. His passages through the dormitory have occurred very quickly, in the last restlessness of a feverish awakening. He now feels incapable of taking another step. Moreover, he could not go out carrying his big box without awakening or reinforcing futile suspicions; his recent behavior has made him only too noticeable already. He scarcely takes the time to wrap his feet and legs in one of the blankets before stretching out again, spreading the second blanket over his whole body as well as he can. And once more he is walking in the snow through the empty streets along the high, flat housefronts which succeed each other indefinitely, without variation. His route is punctuated by black lampposts with stylized ornaments of old-fashioned elegance, their electric bulbs shining with a yellow luster in the leaden daylight.

The soldier walks as fast as he can without running, as though he feared someone might be pursuing him and that all the same too evident a flight might arouse the suspicion of passers-by. But no figure appears as far as the eye can see toward the gray end of the straight street, and each time the soldier turns around to look back, continuing straight ahead without slowing down, he can see that no pursuer threatens to catch up with him: the white sidewalk stretches behind him as empty as in the other direction, with only the line of footprints made by his hobnail boots, slightly distorted each time the soldier has turned around.

He was waiting on a street corner near a lamppost. He was looking at the corner of the house opposite him on the other side of the street. He had already been looking at it for some time when he noticed that there were some people in a room on the third floor. This was a rather large room with no visible furniture and two windows; the figures came and went from one window to the other, but without coming near the panes, which had no curtains. The soldier particularly noticed their pale faces in the room's half-darkness. The room must have had dark walls to make these faces stand out so clearly. The people seemed to be talking to each other, consulting each other; they made gestures, as the relative whiteness of their hands indicated. They were looking at something in the street, and the subject of their discussion seemed of some importance. Suddenly the soldier realized that this could only be himself. There was nothing else outside those windows on the sidewalk or in the street. To disguise his intentions the soldier began examining his surroundings, staring at the horizon first in one direction, then the other. Not exactly to disguise his intentions, but to show that he was expecting someone and was not concerned with the house in front of which he merely happened to be standing.

When he again glanced furtively toward the third floor windows, the pale faces had come noticeably closer to the bare panes. One of the figures was obviously pointing at him, hand outstretched; the other faces were grouped around the first at various levels, as if some of their possessors were standing, some crouching, others on tiptoe or even on chairs; the other window was empty.

"They think I'm a spy," the soldier decided. Preferring not to have to refute this accusation, which risked being formulated in a more immediate way, he pretended to consult a non-existent watch on his wrist and walked off without further thought down the next cross street.

After about ten steps he decided his behavior was foolish: it merely confirmed the suspicions of his observers, who would lose no time following him. Instinctively he began to walk faster. Imagining he heard behind him the sound of a window being flung open, he even had difficulty keeping himself from running.

The soldier turns around once more to look behind him: there is still no one. But as he turns back in the direction he is walking, he now sees the boy who seems to be waiting for him as he passes, half hidden behind the corner of a house at the next crossroad.

This time the soldier stops short. The door of the apartment house on his left is half-open, revealing a dark hallway. Farther on, at the crossroads, the child has stepped back a little so that he is entirely concealed by the stone corner of the building. The soldier suddenly turns into the door and finds himself in the hallway. At the far end, without losing a minute, he begins climbing the short flights of the narrow staircase which turns at right angles, each flight separated from the next by a small square landing.

On the top floor, there is the room sealed behind its thick curtains. The shoe box wrapped in brown paper is lying on the chest, the dagger-bayonet on the marble mantlepiece. The dust has already covered the heavy double-edged blade with a thin layer which dims the metal's luster under the shaded light from the lamp on the table. The shadow of the fly on the ceiling continues its circuit.

To the right of the large luminous circle whose circumference it regularly follows, there is, at the corner of the ceiling, a slender black line about an inch long and scarcely noticeable: a crack in the plaster, or a spider web covered with dust, or some trace of a bump or scratch. This imperfection in the white surface, moreover, is not equally visible from every point in the room. It is particularly apparent to an observer near the base of the wall to the right, at the other end of the room, looking up along what is virtually the diagonal of this wall, as is normal for someone lying on the bed, his head resting on the bolster.

The soldier is lying on his bed. It is probably the cold which has awakened him. He is on his back, in the same position he was in when he first opened his eyes; he has not moved since. In front of him the windows are wide open. On the other side of the street there are other windows identical to these. In the room all the men are still lying down. Most of them look as if they are sleeping. Nor does he know what time it is now. His immediate neighbors, to the right and left, are wrapped as closely as possible in their blankets; one of them, who has turned toward him, has even covered part of his face, leaving only his nose sticking out, while a flap of material pulled over his head covers his eyes as well. Although it is difficult to tell what kind of clothes the sleepers are wearing, it appears that none of them has undressed for the night, for there are no clothes to be seen hanging somewhere or folded up or thrown down at random. Moreover, there are no closets or shelves or cupboards of any kind, and only the bed ends could be used to hang coats, jackets, and trousers on; but these bed ends, made of metal rods painted white, are all as unencumbered at the foot as at the head. Without moving his body, the soldier pats his bolster behind him in order to make sure his box is still there.

He must get up now. If he does not succeed in giving this package to its intended recipient, he at least has the chance of getting rid of it while there is still time. Tomorrow, tonight, or even in a few hours, it will be too late. In any case, he has no reason to stay here doing nothing; a prolonged stay in this pseudo-barracks, or infirmary, or hospitalization center, can only make new complications for him, and he may thereby be compromising his last chances of success.

The soldier tries to raise himself on his elbows. His entire body is paralyzed. Having slipped only a few inches on his back toward the head of the bed, he lets himself fall back, his shoulders leaning against the vertical iron rods supporting the upper, thicker bar against which his head rests. The box, luckily, is in no danger of being crushed. The soldier turns his face to the right, where there is a door through which he should be leaving.

Next to the man whose face is hooded in a flap of the

213

coarse brown blanket, the sleeper beyond has one arm outside his blankets, an arm wearing the khaki sleeve of a military jacket. The reddish hand hangs over the edge of the mattress. Farther along, other bodies are lying stretched out or curled up. Several have kept their field caps on.

At the end of the room, the door has opened noiselessly and two men have come in, one behind the other. The first is a civilian, wearing hunting clothes: heavy leather boots, narrow riding breeches, a thick duffle-coat, and a long muffler around his neck. He has kept on a faded felt hat, shapeless with age and wear; his entire outfit is worn, tattered, and even rather dirty. The second man is the one from the evening before, wearing his jacket and corporal's cap with its unsewn stripes. Without stopping at the first beds, without even glancing at them in passing, they have advanced down the central space to one of the sleepers in the opposite row under the second window. Stopping at the foot of the bed, the two men speak together in low voices. Then the civilian in the felt hat approaches the pillow and touches the body near the shoulder. At once the body, wrapped in blankets, sits up and a pale face appears, the eyes deep in their sockets, the hollow cheeks blackened by several days' growth of beard. Startled out of his sleep, the man takes some time to get his bearings, while the two others stand motionless beside him. He passes one hand over his eyes, across his forehead, and through his short, grayish hair. Then he begins to lean back and suddenly collapses on his mattress.

The civilian must be some kind of doctor or hospital attendant, for he then carefully grasps the man's wrist and holds it between his fingers for some time, as if he were taking the man's pulse, although without consulting any watch. He then lays the inert arm alongside the prone body. He exchanges a few more words with the man accompanying him; after which the two of them cross the width of the room diagonally to reach the patient whose red hand sticks out of the blankets and hangs over the edge of the mattress. Leaning forward in order not to move the sleeper's hand, the attendant grasps it as he did the one before, without in this case producing the slightest reaction. The examination lasts a little longer this time, and afterwards the two men have a longer conversation in low voices. Finally they move away from the bed without having awakened the patient.

The attendant now glances around the rest of the room; he stops at the newcomer, who, unlike his comrades, is half sitting up on his bed. The corporal with the unsewn stripes gestures with his chin to indicate him and says something like: "arrived last night." They come closer. The corporal remains at the foot of the bed. The other man comes to the pillow. The soldier mechanically holds out his wrist, which the attendant grasps firmly without asking any questions. After a few seconds he declares in a low voice, as if he were talking to himself: "You have fever."

"It's nothing much," the soldier says, but his own voice, weak and hoarse, surprises him.

"A high fever," the other man repeats, letting go of his hand.

The hand falls back, inert, on the mattress. The corporal has taken a black notebook and a short pencil out of his pocket and writes some information which the soldier has no difficulty making out: the day and hour of his arrival, the serial number on his overcoat collar, this number 12,345 which has never been his.

"Has it been long?" asks the attendant in the felt hat.

"Long since I've been here?"

"No, since you've had fever."

"I don't know," the soldier says.

The man turns back to his colleague and they step toward the windows for a short discussion which the soldier cannot hear, nor can he read the words on their lips, for he does not see their faces. But the attendant comes back toward him; he leans over and with both hands at once

215

feels each side of his chest through the various layers of clothing:

"Does it hurt when I press?"

"No . . . not any more."

"You've been sleeping like this?"

"What do you mean like this?"

"With a wet coat."

The soldier now pats the stiff, rough material that is still somewhat damp. He says: "It must be the snow . . ."

His words are so faint that they disintegrate before he has spoken them; afterwards he even doubts whether he has actually pronounced them at all.

The attendant now addresses his colleague: "It would be better to change him."

"I'll go see if I have something," the other man says, and he immediately walks to the door, his steps soundless.

Remaining alone, the attendant buttons his dun-colored canvas duffle-coat that is faded and spotted down the front, forcing the three braided-leather buttons into their loops; all three are damaged, the bottom one split by a large scratch halfway through its width, leaving a strip of leather that protrudes about a quarter of an inch. The attendant has put his hands in his shapeless side pockets. He stares at the soldier for a moment and asks:

"Aren't you cold?"

"No . . . Yes . . . A little."

"We can close this now," the man says, and without waiting for his interlocutor's agreement, he moves toward the left end of the dormitory to close the last window. Then he moves along the wall toward the right, slipping between the wall and the iron rods that form the heads of the beds, and continues the operation, coming closer and closer, pulling in the French windows and closing the fastenings which he is obliged to force, making several attempts. As he advances, the daylight wanes in the large room, the darkness increasing from the left and gradually thickening.

There are five windows. Each has two leaves with three

square panes in it. But these panes are visible only when the window is open, for the inner side is covered with dark, translucent paper pasted neatly over the entire surface of the pane. When the man is through, the entire room is plunged into half-darkness, the five rectangular openings are replaced by five series of six purplish, vaguely luminous panes through which filters a light like those of the blue night lamps, all the more inadequate since it succeeds the bright daylight without any transition. The man in the duffle-coat and the felt hat at the right end of the room is only a black silhouette, motionless against the lighter wall, near the outside door.

The soldier supposes that the visitor is about to leave the room, but instead he turns toward his bed:

"There," he says, "now you won't be so cold." And, after a silence: "They'll bring you other clothes. But you have to stay in bed."

He stops talking again; then he resumes: "The doctor will come soon, maybe this afternoon, or later this morning, or tonight . . ." At times he speaks so low that the soldier has trouble hearing him.

"Meanwhile," he continues, "you'll take the pills they give you . . . You mustn't . . ." The end of his sentence is inaudible. He has taken a pair of heavy fur-lined gloves out of his pocket and slowly pulls them on, still adjusting them as he moves away. After several yards all that can be seen of him is a vague shadow; and even before he has reached the door he disappears altogether. Only his heavy boots can be heard continuing on their way with slow steps.

There is no longer light enough to make out the positions of the sleepers. The soldier imagines that this will make it easier for him to leave the dormitory without being seen. He will get a drink as he leaves, from the latrines down the hall.

He makes another effort to sit up and this time succeeds. But he is still leaning against the metal bar behind him. In order to make his position more comfortable he raises the bolster behind him and puts it on top of the box. Then he leans to the right, his hand reaching toward the floor for his boots. At this moment he notices a black silhouette in front of him whose head and bust are outlined against the luminous panes of mauve paper. He recognizes his host of the night before, the corporal without stripes, with his pointed field cap. The soldier's right hand returns to its place on the mattress.

The man puts something that looks like a heavy overcoat across the iron crosspiece at the foot of the bed. Then he steps forward between the two beds and hands the soldier a glass three-quarters full of a colorless liquid.

"Drink this," he says, "it's water. There are pills in the bottom. Afterwards you'll have coffee along with the others."

The soldier seizes the glass and drinks greedily, but the half-dissolved pills which he swallows with the last mouthful stick in his throat and there is no more water to help him get them down. There is a kind of bitter granular deposit which stays in his throat and makes him feel as though it were stripped raw. He feels even thirstier than before.

The man has taken back the empty glass. He observes the whitish streaks which have remained on the sides. Finally he goes away after pointing at the foot of the bed: "I've brought you another overcoat," he says, "put it on before you lie down again."

An indeterminable period after the silent shadow has vanished, the soldier decides to get up. He pivots his legs carefully and sits on the edge of the bed, his knees bent, his feet resting on the floor. Letting his body settle a little, he waits for a long time, at least so it seems to him.

Before going any further he throws off his blankets, which now form a pile on the mattress. Then, leaning down, he gropes about for his boots; having found them under his fingers, he pulls them on, one after the other, and begins lacing them up. Mechanically he unrolls his leggings and wraps them around his calves.

But he has considerable difficulty standing up, as if the weight and burden of his body had become those of a diving suit. Then he begins walking without too much difficulty. Trying to avoid making loud noises with his hobnail boots on the floor, he leaves the row of beds, and without hesitating more than a few seconds, turns right toward the door. He immediately changes his mind and turns back to inspect the overcoat left by the corporal. It is virtually the same as his own, perhaps less worn. The distinctive mark of the regiment—a felt diamond bearing the serial number—has been unsewn from the collar tab on each side.

The soldier lays the garment across the end of the bed and examines it in the darkness, his mind a blank, supporting himself with one hand on the horizontal iron bar. At the other end of the bed he sees the box, still under the bolster. He moves to the head of the bed, rolls back the bolster, picks up the box, puts it under his left arm. At its touch, he feels the dampness of the wool cloth. He puts both hands in his pockets. The lining is wet and cold.

Coming back to the dry overcoat, in the same spot as before, he waits for another moment before leaving. If he exchanges coats, he will not have to unsew the red felt diamonds on his collar. He takes his hands out of his pockets, puts the box down on the bed, slowly unbuttons the overcoat he is wearing. But at first he cannot extricate his arms from the sleeves, because the joints of his shoulders have become so stiff. When he is finally rid of the wet coat, he lets himself rest a minute before continuing the operation. The two coats are now beside each other across the metal bar. In any case, he must put one of them back on. He picks up the new one and slips into the sleeves quite easily, buttons up the four buttons, picks up the box again, puts it back under his left arm, thrusts his hands into the pockets.

This time he has not forgotten anything. He walks carefully toward the door. At the bottom of his right pocket, his hand encounters a round, hard, smooth, cold object the size of a large marble.

In the lighted hallway he passes the corporal who stops to watch him go by, seemingly on the point of speaking when the soldier goes into the latrine—normal behavior, after all; the corporal may think he has taken his package with him because it contains toilet articles.

When he comes out again, having drunk a great deal of cold water from the tap, the corporal is no longer there. The soldier continues down the hall to the stairway; he begins to walk down, holding onto the railing with his right hand. Although he watches his movements carefully, the stiffness of his knees forces him to advance both heavily and mechanically, and the impact of his heavy boots echoes against the wooden steps, one after the other. At each landing the soldier stops; but as soon as he begins going down again, the noise of his hobnail boots on the steps resumes—regular, heavy, isolated, echoing through the house, as in an abandoned building.

At the foot of the staircase, in front of the last step of the last flight, the lame man is leaning on his wooden crutch. The crutch is thrust forward against the steps; the whole body leans forward in what seems a precarious balance; the face is raised, frozen in a forced smile of welcome.

"How are you," he says. "Slept well?"

The soldier too is motionless now. His package under one arm, the other hand on the railing. He is standing at the edge of the first landing between flights, seven or eight steps higher than his interlocutor. He answers: "I'm all right," in a hesitant tone of voice.

In his present position, the lame man is standing in his way. The soldier would have to shove him aside in order to step off the stairs and reach the door to the street. The soldier wonders if this is the same person as the man he met in the apartment of the woman with pale eyes. The man, as a matter of fact, who told him of the existence of this pseudo-barracks for invalids. If it's not the same man, why should he speak to the soldier as if he knew him? If it is the same man, how did he get here on his crutch through the snow-covered streets? And why?

"Is the lieutenant up there?"

"The lieutenant?"

"Yes, the lieutenant! Is he up there?"

The soldier hesitates to answer. He moves closer to the railing in order to lean on it, but he does not want to show how tired he is, stands as straight as possible, and speaks as clearly as he can: "Which lieutenant?"

"The one in charge of this place. You know!"

The soldier realizes that he should at least pretend to know what the man is talking about: "Yes," he says, "he's up there."

He wonders how the lame man will manage to climb the stairs with his crutch, which he generally uses so skillfully. Perhaps he has stopped at the bottom of the stairs because it is impossible for him to climb them. In any case, he is not making the slightest gesture now, merely staring at the soldier, neither stepping back to let him pass nor advancing to meet him.

"I see you've unsewn your number."

The smile on the raised face has grown broader, twisting the mouth and the whole side of the face.

"That was a good idea," the man continues, "in any case it's safer."

To cut short the conversation, the soldier decides to step forward. He comes down one step, but the lame man has not moved an inch, so that the soldier's second foot now stops beside the first, instead of moving down to the next step.

"Where are you going now?" the lame man asks.

The soldier shrugs evasively: "I have things to do."

"And what have you got in your box?" the lame man asks.

Starting down the stairs without stopping this time, the soldier grumbles an irritated answer: "Nothing much." Standing opposite the man, he suddenly flattens himself against the railing. Nimbly the lame man shifts his crutch and moves toward the wall. The soldier passes in front of him and continues down the hallway. He has no need to turn around to know that the lame man is staring after him, leaning forward on his crutch.

The door to the street is not locked. As he is turning the handle the soldier hears the bantering, vaguely threatening voice behind him: "You seem to be in a hurry this morning." He goes out the door and closes it behind him. On the stamped metal plaque fastened to the jamb he reads: "Headquarters, Military Stores of the North and Northwest Regions."

It is so cold in the street that the soldier is shocked. Yet he feels that the cold is doing him good. But he would like to sit down. He must content himself with leaning against the stone wall, setting his feet on the strip of fresh snow between the housefronts and the trampled, yellowish path. In his overcoat pocket his right hand again comes in contact with the large, smooth marble.

It is an ordinary glass marble about an inch in diameter. Its entire surface is completely regular and highly polished. The interior is colorless and transparent except for a central opaque nucleus the size of a pea. This nucleus is black and round. From whatever angle the marble is examined, the nucleus appears as a black disc a fraction of an inch across. Around it the mass of limpid glass reveals only unrecognizable fragments of the red-and-white pattern of which it occupies a circular fraction. Beyond this circle extends on all sides the checkerboard pattern of the oilcloth covering the table. But in the surface of the marble is also reflected, pale and distorted and greatly reduced in scale, the furnishings of the café.

The child rolls the marble gently across the red-and-white checked oilcloth, not pushing it hard enough to make it move beyond the edges of the rectangular surface. It crosses the latter diagonally, follows the long side, returns to its point of departure. Then the child picks it up, stares at it a long time, turning it round and round. Then his large serious eyes shift to the soldier: "What's inside it?" he says, in his voice which is too low to be a boy's.

"I don't know. Glass too, probably."

"It's black."

"Yes, it's black glass."

The child examines the marble again and asks: "Why?" And when the soldier does not answer he repeats: "Why is it inside?"

"I don't know," the soldier says, then after a few seconds: "To look pretty probably."

"But it's not pretty," the child says.

He has lost almost all his mistrust now, and although his voice still has its grave, almost adult timbre, he speaks with a childish simplicity, sometimes even with a naïve abandon. He is still wearing his black cape over his shoulders, but he has taken off his beret, revealing his short blond hair parted on the right.

This boy is the one from the café, apparently, who is not the same as the one who took the soldier (or who will take him, afterwards) to the barracks—from which, as a matter of fact, he has brought back the marble. In any case, it is this boy who has brought the soldier into the café run by the large, thickset, taciturn man, where he has drunk a glass of red wine and eaten two slices of stale bread. He felt stronger after this snack, and to thank the child he has given him the glass marble that was in his overcoat pocket.

"Are you really giving it to me?"

"Yes, I told you so."

"Where does it come from?"

"From my pocket."

"And before that?"

"Before that? I don't know about before that," the soldier says.

The child glances at him inquisitively, and probably incredulously. He immediately becomes somewhat more reserved again and his voice is much colder when he remarks, his eyes fixed on the overcoat collar:

"You've unsewn your number."

The soldier tries to make a joke of the matter. "It's no use any more, you know."

The child does not smile. He does not look as if the explanation were satisfactory.

"But I know it," he says. "It was 12,345."

The soldier does not answer. The boy continues:

"Is it because they're going to come today that you took it off?"

"How do you know they're going to come today?"

"My mother . . ." the boy begins, but he goes no further.

To say something, the soldier asks: "And she lets you run around the streets?"

"I don't run around. There was an errand to do."

"Is she the one who sent you?"

The child hesitates. He looks at the soldier as if he were trying to guess what is coming next, where he is being led to, what kind of trap is being set for him.

"No," he says finally, "she's not."

"So it was your father?" the soldier asks.

This time the boy decides not to answer. The soldier himself has been speaking more slowly during the last few remarks. The slight animation the wine had given him has already vanished, and his fatigue gradually masters him again. Probably he still has fever; the effect of the pills has not lasted long. Nevertheless he continues, his voice lower:

"I ran into him this morning, I think, as I was leaving

the barracks. He does pretty well on his bad leg. Yes, I'm
sure that's who it was. So he wasn't at home . . ."

"He's not my father," the child says, and he turns his
head toward the door.

The two workers at the next table have broken off their
conversation, perhaps some time ago. The man whose
back was turned has pivoted on his chair without letting go
of his glass or raising it from the table, and he has remained in this position, his body half turned to look behind him toward the soldier, or toward the child. The
latter has moved away. At least he is now some distance
from the soldier to the left, near the wall where the white
bulletins are posted announcing the military evacuation of
the city. Complete silence has fallen in the room.

The soldier has remained in the same position: his elbows and forearms in front of him, his grease-spotted hands
lying near each other about four inches apart, the right
hand still holding the empty glass.

The bartender, a tall, thickset figure, has returned to
the room and is standing behind his bar at the far right.
He is motionless too, leaning slightly forward, his arms
wide apart, his hands grasping the edge of the bar. He too
is looking at the soldier, or at the child.

The child has put his beret back on his head. He has
pulled both sides far down in order to cover his ears as
much as possible, and he has pulled the cape around his
body, holding it closed with both hands from inside. At the
other end of the room, the bartender has not moved either.
When he served the soldier just now, he told him that
when he had first seen him through the glass, then crossing
the threshold, he had taken him, in this city where no soldiers circulated any longer, and where everyone expected
to see the newcomers appear at any moment—he had taken
him for one of the latter. But this was only the effect of
surprise, and once the soldier had come in, the bartender
had immediately recognized the familiar uniform with the
long overcoat and the leggings.

225

The boy had then closed the door behind this unexpected customer. The bartender standing at his post, the customer in middle-class clothes standing near the counter, the two workers sitting at their table, all stared at him without saying anything. It was the boy who had broken the silence, his low voice sounding so little like a child's that the soldier had supposed one of the four men watching him come in had spoken. The child was still standing near the door at this moment, behind him. But the others facing him remained motionless, mouths closed, lips motionless; and the sentence, without someone to have spoken it, seemed to be a title underneath a picture.

Afterwards the soldier, his glass of wine finished, has remained no longer in this silent café. He has picked up his package from under his chair and has left the room, accompanied as far as the door by the stares of the bartender and the two workers. After quickly readjusting the distended white string, he has put the package wrapped in brown paper back under his left arm.

Outside, the cold has shocked him once again. This overcoat must not be as thick as the other, unless the temperature has dropped a great deal during the night. The snow, hardened by repeated trampling, grates under his hobnail boots. The soldier walks faster in order to warm himself; urged on by the regularity of the noise his boots make as he walks, he advances without looking where he is going, as though aimlessly, through the deserted streets. When he decided to continue on his way, it was because of the notion that there still remained something to be done in order to get the box to its proper recipient. But when he found himself on the sidewalk again, having closed the café door behind him, he no longer knew which way to turn: he simply tried to proceed to the first meeting place (where he had not been met), without, moreover, losing any time thinking out the best way to get to it, since the man was no longer waiting for him there, now, in any case. The soldier's only hope is that the man lives in the vicinity and that he will meet him on his way. At the first crossroad he has found the lame man again.

Approaching the crossroad where the man is standing, at the corner of the last house, he realizes that it is not the lame man but the man in middle-class clothes who was drinking at the bar just now; he is not leaning on a crutch, but on an umbrella which he is holding in front of him, its tip stuck in the hard snow. His body leans forward slightly. He is wearing spats over his well polished shoes, narrow trousers, and a short overcoat which is probably fur-lined. He has no hat on his head, which is bald in front.

Just before the soldier reaches him, the man bows quickly, his umbrella remaining stuck at an angle in the snow in front of him. The material of the umbrella, rolled tight, is protected by a black silk sheath.

The soldier answers the bow with a nod and attempts to continue on his way, but the other man makes a gesture with his free hand, and the soldier imagines that the man is about to speak to him. He turns toward him and stands still, raising his eyebrows with the look of someone expecting to be spoken to. The man, as if he had foreseen nothing of the kind, then lowers his eyes toward the end of his umbrella stuck at an angle in the hard yellow snow. Yet he has kept his left arm half raised, elbow bent, hand open, thumb up. On his third finger he is wearing a heavy signet ring with a gray stone in it.

"Nasty weather, isn't it?" he says at last, and turns his head toward the soldier. The latter thus finds his expectation justified: he has the feeling again, very distinctly, that this little remark is only a prelude to more personal information. He therefore merely answers it by a vague acquiescence, a kind of grumble. He is still preparing to listen to what follows.

There is a considerable lapse of time, nevertheless, before the man with the umbrella and the fur-lined coat makes up his mind to ask: "Are you looking for something?" Is this the signal?

"I was supposed to meet . . ." the soldier begins.

Since the rest is too long in coming, the other man finishes the sentence himself: "Someone who never showed up?"

"Yes," the soldier says. "It was yesterday . . . I mean the day before yesterday . . . It was supposed to be at noon . . ."

"And you came too late?"

"Yes . . . No. I must have come to the wrong place. A street corner . . ."

"It was a crossroads like this one? Under a lamppost?"

A black lamppost, its base embossed with a garland of stylized ivy whose pattern the snow accentuates . . . Immediately the soldier goes into a more detailed explanation; but no sooner has he begun than he is overcome by doubt and decides to confine himself, out of caution, to a series of incoherent phrases without apparent connection, for the most part incomplete and in any case quite obscure to his interlocutor, in which he himself, moreover, becomes more involved at each word. The other man does not show any sign that his attention is flagging; he listens with polite interest, his eyes squinting slightly, his head tilted to the left, showing no more comprehension than astonishment.

The soldier no longer knows how to stop. He has taken his right hand out of his pocket and moves it forward, clenching his fingers like someone afraid of losing some detail of a memory he thinks he is about to recapture, or like someone who wants to be encouraged, or who does not manage to be convincing, and he continues talking, losing himself in a plethora of increasingly confusing specifications, suddenly conscious of this, stopping at almost each step in order to start again in a different direction, convinced now, but too late, of having blundered from the beginning, and not seeing any means of extricating himself without planting still deeper suspicions in this anonymous pedestrian who merely mentioned the temperature or some banal subject of the sort, or who even asked him nothing at all—and who, moreover, continues to say nothing.

Even while struggling in his own nets, the soldier tries to reconstitute what has just happened: it must have occurred to him (but this now seems incredible) that the man he has been running after since his arrival in the city was perhaps this very man, with his silk-sheathed umbrella, his fur-lined coat, his big ring. He has wanted to allude to what he expected of him, yet without revealing his true mission, permitting the man, all the same, to determine it, if he was actually the man for whom the box wrapped in brown paper was intended, or at least the man who could say what must be done with it.

The man in gray spats and shiny black shoes, on the contrary, no longer gave the slightest sign of complicity. The ringed hand had even fallen back and eventually returned to the coat pocket. The right hand, the one holding the handle of the umbrella, was wearing a dark-gray leather glove. The soldier supposed for a moment that this man was keeping silent on purpose: that he was, in fact, the recipient in question but refusing to make himself known, and that having learned what he himself wanted to know he was concealing his identity . . . This was obviously absurd. Either the business had nothing to do with him or else he had not yet realized that what the soldier was trying to tell him was of the greatest importance to him. Since he had not immediately clutched at this straw being offered to him, the soldier had to choose between two solutions: to speak more openly or else to beat an immediate retreat. But he had not had time to choose one course or the other, and he had persisted in both directions at once, which further risked discouraging his interlocutor if he were, in spite of everything, etc. . . .

The soldier must finally have fallen silent, for they are now standing opposite each other again, frozen in the same position as at the start: the soldier has both hands in his overcoat pockets and stares obliquely at the man in the

229

fur-lined coat who half extends his gloveless left hand, a signet ring with a gray stone on the ring finger, while in his right hand he holds his umbrella at arm's length, stuck at an angle in front of him into the hard-packed snow on the sidewalk. About three yards behind him is the cast-iron lamppost, a former gas light with old-fashioned ornamentation, now equipped with an electric bulb that shines with a yellowish luster in the leaden daylight.

Yet the man has derived some information from the soldier's fragmentary and contradictory stammerings, for after a moment's thought, probably quite a long moment, he asks: "Then someone was supposed to meet you not far from here?" And he adds a moment later, as though to himself: "A man, in the street, these last few days."

Then without waiting for confirmation or asking a complementary question, he begins explaining that he himself, it seems most likely, has seen the person in question: a bare-headed man of medium height, wearing a long brown coat, who was standing at the foot of a corner apartment house. He had noticed him there on several occasions—at least two—when he had passed by: this morning, yesterday as well, and even the day before perhaps. This solitary person, dressed in dark brown, who had been standing in the snow for a long time judging by his position—his hip and shoulder leaning against the cast-iron shaft like a man who is tired of standing—yes, he remembered perfectly having noticed him.

"How old?" the soldier asks.

"About thirty . . . or forty."

"No," the soldier says, "that wasn't the one. He was supposed to be over fifty and dressed in black . . . And why would he have come back like that, several days in a row?"

The last argument hardly stands up, he realizes, for he himself has returned on many occasions, as a matter of fact—and again this morning—to what he supposed was the meeting place, however variable. Moreover, his interlocutor points out that a change in the clothes agreed upon might have been compelled by the snow then falling so thickly; as for the age, he is not certain of that, having glimpsed this figure at some distance, especially the second time.

"Besides," the soldier says, "it might have been me."

But the man assures him he would not have confused an infantry uniform with civilian clothes. He urges the soldier to examine the place he indicates, at least to give it a look: it is so close by it is worth the trouble, particularly if the matter is an important one.

"That box you have under your arm, you were saying it . . ."

"No," the soldier interrupts. "That has nothing to do with it."

Since he has virtually no other resources, he decides, despite his certainty of the uselessness of such a procedure, to go to the crossroads in question: he must turn right at the third street, then go to the end of the block of houses, if not to the next cross street. He has set off without turning back, leaving the stranger behind him still leaning on his umbrella. This prolonged delay has frozen his body through. Although all his joints are numb with fever and fatigue, he experiences a kind of relief in walking again, particularly since he has the prospect of a precise and not too distant goal. Once he has ascertained the futility of this last hope (which is not even that), there will be nothing left to do but get rid of his burdensome package.

It would obviously be best to destroy it, the contents in any case, since the box itself is made of iron. But if it is easy to burn the papers inside it, or to tear them up into tiny pieces, there are also other objects more difficult to tear up—the exact nature of which, moreover, he has never checked. He will have to get rid of the whole thing. To throw away the package without even unwrapping it would be the simplest solution from every point of view. As he crosses a side street, the soldier happens to notice a sewer mouth in front of him near the rounded curb of the sidewalk. He approaches it and, despite the stiffness of his joints, leans down in order to make sure the box is not too large to pass through the arched opening in the stone curb. Fortunately the layer of snow is not thick enough to impede the operation. The box will just fit. All he needs to do is to push it through horizontally until it falls over onto the other side. Why not get rid of it right away?

At the last minute, the soldier cannot make up his mind to do it. Having reassured himself by twice checking that the operation can be accomplished without difficulty, he straightens up at the crucial moment and begins walking straight ahead in order to look over there first, to see whether by some chance . . . But the mere fact of having to step over the curb of the sidewalk, some eight inches, keeps him motionless for a moment, so greatly has the insignificant effort he has just made exhausted him.

As soon as he stops moving, the cold becomes unbearable. He crosses the gutter and takes another two steps. Suddenly he is so exhausted that he can manage to go no farther. He leans his hip and shoulder against the cast-iron shaft of the street light. Was it here that he was supposed to turn right? To see if the man with the gray ring has not remained where he was, leaning forward on his umbrella, in order to show him from a distance the place where he is supposed to turn, the soldier glances behind him. Twenty yards away, walking in his tracks, is the boy.

The soldier, who has immediately turned his head away, has begun walking again. After five or six steps he looks behind him again. The boy is following him. If he were able to, the soldier would begin running. But he is completely exhausted. And probably this child has nothing against him. The soldier stops and turns around once again.

The boy has stopped too, his wide, serious eyes staring at the soldier. He no longer has his beret on his head. He is no longer holding his cape closed around him.

The soldier now moves toward the boy, almost without

moving his body, his steps extremely slow, as if he were frozen stiff. The boy does not back away.

"Do you have something to tell me?" the soldier asks in a tone of voice meant to be threatening but which scarcely escapes his lips.

"Yes," the boy answers.

However he does not say anything more.

The soldier looks at the snow-covered stoop two yards to his right, beneath a closed door. He would feel the cold less if he could take shelter in the doorway. He takes a step. He murmurs:

"Well, I'm going to sit down a little."

Having reached the doorway, he leans in the corner, half against the wood, half against the stone jamb.

The child has pivoted to watch the soldier. He has opened his mouth slightly. He examines the face with the black growth of beard, the body slumped backward, the package, the heavy boots a few inches apart on the stoop. Gradually the soldier lets himself slide down against the door, bending his knees until he is sitting in the snow which has accumulated in the right side of the doorway on the narrow stoop.

"Why did you want to throw away your box?" the child says.

"No, I . . . I wasn't going to throw it away."

"Then what were you doing?"

His low voice is now without mistrust, his questions are not hostile.

"I wanted to see," the soldier says.

"To see? . . . To see what?"

"If it would go through."

But the child does not seem to be convinced. He grasps the edges of his open cape, one in each hand, and sways his arms in cadence, back and forth, back and forth. The cold still does not seem to bother him. At the same time, without coming any closer, he continues his careful scrutiny: the brown package now hugged between chest and thighs, the overcoat collar with the insignia removed, the legs bent, the knees pointing under the flaps of khaki material.

"Your coat," he says at last, "isn't the same as yesterday."

"Yesterday . . . Did you see me yesterday?"

"Of course. I've seen you every day. Your coat was dirty . . . Did they clean it for you?"

"No . . . Yes, I guess so."

The child pays no attention to the answer.

"You don't know how to wrap your leggings," he says.

"All right . . . you'll teach me."

The child shrugs his shoulders. The soldier, exhausted by the conversation, fears still more that his companion will run away, abandoning him in the empty street where night will soon fall. Is it not the same boy who has already taken him to a café that was still open and to a barracks dormitory? The soldier forces himself to ask in a friendlier tone of voice:

"Was that what you wanted to tell me?"

"No," the boy answers, "that wasn't it."

Then they heard the distant sound of the motorcycle.

No. It was something else. It is dark. There is another attack, the dry, staccato sound of automatic rifles quite close behind the little woods, and on the other side too, now and then, against a low, rumbling background. The dirt path is now as soft as if it had been plowed. The wounded man grows heavier and heavier, can no longer lift his shoes, is unable to walk any farther. He must be supported and dragged at the same time. Both men have abandoned their knapsacks. The wounded man has also dropped his rifle, but the other man has kept his, although its strap has broken and he is forced to carry it in his hand. It would have been better to take another one: there was no lack of rifles to choose from. He has preferred to keep the one he was accustomed to, though it is useless and awkward. He carries it horizontally, in his left hand. His right arm is around the waist of his wounded comrade, whose left arm is crooked around his neck. In the darkness they stumble at each step on the soft earth; there are many ruts and furrows, and only fleeting gleams of light.

Afterwards he walks alone. He has neither knapsack nor rifle nor comrade to carry any more. All he is carrying now is the box wrapped in brown paper under his left arm. He advances through the night across the fresh snow covering the ground, and his footsteps appear one after the other in the thin, uniform layer of snow, making a sound regular as clockwork. Having reached the crossroads under the yellow light of the street light, he approaches the gutter and bends down, one foot on the edge of the sidewalk, the other in the street. The stone arch of a sewer mouth appears between his stiff legs; he bends over farther and holds the box toward the black opening, where it immediately disappears, swallowed up by the void.

The next image shows the dormitory of a barracks, or more precisely, of a military hospital. The rectangular box, which is the size and shape of a shoe box, is lying on the kit shelf next to an aluminum cup, a mess-tin, some neatly folded khaki clothes, and various other small objects. Beneath, in the white-painted metal bed, a man is lying on his back. His eyes are closed; the lids are gray, as are the forehead and the temples; but the two cheekbones are bright pink; over the hollow cheeks, around the half-open mouth, and across the chin there is a black beard of four or five days' growth. The sheet, pulled up to his chin, rises periodically with the wounded man's slightly wheezing respiration. One reddish hand sticks out of the brown blankets on one side and hangs over the edge of the mattress.

235

To the right and left, other bodies are lying on other identical beds lined up against one bare wall, along which, a yard above their heads, is attached the shelf filled with knapsacks, wooden boxes, folded clothes either khaki or olive drab, and aluminum dishes and cups. A little farther along among the toilet utensils is a large round alarm clock —doubtless stopped—whose hands indicate a quarter to four.

In the next room, a considerable crowd has gathered: men standing, mostly in civilian clothes, talking in small groups and making many gestures. The soldier tries to clear a path but without success. Suddenly someone he saw only from the rear, standing in his way, turns around and motionlessly stares at him, his eyes squinting slightly, as though with a great effort of attention. Gradually the men nearby turn to look at him, all suddenly motionless, silent, squinting slightly. He soon finds himself in the center of a circle which grows progressively larger as the figures step back, only their pale faces still visible, farther and farther apart, at equal intervals, like a series of street lights along a straight street. The row sways slightly, becoming a receding perspective: the shafts of black cast-iron stand out sharply against the snow. In front of the nearest one is the boy, who stares at him wide-eyed:

"Why are you staying there like that?" he says. "Are you sick?"

The soldier makes an effort to answer:

"I'll be all right."

"Did you lose your barracks again?"

"No . . . I'm going back now."

"Why don't you wear a cap? All the soldiers wear caps . . . or helmets."

After a pause, the child continues, his voice still lower: "My father has a helmet."

"Where is your father?"

"I don't know." Then loudly, carefully articulating each word: "It's not true that he deserted."

The soldier looks up at the boy again: "Who says he did?"

In answer, the child takes a few steps with a limping gait, his legs stiff, one arm stretched alongside his body, grasping a crutch. He is now only a yard away from the door. He continues:

"But it's not true. And he said you're a spy. You're not a real soldier: you're a spy. There's a bomb in your package."

"Well, that's not true either," the soldier says.

Now they have heard the distant sound of the motorcycle. The boy has cocked his head first; he has opened his mouth a little wider and his head has gradually pivoted from street light to street light toward the gray end of the street, already vague in the twilight. Now he has looked at the soldier and then at the end of the street again, while the noise was growing rapidly louder. It was the sputtering of a two-cylinder motor. The child has drawn back toward the doorway.

But the noise has begun to diminish, soon becoming almost inaudible.

"I have to go back," the child says.

He has looked at the soldier and repeated: "I have to go back home."

He has approached the soldier, he has held out his hand. Hesitating at first, the soldier has grasped his hand and has managed to stand up, leaning one shoulder against the door.

The same sputtering of a motor has begun again in the silence, swelling in volume, this time much more distinctly. The man and the child have stepped back together into the doorway. The noise has soon come so close that they have stepped up onto the stoop and are flattened against the wood of the door beside each other. The staccato racket echoing in all directions against the housefronts unmistakably came from the adjacent street, the one forming the crossroads some ten yards from their hiding place. They have flattened themselves even more against the door. The motorcycle has appeared at the edge of the vertical wall, at the corner of the house. It was a side car with two helmeted soldiers in it; it was advancing slowly down the middle of the street, in the fresh snow.

The two men appear in profile. The driver's face, situated slightly forward, is above his companion's. They seem to have the same features: regular, drawn, perhaps shrunken by fatigue. Their eyes are hollow, their lips tight, their skin grayish. The color and shape of their jackets are like those of the familiar uniform, but the helmet is larger, heavier, protecting the ears and the back of the neck. The motorcycle itself is dirty and half covered with dry mud; it seems to be a rather old model. The man driving it sits stiffly on his seat, his gloved hands grasping the handle bars. The other man looks alternately right and left, but only ahead of the motorcycle, almost without moving his head. On his knees he holds a black machine gun whose barrel sticks out of the iron-plated car.

They have passed without turning back and have continued straight ahead past the crossroad. After about twenty yards, they have disappeared behind the corner of the apartment house forming the opposite corner.

A few seconds later the sound has suddenly stopped. Apparently the motor was turned off. Complete silence followed the racket. There remained only the two parallel lines left in the snow by the three wheels of the vehicle, drawn straight across the field of vision between the two planes of vertical stone.

Since this was taking too long, the child has lost patience and has left his hiding place. The soldier has not noticed this immediately, for previously the child had been huddled behind him; the soldier has just seen him in the middle of the sidewalk and has gestured to him to come back. But the child has taken another three steps forward, so that he is now standing against the street light, which is supposed to conceal him.

The silence persisted. The boy, who quickly grew bolder as time passed, has advanced several yards towards the crossroads. For fear of attracting the attention of the invisible motorcyclists, the soldier has not dared call him to keep him from going farther. The child has continued to the point from which he can see the entire cross street; sticking his head out, he has glanced in the direction the side car had vanished. A man's voice, some distance away, in this area, has shouted a short command. With a start, the child has turned around and begun running; he has passed the soldier again, his cape fluttering over his shoulders. Before realizing what he was doing, the soldier was already following him when the two-cylinder motor started up again, suddenly filling the air with its sputtering. The soldier too has begun running, laboriously, while the child has turned the corner of the next street.

Behind him, the racket has quickly become deafening. Then came a long grating sound: the motorcycle taking too sharp a turn and skidding on the snow. At the same time the motor stopped. The harsh voice shouted: "Halt!" twice, without the slightest trace of an accent. The soldier almost reached the corner of the street where the child himself had turned a few seconds before. The motorcycle has started up again, drowning out the powerful voice which was repeating "Halt!" for the third time. And immediately afterwards, the soldier recognized the dry staccato crackling of the machine gun which mingled with the uproar.

He has felt a violent shock on the heel of his right boot. He has kept on running. Bullets have struck the stone wall near him. Just as he was turning the corner, there was a new burst of firing. A sharp pain has pierced his left side. Then everything stopped.

He was out of reach, protected by the wall. The crackling of the machine gun had stopped. The motor had probably stopped a few seconds before. The soldier no longer felt his body, he was still running along the stone wall. The apartment house door was not closed, it opened easily when the soldier pushed it. He has gone in. He has closed it behind him gently; the bolt, as it falls back into place, has made a slight click.

Afterward he lay down on the floor in the darkness, curling up with the box in the hollow of his stomach. He has felt the back of his boot: there was a deep diagonal rent along the back and side of the heel. His foot was not touched. Heavy steps and noisy voices have echoed in the street.

The steps drew closer. A muffled blow has resounded against the wood of the door, then the voices again, rough, rather jovial, speaking an incomprehensible language with drawling intonations. The noise of one man's steps has faded away. The two voices, one quite near, the other somewhat farther away, have exchanged three or four short sentences. Someone has knocked on something, probably another door, and on this one again, with a fist, several times, but apparently without conviction. The more distant voice has shouted foreign words again and the nearer voice has begun laughing loudly. Then the other voice burst into laughter too.

And the two heavy treads have faded away together, accompanied by bursts of laughter. In the ensuing silence the sound of the motorcycle has begun again, then gradually diminished until it is no longer audible.

The soldier has wanted to change position. A sharp pain has pierced his side. A very violent but not unbearable pain. Most of all he was tired. And he felt like vomiting.

Then he heard the boy's low voice quite near him in the darkness, but he did not understand what it was saying. He felt he was losing consciousness.

A considerable crowd has gathered in the room: men, mostly in civilian clothes, talking in small groups and making many gestures. The soldier tries to make his way through them. He finally reaches a less crowded area where the people sitting at tables are drinking wine and arguing, still with many gestures and exclamations. The tables are very close together and circulation between the benches, chairs, and human backs is still difficult; but it is easier to see where one is going. Unfortunately all the chairs seem to be occupied. The tables—round, square, or rectangular —are set facing in every direction, without discernible order. Some have no more than three or four drinkers around them; the larger ones, which are long and have benches, can serve fifteen. Beyond is the bar behind which the bartender is standing, a tall, heavy-set man, made even more noticeable by his slightly raised position. Between the bar and the last tables, a very narrow space is obstructed in the center by a group of standing drinkers who are more luxuriously dressed in short overcoats or fur-collared cloaks, and whose glasses, set down within arm's reach in front of the bartender, are partially visible in the openings left here and there between the bodies and the arms in their demonstrative attitudes. One of these men, to the right and a little to the rear, instead of participating in his friends' conversation, is leaning back against the edge of the bar in order to look at the room, the seated drinkers, the soldier.

The latter finally glimpses, not far away, a small, relatively accessible table at which only two other soldiers are sitting: an infantry corporal and a cavalry corporal. Motionless and silent, both men's reserved appearance contrasts with that of the men around them. There is an unoccupied chair between them.

Having succeeded in reaching it without too much difficulty, the soldier rests one hand on its back and asks if he may sit down. It is the infantry corporal who replies: they were with a friend, but the latter, who has gone away for a minute, doesn't seem to be coming back; he has probably met someone he knows somewhere else. Why not take his place until he comes back. This is what the soldier does, pleased to find a seat free.

The two others say nothing. They are not drinking; they do not even have glasses in front of them. The racket of the room around them does not seem to affect them; they keep their eyes fixed straight ahead, as though they were sleeping without lowering their lids. If not, they are certainly not both looking so fixedly at the same thing, for the man on the right is facing the left wall, which is quite bare at this point, since the white bulletins are posted farther forward, and the man on the opposite side is facing the bar.

Halfway from the bar, over which the bartender's thickset body is leaning between his widespread arms, a young waitress is passing among the tables with her loaded tray. At least she is looking around to find a place where she is needed: having stopped for a moment, she pivots in order to glance in all directions; she moves neither her feet, her legs, nor the lower part of her body beneath the full-pleated skirt, but only her head (with its black hair in a heavy bun) and the upper part of her body; her two outstretched arms, which are holding the tray at eye level, leave the latter in virtually the same place when she turns in the other direction, remaining twisted in this way for some time.

Judging from the direction of her gaze, the soldier supposes she has noticed his presence and will therefore approach this newcomer's table to take his order, or even that she will serve him at once, for on her tray she is carrying a bottle of red wine which, moreover, she is tilting dangerously, at the risk of letting it fall off the tray, which she is not keeping horizontal. But below, in the trajectory of an imminent fall, the old, bald worker apparently suspects nothing, continuing to address the man at his right, or appealing to him, or calling him to witness, while brandishing in his right hand his still full glass, whose contents are on the point of spilling.

The soldier then remembers that there is not one glass on his own table. Yet the tray holds only the one bottle and nothing which might satisfy a new customer in the way of a glass. The waitress, moreover, has not discovered anything to attract her attention in this area, and her glance now completes its circuit of the room, having passed the soldier and his two companions, now sweeping over the other tables along the wall where the small white bulletins are attached by four tacks, then the window with its pleated curtain at eye level and its three enamel balls outside the glass, then the door, also partially curtained and with the word "Café" showing in reverse, then the bar in front of it with the five or six men in middle-class clothes, and at the far right the last of these men who is still looking toward the soldier's table.

The latter continues staring straight ahead. The cavalry corporal now fixes his eyes on the collar of the soldier's coat where the two diamonds of green felt showing the serial number are sewn.

"So you were at Reichenfels?" And at the same time his chin points forward with a short, quick movement.

The soldier replies: "Yes, I was in the area."

"You were there," the cavalry corporal corrects, repeating his gesture as though to prove the fact by indicating the regiment's distinctive insignia.

"The other one was too," the infantry corporal says. "The man who was sitting here just now."

"But he did some fighting," the cavalry corporal snaps.

Then, since he receives no answer: "I hear there were some who weren't up to it."

He turns toward the cavalry corporal who makes a vague gesture of ignorance or agreement.

"No one was up to it," the soldier says.

But the cavalry corporal protests: "Yes, some were! Ask the little guy who was sitting here before."

"Maybe you're right," the soldier admits, "it all depends what you mean by 'up to it.' "

"I mean what it means. There were some who fought and some who didn't."

"They all got out of it eventually."

"They were ordered to! Keep it straight."

"Everyone stopped fighting on orders," the soldier says.

The cavalry corporal shrugs his shoulders. He looks at the infantry corporal as though he had expected support from him. Then he turns toward the large window looking out on the street. He murmurs: "Rotten officers!"

And again, after a few seconds: "Rotten officers, that's what it was."

"I'm with you there," the infantry corporal agrees.

The soldier tries to see, to his right or farther back, if the young waitress has not started to come over to their table, but even though he half rises from his chair to see over the heads of the drinkers surrounding it, he cannot catch sight of her anywhere.

"Don't worry," the infantry corporal says, "you'll see him soon enough when he comes back." He smiles rather pleasantly and adds, still supposing that the soldier is looking for the absent friend: "He must be over there, in the poolroom. He must have found someone he knew."

"You can ask him," the cavalry corporal continues with a thrust of his chin. "He was in the fighting. You can ask him."

"All right," the soldier says, "but he's here all the same, now. He had to come here just like everyone else."

"He was ordered to, I tell you," and after a moment of silent reflection he concludes, as though to himself, "Rotten officers, that's what it was!"

"I'm with you there," the infantry corporal agrees.

The soldier asks: "Were you at Reichenfels?"

"Oh, no," the infantry corporal answers, "we were both farther west. We fell back to keep from being taken when they broke through from the rear."

"We were ordered to. Remember that. Keep it straight," the cavalry corporal corrects.

"And we moved fast," the infantry corporal says. "It was no use hanging around: the Twenty-eighth, on our left flank, waited too long and got picked off like flies."

"Anyway," the soldier says, "it all comes down to the same thing now. Sooner or later they'll get us."

The cavalry corporal glances at him, but prefers to address his remarks to an imaginary interlocutor sitting on the opposite side: "Nobody's proved that. We're not through yet."

Now the soldier shrugs his shoulders. This time he stands up completely to try to attract the waitress' attention and get something to drink. As he does so, he overhears a random sentence from the conversation at the next table: "I tell you there are spies everywhere!" A relative silence follows this declaration. Then, from the other end of the same table, comes a longer commentary in which only the words "firing squad" can be heard. The rest is lost in the general confusion. And another phrase stands out just as the soldier sits down again: "Some fought, others didn't."

The cavalry corporal immediately begins examining the green diamonds on the soldier's overcoat collar. He repeats: "We're not through yet." Then, leaning toward the infantry corporal, he says as though in confidence: "They say there are enemy agents paid to sabotage morale."

The other man shows no reaction. The cavalry corporal, who has vainly expected a reply, leaning forward across the red-and-white checked oilcloth, finally straightens up in his chair. A little later he says again: "Should take a look," but without explaining himself further, and in so low a tone that he can scarcely be heard. Both men are now silent, motionless, each one staring straight ahead into space.

The soldier has left them, intending to find the young woman with the heavy dark hair. Yet once he is on his feet among the crowded tables, he has decided he was not so thirsty after all.

On the point of leaving, already not far from the bar and the group of middle-class drinkers, he has just remembered the soldier who was also at Reichenfels and who, for one, had fought so gloriously. The important thing was to find him, to talk to him, make him tell his story. The soldier immediately turns around and crosses the room in the opposite direction between the benches, the chairs, and the backs of the seated drinkers. The two men are still alone in the same positions in which he left them. Instead of proceeding to their table, he turns directly toward the back of the room to reach an area where everyone is standing: a crowd of men gesturing and shouldering each other toward the left, but advancing very slowly because of the narrowness of the passage, which they nevertheless gradually approach, between a projecting angle of the wall and three large, loaded, circular coat racks standing at the end of the bar. While the soldier too is moving forward along with the crowd—even more slowly since he is on the edge—he wonders why it suddenly seemed so urgent to talk to this man who could only tell him what he already knows. Before reaching the next room where there are probably more drinkers, a pool table concealed under its tarpaulin cover, the black-haired waitress, and the hero of Reichenfels, he has given up his project.

It is probably here that the scene occurs: the silent gathering wihch steps back in every direction around him, the soldier finally remaining alone in the center of a huge circle of pale faces . . . But this scene leads to nothing. Besides, the soldier is no longer in the center of a crowd, neither silent nor noisy; he has left the café and is walking in the street. It is an ordinary kind of street; long, straight, lined with identical houses with flat façades and uniform doors and windows. It is snowing, as usual, in close, small, slow flakes. The sidewalks are white, as are the street, the window sills, the stoops.

When a door is not closed tight, the snow which the wind drove into the doorway during the night has been wedged into the narrow vertical slit for several inches, remaining caked against the jamb when the soldier opens the door wide. A little snow has even accumulated inside, forming on the ground a long, tapering streak which has partially melted, leaving a moist black border on the dusty wood of the floor. Other black marks occur along the hallway at intervals of about two feet, growing fainter as they continue toward the staircase, whose first steps appear at the end of the hallway. Although the shape of these puddles is uncertain, changeable, and occasionally fringed with intermediary zones, it is likely that they are footprints left by small shoes.

On the right of the hallway as on the left are lateral doors at equal and alternating intervals, one to the right, one to the left, one to the right, etc. . . . The series continues as far as the eye can see, or almost, for the first steps of the staircase are still visible at the end of the hallway, lit by a brighter gleam. A small silhouette, a woman or a child greatly reduced by the considerable distance, rests one hand on the large white sphere where the banister ends.

The more the soldier advances, the more he has the impression that this figure is retreating. But one of the doors has been opened on the right. Here, moreover, the footprints stop. Click. Darkness. Click. Yellow light revealing a narrow vestibule. Click. Darkness. Click. The soldier is once more in the square room furnished with a chest, a table, and a day bed. The table is covered with a checkered oilcloth. Above the chest the photograph of a soldier in battle dress is fastened to the wall. Instead of sitting at the table drinking wine and slowly chewing his bread, the soldier is lying on the bed; his eyes are closed, he seems to be sleeping. Around him are standing three motionless

247

people, who are looking at him without speaking: a man, a woman, and a child.

Right next to his face, at the head of the bed, the woman is bending forward slightly, examining the sleeper's drawn features, listening to his laborious breathing. Behind her, near the table, stands the boy, still wearing his black cape and beret. At the foot of the bed, the third person is not the lame man with the wooden crutch, but the older man whose head is bald in front, wearing a short fur-lined overcoat and well-polished shoes protected by spats. He has kept his fine gray leather gloves on; the one on his left hand is distended, on the third finger, by the stone of his signet ring. The umbrella must have remained in the vestibule leaning against the coat rack, with its ivory handle and its silk sheath.

The soldier is lying on his back, fully dressed, with his leggings and his heavy boots. His arms are at his sides. His overcoat is unbuttoned; underneath it, his uniform jacket is spotted with blood on the left side, near the waist.

No. Actually it is another wounded man who occupies the scene, outside the door of the busy café. The soldier has no sooner closed the door behind him than he sees a young man coming toward him, a soldier drafted the year before whom he has met several times during the retreat and again this morning at the hospital, who is also about to go into the café. For a second, the soldier imagines he has before his eyes the valiant fighter referred to inside, the man whose conduct the cavalry corporal had just been praising. He immediately realizes the impossibility of such a coincidence: the young man happened to be at Reichenfels during the enemy attack, but in his own regiment, as the green diamonds on his uniform attest; yet this unit did not include a single hero, as the cavalry corporal had clearly implied. As the soldier is about to pass his comrade, merely nodding to him, the latter stops to speak to him: "Your friend you went to see this morning in surgery," he says, "is pretty bad. He's been asking for you several times."

"All right," the soldier says. "I'll go back."

"You better hurry. He won't last long."

The young man has already put his hand on the brass doorknob when he turns to add: "He says he's got something to give you." After a moment's thought: "But maybe it's just delirium."

"I'll go see," the soldier says.

He immediately begins walking quickly, taking the shortest route. The setting he passes through is no longer that of the great symmetrical and monotonous city with its straight roads intersecting each other at right angles. And there is no snow yet. The weather is even rather mild, for the season. The houses are low, old-fashioned, vaguely baroque, over-ornamented with volutes, molded cornices, columns with carved capitals framing the doors, balconies with sculptured brackets, complicated cast-iron railings. All of which corresponds to the lampposts on the street corners, former gas lights that have been converted, consisting of a cast-iron column widening at the base and supporting, three yards from the ground, a lyre-shaped structure with twining branches, from which is suspended the globe containing the large electric bulb. The shaft itself is not uniform, but girdled with many rings of varying shapes and sizes, indicating at various heights changes in diameter, swellings, constrictions, circular or spindle-shaped bulges; these rings are particularly numerous toward the top of the cone which constitutes the foot of the structure; around this cone spirals a garland of stylized ivy embossed on the metal and reproduced identically on each lamppost.

But the hospital is only a military building of classic construction, at the rear of a large, bare, gravel courtyard separated from the boulevard and its leafless trees by a high iron fence whose gate is wide open. On each side the sentry boxes are empty. In the center of the huge courtyard one man is standing, a non-commissioned officer with belted tunic and kepi; he is standing perfectly still. He seems to be thinking; his black shadow lies at his feet across the white gravel.

As for the room where the wounded man is, it is an ordinary hall whose metal beds have been painted white— a decor which also leads to nothing, if not to the box wrapped in brown paper lying on the kit shelf.

Hence it is with this box under his arm that the soldier walks through the snowy streets along the high, flat house-fronts when he is looking for the meeting place, hesitating among several similar crossroads, deciding that the description he has been furnished is quite inadequate to determine the exact place with any certainty in this huge city arranged so geometrically. And finally he goes back to an apparently uninhabited apartment house, pushing open a door that has remained ajar. The hallway, painted dark brown halfway up the wall, has the same deserted aspect as the streets themselves: doors with neither door mat nor calling card, absence of the usual household utensils left here or there which usually show that a house is inhabited, and walls completely bare save for the compulsory civil defense bulletin.

And then comes the side door which opens onto a narrow vestibule where the black-sheathed umbrella is leaning against an ordinary coat rack.

But another entrance makes it possible to leave the apartment house without being seen by someone watching for you at the doorway: it opens onto the cross street at the end of the secondary hallway perpendicular to the first, to the left of the staircase ending the latter. Moreover, this street is in every way similar to the preceding one; and the child is here at his post, waiting for the soldier at the foot of the lamppost in order to lead him to the military offices which serve as a kind of barracks and hospital.

In any case they have set out with this intention. However the crossroads and sudden changes in direction increase in number, and the interminable walk through the night continues. Since the boy goes faster and faster, the soldier is soon no longer able to follow him and is alone again, with no other recourse than to seek some shelter in which to sleep. He doesn't have much choice, and must content himself with the first door he finds open. This is once again the apartment of the young woman in the gray apron with the black hair, the pale eyes, the low voice. Yet he had not noticed, at first, that the room where he had been given bread and wine, under the framed photograph of the husband in battle dress fastened to the wall over the chest, contained a day bed as well as the rectangular table covered with a checkered oilcloth.

At the top of the wall opposite this bed, almost at the angle of the ceiling, there is a small, sinuous black line a little over four inches long, which may be a crack in the plaster, perhaps a dusty spider web, perhaps merely a defect in the white paint emphasized by the harsh lighting of the electric light bulb hanging at the end of its wire swaying back and forth in a slow, oscillating movement. In the same rhythm, but in the opposite direction, the shadow of the man with the unsewn chevrons and the civilian trousers (is this the man whom the lame man called the lieutenant?), the shadow on the floor sways left and right against the closed door on either side of the motionless body.

This pseudo-lieutenant (but the insignia missing from his jacket were those of a corporal, their outline remaining clearly visible on the brown material), this man who took in the wounded or the sick must have first leaned out of a second floor window, probably the one just over the door, in order to try to see, in the darkness, who wanted to come in. However this does not resolve the main problem: how had he known that there was someone on the doorstep? Had the boy knocked on the closed door when he got there? Therefore, the soldier, having finally caught up with his guide after a considerable delay, since he had no longer been following him for some time now save by his tracks, had not suspected that his presence would already be announced and that while he was perched on the narrow stoop vainly trying to decipher the inscription stamped on the polished plaque by passing his fingertips back and forth across it, his host, three yards above him, was minutely observing part of his overcoat which stuck out beyond the doorway: a shoulder, a stained sleeve hugging a package whose shape and size resembled those of a shoe box.

Yet no window was lighted, and the soldier had thought this house, like the others, deserted by its inhabitants. Having pushed open the door, he had soon realized his error: a large number of tenants were still there (as everywhere else, too, no doubt), and appeared one after the other on all sides, a young woman flattening herself at the rear of the hallway against the corner of the staircase, another woman suddenly opening her door on the left, and finally a third, on the right, revealing, after some hesitation, the vestibule leading once again to the square room where the soldier is now lying.

He is lying on his back. His eyes are closed. The lids are gray, as are the forehead and the temples, but the cheekbones are bright pink. Across the hollow cheeks, around the half open mouth and over the chin, there is a four or five days' growth of black beard. The sheet, pulled up to the chin, rises periodically with the slightly wheezing respiration. One reddish hand with black stains at the joints of the fingers sticks out at one side and hangs over the edge of the bed. Neither the man with the umbrella nor the boy is in the room any longer. Only the woman is here, sitting at the table, but at an angle, so that she is facing the soldier.

She is knitting a garment out of black wool; but her work

is not yet far along. The heavy ball of yarn is lying near her on the red-and-white checked oilcloth which hangs over the edge of the table in wide, stiff folds at the corners. The rest of the room is not quite as the soldier has remembered it; not counting the day bed, whose presence he had scarcely noticed on his first visit, there is at least one important thing to be noted: a high window now completely concealed by long red curtains falling from ceiling to floor. Though wide, the day bed might easily have passed unnoticed, for it is placed in the corner concealed from the eyes of someone coming into the room by the open door; afterwards the soldier turned his back to it when he was eating and drinking at the table; and besides, he was paying little attention to the furnishings, his senses dulled by fatigue, hunger, and the cold outside. However he is surprised that his eyes were not caught by what was then, as now, just opposite him: the window, or in any case the red curtains made of some thin shiny material that resembles satin.

These curtains must not have been drawn; for, as they look today, spread out under the light, it is impossible not to be struck by their color. Probably the window itself was then visible, between two narrow vertical red strips that were not clearly lighted and so much less noticeable. But if it had been daylight, what did this window look out on? Was it a street scene which would appear through the panes of glass? Given the monotony of the neighborhood, there would certainly be nothing remarkable about such a view. Or else it was something else: a courtyard, perhaps, so narrow and dark on the ground floor level that it provided little daylight and no view of any interest, especially if thick draperies kept whatever was outside from being seen.

Despite these rationalizations, the soldier is still perturbed by such a gap in his memory. He wonders if anything else in his surroundings might have escaped him and even continues to escape him now. It suddenly seems very important to make an exact inventory of the room. There is the fireplace, about which he has remembered almost nothing: an ordinary black marble mantelpiece with a large rectangular mirror over it; its iron grate is open, revealing a heap of light gray ashes, but no andirons; on the mantelpiece is lying a rather long object, not very tall—only a half an inch, or an inch at the most—which cannot be identified from this angle, not being placed near enough the edge of the shelf (it is even possible that it is much wider than it looks); in the mirror are reflected the satiny red curtains whose folds gleam with vertical reflections . . . The soldier has the impression that all this is nothing: he must take note of other details in this room, details much more important than all the preceding ones, one detail in particular which he had been vaguely conscious of when he came into the room the other time, the day of the red wine and the slice of bread . . . He no longer remembers what it was. He wants to turn around in order to examine the chest more carefully. But he cannot manage to move except in the most insignificant way, a kind of torpor paralyzing his whole body. Only his hands and forearms move with any ease.

"You want something?" the young woman's low voice asks.

She has not changed position, having stopped in the middle of her work, her knitting still held in front of her, her fingers still placed—one forefinger raised, the other bent double—as if they were about to make a new stitch, her face still bent over to make sure it is executed properly, but her eyes raised toward the head of the bed. Her features are anxious, severe, even strained by her application to her work; or else by the anxiety afforded by this wounded man who has appeared so unexpectedly in her apartment; or else for some reason unknown to the latter.

"No," he says, "I don't need anything."

He speaks slowly, in a way that he himself finds surprising, the words abnormally distinct without his making them so intentionally.

"Are you in pain?"

"No," he says, "I can't . . . move . . . my body."

"You mustn't try to move. If you need something, ask me. It's because of the shot the doctor gave you. He'll try to come by tonight to give you another one." She has begun knitting again, her eyes lowered again over her work. "If he can," she says again. "No one can be sure of anything now."

It must also be the shot which gives the soldier this nausea he has been feeling since his awakening. He is thirsty; but he does not want to get up to drink from the faucet in the latrines down the hall. Instead he will wait until the attendant in the canvas duffle-coat and the hunter's boots comes back. No, that's not it: here, it is the woman with the low voice who is taking care of him. It is only at this moment that he is surprised to be back in this room whose setting belongs to a much earlier scene. He distinctly remembers the motorcycle, the dark hallway where he lay down in darkness against the door. Afterwards . . . He no longer knows what comes after: doubtless neither the hospital nor the busy café nor the long walk through the empty streets, now impossible in his condition. He asks:

"Is the wound serious?"

The woman continues knitting as if she had heard nothing.

He repeats: "What kind of wound is it?"

At the same time he realizes that he is not speaking loud enough, that his lips are forming the words, but without adding any force to them. The second time, however, the young woman has raised her head. She sets her work down on the table beside the large black ball of yarn and remains motionless, staring at him in silence, with a look of expectation, or anxiety, or fear. Finally she decides to ask: "Did you say something?"

He repeats his question again. This time weak but distinct sounds come out of his mouth, as if her voice with its extraordinary low intonations were restoring him the use of his own; unless the woman has guessed his words by reading them on his lips.

"No, it's nothing. It will all be over soon."

255

"To get up . . ."

"No, not today, and not tomorrow. A little later."

But he has no time to lose. He will get up tonight.

"The box," he says, "where is it?"

To make himself understood he must start over again: "The box . . . I had with me . . ."

A fleeting smile passes over the watchful face: "Don't worry, it's here. The boy brought it back. You mustn't talk so much. It's bad for you."

"No," the soldier says, "it isn't . . . very bad."

She has now picked up her knitting again; she continues to look at him, her hands resting on her knees. She resembles a statue. Her regular face with its sharp features recalls that of the woman who served him some wine one day, some other time, long ago. He makes an effort to say:

"I'm thirsty."

His lips have probably not even moved, for she neither stands up, nor answers, nor makes the slightest gesture. Moreover, her pale eyes had perhaps not even glanced at him, but at the other drinkers sitting farther away at other tables, toward the back of the room, where her gaze has now passed the soldier and his two companions, moving over the other tables along the wall where the small white bulletins are tacked whose fine-printed text still attracts a knot of readers, then the window with its pleated curtain at eye level and its three enameled balls on the outside of the glass and the snow behind it falling regularly and vertically in slow, heavy, close flakes.

And the new layer which gradually accumulates on the day's footprints, blurring angles, filling depressions, leveling surfaces, has quickly effaced the yellowish paths trampled by the pedestrians along the housefronts, the boy's isolated footprints, the two parallel furrows which the side car has made in the middle of the street.

But first he must make sure the snow is still falling. The soldier decides to ask the young woman about it. Does she even know, in this windowless room? She will have to look outside, to pass through the still open door back through the vestibule where the black umbrella is waiting, and through the long series of hallways, narrow staircases, and more hallways turning off at right angles, where she may easily get lost before reaching the street.

In any case it takes her a long time to come back, and it is now the boy who is sitting in her place at the table. He is wearing a turtle-neck sweater, short pants, wool socks, and felt slippers. He is sitting bolt upright without leaning against the back of the chair; his arms are stiff at his sides, his hands grasping the rattan arms of the chair; his bare legs sway between the front legs of the chair, making equal but opposite oscillations in two parallel planes. When he notices that the soldier is looking at him, he immediately stops moving; and, as if he had patiently waited for this moment to find out about something that is bothering him, he asks in his serious voice, which is not a child's voice at all:

"Why are you here?"

"I don't know," the soldier says.

The child has probably not heard the answer, for he repeats his question:

"Why didn't they put you in the barracks?"

The soldier no longer remembers whether or not he has asked the young woman about this matter. It is obviously not the boy who has brought him here, nor the lame man. He must also ask if someone has brought back the box wrapped in brown paper. The string no longer held, and the package must have come undone.

"Are you going to die here?" the child asks.

The soldier does not know the answer to this question either. Besides, he is amazed that it should even be asked. He tries to find explanations, but he has not even managed to formulate his anxiety when the boy has already turned away and is disappearing as fast as he can down the straight street, without even taking time to circle the cast-iron lamp-posts he passes, one after the other, without stopping. Soon only his footprints remain on the smooth surface of the fresh snow, their outline recognizable although deformed by his running, then becoming increasingly blurred as he runs faster and faster, finally growing quite vague, impossible to distinguish from the other footprints.

The young woman has not moved from her chair; and she answers quite readily, doubtless so that the wounded man will not worry. It is the child who has come to tell her that the soldier she had taken care of the day before was lying unconscious in a hallway a few streets away, curled up, no longer speaking, hearing nothing, moving no more than if he were dead. She had immediately decided to go to him. There was already a man standing beside the body, a civilian who happened to be passing at that moment, he said, but who in fact, seemed to have observed the entire scene from a distance, hidden in another doorway. She described him without any difficulty: a middle-aged man with thin gray hair, well dressed, with gloves, spats, and an ivory-handled umbrella. The umbrella was lying on the floor across the stoop, the door was wide open. The man was kneeling near the wounded man whose inert hand he was holding, grasping the wrist in order to take the pulse; he was a doctor, more or less, although not practicing. It is he who helped carry the body here.

As for the shoe box, the young woman had not noticed its precise location nor even its presence; it must have been nearby, shoved aside by the doctor in order to proceed more conveniently with his brief examination. Although his conclusions were hardly precise, he considered it was advisable in any case to put the wounded man to bed in a suitable place, despite the danger of moving him without a stretcher.

But they did not start out immediately, for no sooner had they decided to do so than the noise of the motorcycle had begun again. The man had quickly closed the door, and they had waited in the darkness until the danger was past. The motorcycle had come and gone several times, passing slowly through the neighboring streets, approaching, going away, approaching again, its maximum intensity soon

diminishing at each passing, however, the machine explor-
ing streets farther and farther away. When the noise was
nothing more than a vague rumble, which they even had
to strain to hear at all, the man opened the door again.

Everything was calm outside. From now on no one ven-
tured out in the streets. A few scattered flakes of snow were
falling through the motionless air. The two of them lifted
the body, the man holding him by the thighs and the woman
by the shoulders, under the arms. It was only then that she
saw the blood which made a large stain on one side of the
overcoat; but the doctor reassured her, declaring that it had
nothing to do with the seriousness of the wound, and he
carefully stepped off the stoop, skillfully carrying his share
of the burden, followed by the young woman, who had more
trouble keeping the soldier in a position she considered the
least uncomfortable, struggling to maneuver this extremely
heavy body, constantly changing her grip, and by doing so
only succeeding in shaking him up more. Three steps ahead
of them the boy was holding the umbrella in its black silk
sheath in one hand and the shoe box in the other.

Then the doctor had to go home in order to get first aid
supplies for the wounded man, until a hospital could take
him (which might be some time, given the general dis-
organization). But when they had reached the young woman's apartment, which luckily was quite nearby, they again
heard the sound of a motor, less distinct but more powerful.
This time it was no longer merely a motorcycle but heavy
cars or perhaps trucks. Therefore the man had to wait a
while longer before daring to go outside again, and the
three of them had remained in the room where they had
laid the still unconscious soldier on the day bed. Standing
motionless, they looked at him without speaking, the woman near the pillow leaning over his face, the man at the foot
of the bed still wearing his gray leather gloves and his fur-
lined coat, the child near the table with his cape and his
beret on his head.

The soldier has also remained fully dressed: overcoat,

leggings, and heavy boots. He is lying on his back, his eyes closed. He must be dead for the others to leave him like this. Yet the next scene shows him in the bed, the sheets pulled up to his chin, half listening to a confused story the same young woman with pale eyes is telling him: a slight difference of opinion having arisen between the kindly doctor with gray gloves and another individual whom she does not describe clearly but who must be the lame man. The latter must have returned to the house—much later, after the first injection—and wanted to do something which the other two, particularly the doctor, objected to. Although the basis of their disagreement is not easy to make out, its violence is sufficiently indicated by the behavior of the antagonists, both of whom make a number of expressive gesticulations, assume theatrical attitudes, and make exaggerated faces. The lame man, leaning one hand on the table, even finishes by brandishing his crutch at the other; the doctor raises his arms to heaven, opening his hands like a prophet preaching a new religion, or a dictator answering the cheers of the crowd. The woman, frightened, steps to one side to avoid the dispute; but without shifting her other foot, she turns toward what she is avoiding in order to follow the last exchanges which threaten to become dramatic, while still hiding her eyes behind her hands which are spread before her face. The child is sitting on the floor near an overturned chair; his legs are lying flat forming a wide V; in his arms, against his chest, he is holding the box wrapped in brown paper.

Then come scenes still less distinct—still more inaccurate, too, probably—violent although generally silent. They take place in vaguer, less characterized, more impersonal areas; a staircase recurs several times; someone is going down it rapidly, holding onto the railing, taking several steps at the same time, almost flying from one landing to the next, while the soldier, in order not to be knocked over, is obliged to step back into a corner. Then he goes more calmly down the stairs himself, and at the end of the long hallway he finds the snow-covered street again; and at the end of the street he finds the busy café again. Inside, everyone is as before: the bartender behind his bar, the doctor with the fur-lined coat in the group of middle-class citizens standing in front of the bar, but a little apart from the others and not participating in their conversation, the child sitting on the floor against a bench filled with drinkers near an overturned chair, still holding the box in his arms, and the young woman in the pleated dress with the dark hair and the graceful walk raising her tray with its single bottle over the heads of the seated drinkers, and finally the soldier sitting at the smallest table between his two comrades, who are ordinary infantrymen like himself, dressed as he is in overcoats buttoned to the neck and field caps, exhausted as he is, looking at nothing, as he is, sitting stiffly in their chairs and, like himself, saying nothing. All three have exactly the same face; the only difference among them is that one is seen from the left profile, the second full face, the third from the right profile; their six hands are resting on the table whose checkered oilcloth falls in rigid, conical folds at the corner of the table.

Does the waitress turn away from their motionless group now, presenting her classical profile toward the right, but with her body already turned in the other direction, in the direction of the man in middle-class clothes situated slightly behind his own group, also seen in profile and from the same side, his features motionless like hers, like theirs? Someone else also has an impassive face amid the agitation of the entire company; it is the child sitting on the floor in the foreground, on the parquet floor resembling that of the room itself, continuing the latter, so to speak, after a brief separation which consists of the horizontal strip of vertically-striped wallpaper and then, lower down, the three drawers of the chest.

The parquet floor extends beyond without further interruption, to the heavy red curtains, above which the fly's threadlike shadow continues its circuit across the white ceiling, now passing close to the dark line that spoils the uniformity of the surface near the angle of the wall in the right corner, just within the field of vision of the man lying on the day bed, the back of his neck supported by the bolster.

He would have to get up in order to see at close range just what this defect consists of: is it actually a crack, or a spider web, or something else? He would probably have to stand on a chair, or even on a ladder.

But once on his feet, other thoughts would quickly distract him from this project: the soldier would first of all have to find the shoe box again, probably put in another room now, in order to deliver it to its recipient. Since there can be no question of such a thing for the moment, the soldier need only remain motionless, lying on his back, his head raised slightly by the bolster, staring straight in front of him.

And yet his mind feels clearer, less drowsy, despite the persistent nausea and the progressive numbing of his entire body, which has grown worse since the second injection. It seems to him that the young woman who is leaning over him to give him something to drink is also looking at him more anxiously.

She speaks to him again about the lame man, against whom she seems to have some kind of grudge, or something even more violent. In her remarks she has already returned several times to this man who shares her apartment, apropos of other subjects, and always with a certain reticence, though at the same time revealing a need to explain her feelings on the matter, as if she were ashamed of this presence she was trying to justify, to destroy, and to minimize. Besides, the young woman never explains the relationship connecting them. She has had to struggle, among other things, to keep the lame man from opening the shoe box: he claimed it was essential to know what was in it. As a matter of fact, she herself has wondered what should be done with it . . .

"Nothing," the soldier says. "I'll take care of it once I'm up."

"But," she says, 'if it's something important and you have to stay here for a while . . ." Suddenly she seems overcome with anxiety, and the soldier supposes he himself is responsible for it and would like to allay it.

"No," he says, "it's not so important."

"But what should be done with it?"

"I don't know."

"You were looking for someone. Was it to give it to him?"

"Not necessarily. To him, or to someone else. He would have told me who."

"Was it important for him?"

"It might be. I'm not sure."

"But what's in it?" She has spoken this last sentence with such vehemence that he feels obliged to tell her, as far as he is able, despite the fatigue this conversation causes him, despite his own lack of interest in this particular point, despite his fear of disappointing her by the insignificance of his answer:

"Not much, I think, I haven't looked, probably letters, papers, personal effects."

"It was for a friend?"

"No, someone I barely knew."

"Is he dead?"

"Yes, he died at the hospital. He was wounded in the stomach."

"And was it important for him?"

"Probably. He had asked for me and I came a few minutes too late. They gave me the box, from him. Then someone called him, on the telephone. I answered. I think it was his father or something. They didn't have the same name. I wanted to know what should be done with the box."

"And he asked you to meet him."

Yes; the man who telephoned has arranged to meet him in his own city, this one, where the soldier could try to go too, each henceforth doing whatever he could among this retreating army. The meeting place was not the man's house, for family reasons or something of that kind, but in the street, since all the cafés were closing, one after another. The soldier found a military truck carrying old uniforms which was going in this direction. Yet he had to come part of the way on foot.

He didn't know the city. He might have lost his way and gone to the wrong place. It was at a crossroads near a street light. He had not heard clearly, or not remembered the names of the streets. He has relied on topographical indications, following the prescribed itinerary as best he could. When he thought he had reached the place, he waited. The crossroads corresponded to the description he had been given, but the names of the streets did not sound like the vaguely remembered consonants. He has waited a long time, he has seen no one.

He was certain of the day, in any case. As for the time, he had no watch. Perhaps he has arrived too late. He has looked around the neighborhood. He has even waited at another crossroads identical to the first. He has wandered through the whole city. He has returned several times to the original place, insofar as he was capable of recognizing it, that day and the days following. In any case it was too late then.

"Only a few minutes. He had just died, before anyone had noticed. I had stayed in a café with some non-coms, men I had never seen before. I didn't know. They told me to wait for a friend of theirs, another man, a recruit. He was at Reichenfels."

"Who was at Reichenfels?" the woman asks. She leans a little closer to the bed. Her low voice fills the whole room as she insists: "Who? In which regiment?"

"I don't know. Someone. The doctor was there too, with his gray ring, leaning on the counter, and the wife, the lame man's wife, the one who poured the wine."

"What are you talking about?"

Her face is quite close to his. Her pale, dark-rimmed eyes are made even larger by the widening of the lids.

"I have to go get the box," he says. "It must be back at the barracks. I forgot it. It's on the bed, behind the bolster . . ."

"Lie still, rest. Don't try to talk any more."

She holds out her hand to pull up the sheet. The palm and the inner surface of the fingers show black stains, as though from paint or grease, which have resisted washing.

"Who are you?" the soldier says. "What should I call you? What's your name? . . ."

But she no longer seems to hear him. She arranges the sheets and the pillow, straightens the blanket.

"Your hand," the soldier says again. This time he cannot proceed further.

"Lie still," she says, "it's nothing. It's from carrying you. The overcoat had fresh stains on the sleeve."

They stumble at every step over the ruts and soft earth, the darkness illuminated only occasionally by fleeting gleams. Both men have abandoned their knapsacks. The wounded man has also left his rifle behind. But the soldier has kept his, even though its strap has just broken and he is obliged to carry it in his hand, horizontally. Three steps ahead, the boy is carrying the umbrella in the same way. The wounded man grows heavier and heavier and clings to the soldier's neck, making it still more difficult for the latter to walk. Now he can no longer move at all: neither his arms nor even his head. He can only look straight ahead at the leg of the table from which the oilcloth has been removed, the table leg now visible all the way to the top: it ends in a sphere supporting a cube, or rather an almost cubical parallelepiped, with square horizontal surfaces but rectangular vertical ones; the vertical surface has a design carved within a rectangular frame following the shape of the surface itself: a kind of stylized floret, its straight stem splitting near the top into two small symmetrical arcs on either side, like a V with curved branches, the concavity toward the bottom, slightly shorter than the terminal portion of the axial stem starting from the same point, and . . . , his eyes no longer able to remain lowered so long, his gaze is obliged to move up the length of the red curtains to the ceiling and the hair-thin, somewhat sinuous crack whose shape also has something distinct and complicated about it which it would be necessary to follow with application from one turn to the next, with its curves, vacillations, uncertainties, sudden changes of directions, inflections, continuations, slight regressions, but it would take more time, a little time, a few minutes, a few seconds, and it is already, now, too late.

On my last visit, the third injection was useless. The wounded soldier was dead. The streets are full of armed soldiers who march by singing in low voices, their songs more nostalgic than joyous. Others pass in open trucks in which the men are sitting stiffly, rifles upright, held in both hands between their knees; they are arranged in two rows, back to back, each row facing one side of the street. Patrols circulate everywhere, and no one may go out after nightfall without a pass. It was necessary to give the third injection, and only a practicing doctor would have had authorization to do so. Fortunately the streets were poorly lit, certainly much worse than during the last few days when the lights were on even in broad daylight. But it was too late for the injection. Besides, they only served to make the dying man's last hours less painful. There was nothing else to do.

The body has remained in the apartment of the sham lame man, who will make the proper declaration, telling the whole story as it actually happened: a wounded man whom they took in off the street and about whom they knew nothing, not even his name, since he had no papers. If the man is afraid his leg will be examined on this occasion and his actual condition discovered, the woman could take the appropriate steps; as for the man, he need only avoid showing himself when they come to get the body: it will not be the first time he has hidden from a visitor.

The woman seems to mistrust him. In any case she has been unwilling to let him deal with the package wrapped in brown paper which he badly wanted to open. He thought it was some secret weapon, or at least its plans. The box is now in safe keeping—on the cracked black marble top of the chest—closed, wrapped up again, retied, but bringing it back here from their place has not been easy on account of the patrols. Luckily it was not very far. Just before the goal was reached, a brief command rang out: "Halt!" shouted in a loud voice from some distance behind. In itself, the box was obviously not very compromising; the sham lame man's notions on this subject were, of course, ridiculous, but the woman was nevertheless afraid that the letters the soldier had mentioned to her might contain information of a non-personal nature, of military or political interest, for instance, the soldier himself having shown in many circumstances an exaggerated discretion in their regard. It would be better, in any case, not to let them be taken, particularly since the dagger-bayonet the woman also returned at the same time might seem quite suspicious. The lack of a pass would have made the bearer's case still worse. The loud, commanding voice has shouted "Halt!" a second time, then a third, and immediately afterward there was a rapid burst of machine-gun fire. But the gun must have been too far away to aim properly, and it was very dark in this area. Perhaps it was even fired into the air. Once past the street corner, there was no longer any danger. The apartment house door had not remained ajar, of course. Nevertheless the key has turned noiselessly in the lock, the hinges have not creaked, the door has closed in silence.

At first glance the letters contain no secret of any kind and are of no general or personal importance. They are ordinary letters, the kind a country girl sends every week to her fiancé, giving news of the farm or the neighbors, regularly repeating the same conventional formulas about separation and return. The box also contains an old gold watch, of no particular value, with a tarnished gilded-brass chain; there is no name engraved inside the lid over the watch face; there is also a ring, a signet ring made of silver or nickel alloy, the kind workers often make for themselves in factories, with "H. M." engraved on it; finally, a dagger-bayonet of the current model, identical in every detail to the one given by the young woman, along with the package whose origin she was unwilling to specify, saying only that she was afraid to keep it at home since the latest regulations concerning the surrender of weapons, but that even so she did not want to turn it in (it is certainly the sham lame man who has forced her to get rid of it). The box is not a shoe box, it is a biscuit box of the same dimensions, but made out of tin.

What is most important about all this is the envelopes of the letters: they are addressed to a soldier—Henri Martin—and give his postal sector. On the back is the name and address of the girl who has written them. It is to her that the box will have to be sent when the mails are functioning again, since it is now impossible to find the father, who is not even named Martin. Besides, he had probably proposed himself as the provisional recipient only for reasons of convenience: even if he knew the contents of the box, he supposed it would be easier, geographically speaking, to reach him than the girl herself. Unless only the letters are intended for the latter, the dagger, the watch, and the ring belonging by rights to the father. It might also be supposed that the letters too should not be returned to their sender; many reasons might readily be suggested in support of this notion.

Rather than send the package through the mails, it would probably be preferable to carry it in one's own hands and return it with the customary considerations. As a matter of fact the girl might not yet have been informed of her fiancé's death. Only the father was notified when he telephoned the hospital; yet supposing that he is not the real father—or not legally the father, or in any case not quite the father—he is not obliged to be in communication with the girl, or even to know of her existence; so there is no reason for him to write her once the mails are functioning again.

The woman who has taken care of the wounded soldier has obtained no information from him as to his comrade who died before he did. Toward the end he talked a good deal, but he had already forgotten most things that had happened recently; besides, he was delirious most of the time. The woman declares that he was already sick before he was wounded, that he had fever, and that he sometimes behaved like a sleepwalker. Her son, a serious-looking boy of about ten, had already encountered him in the street, perhaps even several times, if it is actually the same boy each time, as is likely despite slight contradictions. His role is significant since he is the one who, by his heedlessness, has provoked the actions of the occupants of the side car, but his many appearances are not all decisive to the same degree. The lame man, on the other hand, plays virtually no part at all. His presence in the morning at the Rue Bouvet military offices (transformed into a barracks or hospitalization center) has nothing surprising about it, given the ease with which he maneuvers when no one is there to observe his means of locomotion. Besides, the soldier does not seem to have paid much attention to his remarks. The bartender, for his part, is problematical or insignificant. He does not say a word, does not make a move; this heavy-set bald man might also be a spy or an informer, the nature of his reflections is impossible to determine. The minor characters arguing in front of him with so much animation will, in any case, tell him nothing worth reporting to his eventual chiefs; they are only café strategists who make History over as they please, criticizing the ministers, correcting the generals, creating imaginary incidents which among other things might have permitted a victory at Reichenfels. The soldier sitting in the back of the room at the next to the last table to the right certainly has a more realistic outlook on battles; hence he has nothing to say about them; he must merely be waiting to be served something to drink, between his two comrades whose faces are not entirely visible, the one seen in profile and the other three-quarters from the rear. His first change of uniform can be explained by the general and probably unjustified contempt to which his regiment has been subjected since the defeat; he has preferred wearing less familiar insignia on this trip.

Hence he can mingle with the crowd without attracting attention, and quietly drink the wine the waitress is about to serve him. Meanwhile he stares straight ahead through the large window. The snow has stopped falling. The weather has grown increasingly mild during the course of the day. The sidewalks are still white, but the street, where the trucks have been passing continuously for hours, has already turned black again along its entire central section, the half melted snow having been heaped in the gutters on either side; each time the soldier crosses a side street, he sinks in up to his leggings with a spongy noise, while the scattered drops of fine rain begin to float in the evening air, still mixed with a few moist snowflakes which turn to water even before they have reached the street.

The soldier hesitates to leave the busy café where he has come in to rest for a moment. It is the rain he is staring at through the large window with its pleated curtains and its three billiard balls on the other side of the glass. The child is also watching the rain, sitting on the floor close to the window so that he can see through the thin material. It begins to rain much harder. The umbrella in its black silk sheath is leaning on the coat rack near the fur-lined overcoat. But in the drawing there are so many other garments hanging on top of each other that it is difficult to make out much of anything in the jumble. Just under the picture is the chest with its three drawers whose gleaming front is fitted with two large, tarnished brass knobs. In the bottom drawer is the biscuit box wrapped in brown paper. The rest of the room is unchanged: the ashes in the fireplace, the sheets of paper scattered on top of the table, the burnt cigarette butts filling the ashtray, the table lamp turned on, the heavy red curtains drawn tight.

Outside it is raining. Outside you walk through the rain with your head down, shielding your eyes with one hand while you stare ahead, a few yards ahead, at a few yards of wet asphalt. The rain does not get in here, nor the snow nor the wind; and the only dust that dulls the gleaming horizontal surfaces, the polished wood of the table, the waxed parquet floor, the marble mantelpiece, the cracked marble top of the chest, the only dust comes from the room itself, perhaps from the cracks in the floor, or else from the bed, or from the ashes in the fireplace, or from the velvet curtains whose vertical folds rise from the floor to the ceiling across which the fly's shadow—which is shaped like the incandescent thread of the electric bulb concealed by the truncated conical lampshade—now passes near the tiny black line which, remaining in the half-darkness beyond the circle of light and at a distance of four or five yards, is extremely difficult to make out: first a short, straight segment about half an inch long, followed by a series of rapid undulations, themselves scalloped . . . But the image grows

271

blurred by trying to distinguish the outlines, as in the case of the inordinately delicate pattern of the wallpaper and the indeterminate edges of the gleaming paths made in the dust by the felt slippers, and, beyond the door, the dark vestibule where the umbrella is leaning against the coat rack, then, once past the entrance door, the series of long hallways, the spiral staircase, the door to the building with its stone stoop, and the whole city behind me.

SELECTED BIBLIOGRAPHY

A. *Works by Robbe-Grillet in French*
1. *Les Gommes.* Paris, Les Editions de Minuit, 1953.
2. *Le Voyeur.* Paris, Les Editions de Minuit, 1955.
3. *La Jalousie.* Paris, Les Editions de Minuit, 1957.
4. *Dans le labyrinthe.* Paris, Les Editions de Minuit, 1959.
5. *L'année dernière à Marienbad.* Paris, Les Editions de Minuit, 1961.
6. *Instantanés.* Paris, Les Editions de Minuit, 1962.
7. *L'immortelle.* Paris, Les Editions de Minuit, 1963.
8. *Pour un nouveau roman.* Paris, Les Editions de Minuit, 1963.
9. *La maison de rendez-vous.* Paris, Les Editions de Minuit, 1965.

B. *Works by Robbe-Grillet in translation*
1. *The Erasers.* Translated by Richard Howard. New York, Grove Press, 1964.
2. *The Voyeur.* Translated by Richard Howard. New York, Grove Press, 1958.
3. *Jealousy.* Translated by Richard Howard. New York, Grove Press, 1959.
4. *In the Labyrinth.* Translated by Richard Howard. New York, Grove Press, 1960.
5. *Last Year at Marienbad.* Translated by Richard Howard. New York, Grove Press, 1962.

C. *Books and articles on Robbe-Grillet*

1. Audry, Collette: "La caméra d'Alain Robbe-Grillet," *La Revue des Lettres Modernes,* nos. 36-38 (1958), pp. 131-140.

2. Barnes, Hazel: "The Ins and Outs of Alain Robbe-Grillet," *Chicago Review,* Vol. XVI, no. 3 (Winter-Spring 1962), pp. 21-42.

3. Barthes, Roland: "Littérature littérale: Alain Robbe-Grillet," *Critique,* nos. 100-101 (septembre-octobre 1955), pp. 820-826.

4. ....: "Littérature objective: Alain Robbe-Grillet," *Critique,* nos. 86-87 (juillet-août 1954), pp. 581-591.

5. Berger, Yves: *"Dans le labyrinthe," Nouvelle Nouvelle Revue Française,* no. 85 (janvier 1960), pp. 112-118.

6. Blanchot, Maurice: "Notes sur un roman" [on *Le Voyeur*], *Nouvelle Nouvelle Revue Française,* Vol. III, no. 31 (juillet 1955), pp. 105-112.

7. Bonnot, Gérard: "Marienbad ou le parti de Dieu," *Les Temps Modernes,* no. 187 (decembre 1961), pp. 752-768.

8. Brée, Germaine: "Jalousie: New Blinds or Old?" *Yale French Studies,* no. 24 (1960), pp. 87-91.

9. Champigny, Robert: "In Search of the Pure Récit," *American Society of the Legion of Honor Magazine* (Winter 1956-1957), pp. 331-343.

10. Dort, Bernard: "Sur les romans de Robbe-Grillet," *Les Temps Modernes,* no. 136 (juin 1957), pp. 1989-1999.

11. Friedman, Melvin: "The Neglect of Time," *Books Abroad,* Vol. XXXVI, no. 2 (Spring 1962), pp. 125-130.

12. Goytisolo, Juan: *Problemas de la novela*. [Chapter on Robbe-Grillet]. Barcelona, Seix Barral, 1959.

13. Hahn, Bruno: "Plan du Labyrinthe de Robbe-Grillet," *Les Temps Modernes,* no. 172 (juillet 1960), pp. 150-168.

14. Labarthe, André S.: "Marienbad Année Zéro," *Cahiers du Cinéma,* no. 123 (septembre 1961), pp. 28-31.

15. Labarthe, André and Jacques Rivette: "Entretien avec Resnais et Robbe-Grillet," *Cahiers du Cinéma,* no. 123 (septembre 1961), pp. 1-8.

16. Lefebvre, Maurice: *"La Jalousie," Nouvelle Nouvelle Revue Française,* Vol. V, no. 7 (juillet 1957), pp. 146-149.

17. Mauriac, Claude: *L'allitérature contemporaine.* [Chapter on Robbe-Grillet]. Paris, Editions Albin Michel, 1958.

18. Minor, Anne: *"La Jalousie," The French Review,* Vol. XXXII (April 1959), pp. 477-479.

19. Morrissette, Bruce: "En relisant Robbe-Grillet," *Critique,* no. 146 (juillet 1959), pp. 579-608.

20. ....: "Oedipus and Existentialism" [on *The Erasers*], *Wisconsin Studies in Contemporary Literature* (Fall 1960), pp. 43-73.

21. ....: "Surfaces et structures dans les romans de Robbe-Grillet," *The French Review,* Vol. XXXI, no. 5 (April 1958), pp. 364-369.

22. ....: *Les romans de Robbe-Grillet.* Paris, Editions de Minuit, 1963. [Contains a bibliography].

23. ....: "Roman et cinéma: le cas de Robbe-Grillet," *Symposium,* Vol. XV, no. 2 (Summer 1961), pp. 85-104.

24. Nadeau, Maurice: "Le nouveau roman," *Critique*, nos. 123-124 (août-septembre 1957), pp. 707-722.

25. Ollier, Claude: "Ce soir à Marienbad," *Nouvelle Nouvelle Revue Française*, Vol. XVIII, no. 106 (octobre 1961) and no. 107 (novembre 1961), pp. 906-912.

26. Peyre, Henri: "Monkeys in a Cage" [on *La Jalousie*], *The New York Times* Sunday Book Review, November 22, 1959.

27. Picon, Gaetan: "Le problème du *Voyeur*," *Mercure de France* (octobre 1955), pp. 20-26.

28. Pingaud, Bernard: *"Dans le labyrinthe* d'Alain Robbe-Grillet," *Les Lettres Nouvelles* (7 octobre 1959), pp. 38-41.

29. . . . . : *Ecrivains d'aujourd'hui*. [Chapter on Robbe-Grillet]. Paris, Grasset, 1960.

30. . . . . : "Lecture de *La Jalousie*, *Les Lettres Nouvelles*, no. 50 (juin 1957), pp. 901-906.

31. Rainoird, Manuel: *"Les Gommes* d'Alain Robbe-Grillet," *Nouvelle Nouvelle Revue Française*, Vol. I, no. 5 (juin 1953), pp. 1108-1109.

32. Ricardou, Jean: "Description et Infraconscience chez Robbe-Grillet, *Nouvelle Nouvelle Revue Française,* Vol. VII, no. 11 (novembre 1960), pp. 890-900.

33. Stoltzfus, Ben F.: *Alain Robbe-Grillet and the New French Novel*. With a preface by Harry T. Moore. Carbondale (Ill.), Southern Illinois University Press, 1964. [Contains a bibliography].